The Ghost
of
Tobacco Road

Dale J. Young

Copyright © 2015 Dale J. Young

Niner 8 Books

ISBN 978-0-9913710-6-8

To my Southern Belle

1

September, 1937

A harvest moon hung low in the sky just above the tree line as Franklin Cain walked slowly down the row between the waist-high tobacco plants. The yellow leaves shimmered in the moonlight as a warm breeze rolled across the field. His muscles ached and his joints were stiff from the long day of picking leaves and stacking them on the carts. Even with the help of his wife, their five children and his mules the work never seemed to end. Tomorrow at dawn they would be at it again. And tomorrow night he would be just as tired and worn out as he was right now.

But even though it was exhausting work, Franklin always liked to walk the rows by himself at the end of the day. The smell of the tobacco leaves combined with the smoke from the chimney of his sharecropper's house always gave him the strength to carry on. He had a family to feed and he knew the only way he could do that was to make sure the harvest was successful. Times were tough and the promise of a share of the crop in the field was all he had. Tobacco farming was his life.

Tonight Franklin walked farther from the house than usual. The night was clear and the soft breeze brought comfort to his tired soul. His wife had made him promise to stay close to the house, but as he walked slowly down the row he thought about how his wife always worried too much about things. But Franklin knew why his wife had warned him not to go too far into the fields by himself. Superstitions about the harvest moon ran deep in Starlight, ever since the first grisly murder in 1931.

When Franklin reached the end of the row he stopped and listened as the breeze combed through the tobacco leaves. The rustling sound was like a whisper in the night and made Franklin feel as if the plants were talking to him, telling him that their leaves would bring a fair price at the market and would enable him to feed his family through the winter. He breathed a tired sigh of relief as he listened to the sound. Then he slowly began to make his way up the next row.

Midway through the row Franklin paused and dropped down on one knee. He reached over with a hand and felt of the bare stalk of the closest tobacco plant. Most of the leaves were gone with the exception of the leaves near the top of the plant. Tobacco leaves are picked from the bottom to the top of the plant as they ripen, and the absence of the leaves on the lower portion of the plant reminded Franklin that the harvest was almost over. Just a few more days of picking and the plants would be nothing more than naked stalks. Then it would be time to dry and cure the leaves in the barn to ready them for sale at the market.

The yellow disk of the harvest moon floated in the sky just over Franklin's shoulder. The light from the moon cast deep shadows down the rows between the plants, and made it appear as if the large, flat tobacco leaves were floating on top of a sea of darkness. Franklin's body was barely visible in the shadows as he rested himself on one knee beside the plants.

Franklin ran his hand down to the base of the tobacco plant and stuck his fingers into the sandy soil. Heavy rains had delayed planting in the previous spring but the summer had been dry. He was thankful that the crop had survived and was glad the harvest would be over soon. Normally he would have already completed the harvest, but this year his crop was running late because of the delay in planting.

Suddenly a strong breeze rushed across the field, causing the tobacco plants to sway in unison. The sound of the wind sifting through the plants prevented Franklin from hearing the footsteps in the dirt as the dark figure approached him from behind.

As Franklin turned on his knee his eyes grew wide with terror. Unable to catch his balance he fell backwards onto his back as he raised his tired arms in a futile attempt to stop the blade of the tobacco axe as it arced down towards his body. He rolled to his side as the blade dug into the dirt, barely missing his shoulder.

Franklin tried to yell out but his lungs failed him. He rolled over onto his stomach and tried to crawl away from the killer. The muscles in his body screamed in protest as he tried to claw at the dirt to pull himself down the row, but he was so tired and exhausted that his body was slow to respond to his commands. Just then his right hand found the bare stalk of a tobacco plant and he was able to pull himself down the row. A brief glimmer of hope rushed through his body but in his mind he knew there would be no escape.

Franklin screamed out in agony as the blade of the axe sliced through his lower leg just above his ankle, completely severing his foot from his leg. A white-hot flash of pain bolted up his leg as he rolled onto his back. He could see the shadowy figure silhouetted against the night sky, the tobacco axe raised high in the air. Franklin instinctively lifted his hands and crossed his arms over his face. He knew his time had come, and the last thought to go through his mind was of his family and how hard it would be for them to survive without him.

The axe came down in a violent arc and buried itself in middle of Franklin's chest, slicing through his ribcage and into his heart. The world then went black for Franklin Cain. But the killer was not finished with him. His death was not enough. Now it was time for the mutilation. As the axe was raised again and again, Franklin Cain's tired, worn-out body was hacked and chopped until he looked like nothing more than the bloody carcass of a slaughtered hog.

The sharp blade split Franklin's forehead in two and cut a path down through his face to his lower jaw. Blood splattered onto the surrounding leaves as the blade of the tobacco axe was yanked out of his skull, raised into the air and then brought down again, and again, and again until Franklin's head and face were chopped into an unrecognizable mound of flesh and bone.

Then as quickly as it began, it was over. As the harvest moon hung like an eyeball in the sky, the tobacco plants continued their gentle dance in the breeze, unaffected by the carnage that had just taken place in the field.

Franklin's dead, mutilated body in his blood-soaked and ruined overalls would be found several hours later by his wife and son who had finally set out to find him when he had failed to return to the house that evening.

2

Logan Shaw peered through the blinds of the office on his small car lot as a smile crept onto his face. He watched as the young man walked around the red Toyota sedan while rubbing his chin, clearly interested in the car. Logan knew the best thing to do was to let the guy think about it for a few more minutes and then go out and make the deal. And Logan needed to make the deal. Here it was the second week of the month and he still had not booked a sale. If he sold this red Toyota he would be able to eat and pay his rent for the rest of the month. As for next month, he'd worry about that when the time came.

"Good afternoon," Logan said as he walked up to the young man peering through window of the red Toyota. "She's a beauty, ain't she?" The two men then shook hands. "I'm Logan Shaw. Pleased to meet you."

The young man, probably in his early twenties and purchasing his first car on his own without the help of his parents, smiled nervously at Logan. He had heard stories about used car salesmen. Still, the red Toyota had caught his eye several times when he had ridden past the lot on the city bus and he wanted to know more about it. He had just graduated from college and needed a car but money was tight and he knew he couldn't afford anything on the lots of the big, name-brand dealerships. He knew the high-mileage cars found on small used car lots were about the only thing he could afford. All he had to do was get something for the time being and in a year or two he'd be able to upgrade to a better car. But right now he needed something to get himself back and forth to work. He had only been at his new job for about a month and was already sick of riding the city bus to work. And was he also tired of bumming rides from his friends on the weekends. And to make matters worse, it seemed that no girl wanted to date a guy without a car. He had learned this the hard way over the past few weeks.

"My name is David. Pleased to meet you too."

Logan nodded his head and then launched into his practiced routine, honed from years of hocking cars on his lot. He knew he would not let this David kid leave unless he was riding in the red Toyota or one of the other cars on the lot.

"This red beauty is a one-owner car, an elderly woman. Yep, she said her cataracts were getting so bad that she was afraid to drive any longer. She took good care of this baby. In fact, I was thinking about just keeping it for myself but I figured that I make my living by providing great cars at great prices so I would be ashamed of myself if I didn't pass this vehicle on to one of my customers. It just wouldn't seem right to keep it all to myself."

In reality, Logan had bought the car at auction less than a month ago. It had been repossessed from a young girl who was the third owner of the car.

David smiled and knew he was probably being fed a line of bullshit. But just like everyone else that bought cars on small used car lots from guys wearing clip-on neckties, there was that tiny flicker of hope in the back of his mind that what he was hearing really was the truth. It was enough hope for David to keep listening. After all, he needed a car and he only had a certain amount of money to spend on one.

Logan kept up the pressure. "I've got the keys right here. Let's take this sweet thing for a ride, how about that?"

"Sure," replied David.

They both got into the car and rode around for about ten minutes. Logan could tell that David liked the Toyota when he started fiddling with the stereo. Logan knew that nowadays most young people didn't know much about what was going on underneath the hood of a car and that the stereo was about the only thing they cared about.

When they returned to the lot, Logan had David park the car near the front door to the office. This was an old car salesman trick. Never let the customer return the car to its original parking spot. Always make them park it near the office. This way it made them feel like the car was that much closer to being theirs.

After the customary haggling, David finally agreed to a price. Little did he know that his down payment was more than the amount that Logan had paid for the car. This was how Logan did business. He would require a down payment that was at least the amount he had invested in the car, hopefully more, and then he would finance the rest of the price of the car at a high interest rate. All the subsequent payments would be pure profit since he had already recouped his investment before the customer ever left the lot with the car. And if they missed a payment down the road he would have the car repossessed and put right back out on his lot to wait for the next fool to come along.

Logan watched as David drove off in the red Toyota. He figured that he would get six or seven payments out of this kid, all profit, before the kid would get tired of the maintenance bills on the car. He would then miss a payment and Logan would have the car repossessed. Then the cycle would begin all over again. Logan knew that if he was lucky he wouldn't get another angry letter from some sue-happy law firm like he usually did. Being sued for his business practices was becoming commonplace for Logan Shaw.

Logan locked the door to his office and sat down at his desk. It was late in the day and he had finally made a sale. The cash he had used to buy the red Toyota at auction was now back in his pocket and then some and he could finally breathe a sigh of relief. Maybe tonight he would stop by the grocery store and buy himself a sirloin steak if he could find one on sale, take it home to his trailer, fire up his little charcoal grill and have himself a barbeque.

Logan leaned back in his chair and closed his eyes. A sirloin steak... How long had it been since he had had one of those? Lately it had been instant noodles in a Styrofoam cup or bologna sandwiches. Cars just weren't moving on his lot the way they used to. And the economy seemed to be getting worse by the day.

Despite his attempts to stop himself, Logan opened his desk drawer and retrieved the small bottle of whiskey he kept for special occasions, like when he sold a car. But lately he had been using the whiskey to take the edge off of the days when he didn't sell anything. But today he knew he could have a shot for celebratory purposes. Hell, maybe two shots. He had just sold the red Toyota, recouped his money, and was by his best estimates looking at probably six months of pure profit payments. Why shouldn't he celebrate?

Logan poured himself a shot of whiskey into his empty coffee cup. He tossed back the cup and swallowed the whiskey in one gulp. He relished the burn as the cheap whiskey cut a hot path down his throat. He closed his eyes and leaned back in his chair and tried to relax. He hadn't eaten since breakfast and as a result he could feel the effects of the whiskey almost immediately. After a few minutes he poured one more shot. After it was down, he placed his cup on his desk and let out a long breath as he placed his feet up on his desk. The second shot of whiskey was causing his face to warm, and he could feel the muscles throughout his body beginning to relax.

The two shots of whiskey gave Logan a light buzz. Outside the sun had set and the blinds were beginning to glow purple from the twilight. Pretty soon he knew he would be sitting alone in the dark.

Logan knew what he really wanted, besides another shot of whiskey, and that was a visit from Sexy Sarah. He liked that name because he knew that she only used it with him. At least that's what she always told him. That made it even better.

Logan had sold Sarah a car about six months ago. It was one of the few times that he had actually sold a halfway decent car to someone. Sarah had walked onto his lot looking for something cheap because she was about to leave her husband. All she wanted to do was get out of town and go somewhere no one could find her. She had found out that her husband was cheating on her with one of the paralegals in his law firm and Logan took pity on her and sold her a rather nice high-mileage BMW that he had bought at auction. He had sold Sarah the car at cost because he wanted to help her, and because he hated lawyers. And since her husband was a lawyer Logan figured that helping Sarah leave the guy was the closest thing he would get to revenge against lawyers. Little did Logan know at the time that Sarah would end up staying with her husband, having formulated a better plan for revenge than just leaving him and skipping town.

But tonight Logan resisted the urge to call Sexy Sarah. It had been too long since he had last sold a car and now that he had finally booked a sale he knew he had to take care of his lot rent or he would be out on the street. He was behind a month already, and he knew that selling the red Toyota would enable him to get right with his landlord. And then after he paid his rent and had that sirloin steak he was dreaming of, if he had any money left for Sexy Sarah he would give her a call.

Logan sat in his chair until his office was consumed by darkness. Then he got up from his desk, gathered his suit coat and locked up. On his way to his trailer he stopped by the grocery store to buy himself the sirloin steak he had been craving. His whiskey buzz had worn off and on the ride home he felt almost good about himself. He had limited himself to only two shots of whiskey to celebrate, and now he was going to have himself a steak grilled on the small patio behind his trailer. Life could be worse. It had been worse, but maybe now things were looking up.

Logan bought the steak, a small bag of charcoal and a large potato. He knew that his purchase would scream "bachelor" to the girl at the checkout counter but there was no use in trying to hide the obvious. He was, after all, a bachelor of almost a year, his first and only wife having left him for a lawyer who worked for one of the prominent law firms in Logan's home town of Wilmington, NC. Yet another reason to hate lawyers, Logan thought to himself as he placed his items on the checkout conveyor. Then he put it out of his mind. He wasn't going to let anything spoil the rest of his night and his celebration of selling the red Toyota.

§§§

Logan's home was a modest, single-wide trailer in a large trailer park near the port of Wilmington. Most of the tenants were merchant mariners whose trailers sat vacant for six months at a time while they were at sea. But the lot rent was cheap, there wasn't a lot of trouble since many of the tenants were gone most of the year, and it was as safe, as safe as a trailer park could be in that part of town. But Logan kept a handgun in his trailer just in case.

After firing up his grill Logan went inside and took a shower while the coals burned down. He put on an old pair of jeans and his favorite T-shirt and grabbed a beer from the refrigerator, put his potato in the microwave and then went outside to grill his steak. The night was warm and he could smell the salt air from the nearby Atlantic Ocean mingling with the smoke from the grill. Just over the treetops, Logan could see the yellow glow from the port lights. The ships came and left at all hours of the day and night and Logan could hear the low rumble of the huge cargo cranes unloading the containers.

As Logan grilled his steak he thought to himself again that things could be worse, and had been worse more than he cared to remember. Just as he flipped his steak, he heard the metallic clink of a Zippo cigarette lighter.

"Evening neighbor," said a voice in the darkness.

Logan looked to his right and saw an orange pinprick of light flare in the darkness about shoulder height off of the ground. He knew the voice immediately. It was his neighbor Lowell.

"Hey Lowell, didn't know you were home," Logan said as he replaced the dome-shaped cover on his grill. The coals were just right and the steak was coming along nicely.

"Yeah, pulled in this morning from a six-month cruise. Cape Town, over to Sao Paulo and then home. The old lady is inside recovering, if you catch my meaning." Lowell then took a long pull on his cigarette causing the orange tip to glow bright enough for Logan to see part of his face.

"Come on over," Logan said. "Have a beer."

Lowell left the small concrete patio at the foot of the backdoor to his trailer and walked through the darkness over to where Logan was standing. Logan went inside and grabbed the rest of his six-pack from the refrigerator. He had promised himself earlier that after two shots of whiskey in his office that he would only have one beer with his steak. But now all bets were off. He had company, and when men had company they always drank beer. Logan knew he was making excuses but decided that cutting down on his alcohol could be put off until tomorrow.

Logan returned to his patio and handed Lowell a can of beer, then he placed the rest of the six-pack on the small plastic table next to the grill. Lowell popped the top on the beer, took a long pull from the can and then chased it with a drag on his cigarette.

"It was a good cruise. Same old, same old. That was my third time on that route. I'm ready for something new. I'm ready to go past Cape Town and see what's on the other side of Africa. I still haven't seen the Indian

Ocean yet."

"And you call yourself a sailor," Logan replied as he grinned and removed the cover on his grill to flip his steak.

Lowell laughed and took another sip of beer. "Yep, I'm a sailor alright. Yo ho and a bottle of rum and all that shit." Lowell then took the last drag on his cigarette before dropping it to his feet and stepping on the butt.

Logan knew Lowell liked sailing with the merchant marine. He knew part of what Lowell liked was the travel and the other part was that it was basically a six month on, six month off kind of job. Now that Lowell had returned from his cruise he could lie around his trailer and relax for the next six months without having to work.

"Steak?" Lowell said as he watched Logan flip the piece of meat on the grill. "What's the occasion?"

"I sold a car today. First one in almost a month. I was getting worried. You know how Charlie is about the rent. He was beginning to nag about it."

"Fuckin' landlords," Lowell replied as he took a swig of beer. Then he looked over his shoulder at Logan's trailer, the yellow bug light illuminating the rickety stairs that led up to the backdoor.

"Still all by yourself, man?" Lowell didn't want to dig, but he and Logan had been neighbors for a while. He considered Logan his friend.

Logan tapped the leg of the grill with the side of his foot before looking at the backdoor of his trailer.

"Yeah, all by my lonesome. She ain't comin' back. Can't say as I blame her." Logan felt ashamed of himself. He was angry at his wife for leaving him for another man, but deep down inside, just like he had told Lowell, he didn't really blame her. After all, who wants to be married to a used car salesman that lives in a trailer park and can barely buy groceries?

"Fuck her," Lowell replied.

"I used to on a regular basis. Now someone else is fucking her in a big fancy house." Logan laughed half-heartedly at his joke. Lowell only grunted and took another sip of beer.

Just then Lowell's wife opened the backdoor of their trailer and motioned to him with her hand. Lowell turned and smiled at Logan.

"I think she's ready for round three. Thanks for the beer, brother." Lowell then raised his beer can to Logan and walked off towards his trailer and his waiting wife.

Logan smiled and shook his head. Then he removed his steak from the grill and put it on his plate, picked up the beer from the plastic table and went inside. He took his potato from the microwave, fixed it up and then sat down in front of the TV to eat. He thought about Lowell and his wife and what they were probably doing at that very moment and felt a pang of loneliness lance his gut. He knew the cure for that was to finish off the six-pack along with his steak. He was alone tonight, but maybe if he sold just one more car this week or next, he could give Sexy Sarah a call. Her cure for loneliness worked even better than beer or whiskey.

Logan passed out an hour later on his cheap naugahide sofa. He awoke in the morning with the familiar headache that he always woke up with after a night of drinking. It was like a nail being driven into his forehead. His breakfast was hair of the dog, as usual, and after an hour or so and a hot shower he was ready to go to his car lot. Today was a new day and maybe he would get lucky again and sell another car. Logan knew there was a fool born every minute, and maybe another one of them would wander onto his lot before the day's end.

3

Logan pulled onto his car lot and was more than a little surprised to see an older gentleman peering through the window of the lone pickup truck that he had for sale.

"Holy shit," Logan mumbled to himself as he brought his car to a stop near the door to his office. "There's no way I can be this lucky."

Logan tried to comb his hair in his rearview mirror using his fingers in a futile attempt to neaten his appearance. Then he reached for the pack of gum in his console. Despite brushing his teeth he knew the beer was still on his breath and he didn't want it to cause him to lose this sale, if there was going to be a sale. Once he had himself together he stepped out of his car. The morning was cloudy and he could feel random raindrops hitting his arms as he walked towards the gentleman looking at the pickup truck.

The man looking at the pickup truck spoke before Logan could even introduce himself. There was an authoritative tone in his voice.

"Good morning," the man said as Logan approached the truck. "The name's Bill. I need a work truck, don't give a shit if it runs good or not because I know how to work on an engine, and I've already blue booked this truck on my cellphone. So we can skip the sales pitch. What would you take for it?"

Logan could not believe his luck. He didn't have much in the truck. It had been part of deal he had made to trade several cars with a buddy of his in Lumberton who also owned a car lot.

"I'll knock a hundred off the blue book value because you said you need a work truck. I like to help the workin' man get the job done. We can step inside out of this rain if you'd like, or if you'd like to take it for a test drive I can go get the key."

"Five hundred off the blue book and we can skip the test drive. Like I said, I know how to work on an engine. The man then gave Logan a look that signaled he was finished negotiating.

Logan quickly did the math in his head. Five hundred off the blue book would still give him a profit.

"You drive a hard bargain but you've got yourself a deal," Logan said has he rubbed his chin. Let's go inside and sign the paperwork."

Thirty minutes later Logan was sitting behind his desk staring at the stack of hundred dollar bills. He loved when people paid in cash. He turned and looked through the window at the empty spot where the pickup truck had been parked and once again could not believe his luck. He had not sold a car two days in a row in, well, never. The red Toyota would pay his bills for the next month, and now his profit on the old truck could be spending money. Hell, he might even buy himself another steak. Maybe he'd buy three and invite Lowell and his wife over for dinner. And then there was Sexy Sarah. Maybe he'd give her a call later.

Logan grinned at the thought of calling Sexy Sarah. He leaned back in his desk chair and put his feet up on the desk. Then his eyes wandered to the drawer that contained the bottle of whiskey. No, he told himself. He was not going to open that drawer. He felt his mouth begin to water at the thought of having a shot but he knew he had to be strong. He knew the drinking had to stop.

Logan milled around his office for the rest of the morning. He made a few phone calls to some of the repo guys he knew and to several of the banks that he did business with. With the economy in the tank there was no shortage of repossessed cars to choose from. After lining up several cars to go check out, Logan locked up his office. He planned to go look at the cars and then get some lunch on the way back. He didn't worry about missing any business on his own lot. He had already sold the truck and he had never, in his entire time as a used car salesman had this good of a week.

Logan returned to his office with his lunch from a burger joint down the road from his lot. His attempts to make a deal on several of the cars had fallen flat. How did they expect him to make a profit if they wouldn't come down on the price? Logan turned on the small TV next to his desk and enjoyed his lunch. To hell with them anyway, he thought to himself as he bit into his burger. He didn't need their overpriced junk. He had plenty of that already sitting on his lot.

§§§

The mail was delivered around three o'clock that afternoon. Logan waved at the cute girl driving the mail Jeep and immediately felt pity for her. He had a high school friend named Gavin that had gone on to work for the Post Office as a letter carrier after graduation and had been miserable ever since. In fact, Logan could not ever recall knowing anyone that hated their job more than his friend Gavin did. The guy was truly miserable.

Logan walked out to the small mailbox by the entrance to his lot and retrieved his mail. He watched as the cute girl in the mail Jeep drove away and then had a thought about how nice it would be to nail her in her Jeep surrounded by everyone's mail. She had been his carrier now for a little over month and Logan didn't know if she was so friendly towards him because she was new on the job, or if it was because she liked him. He quickly convinced himself she was just being nice as part of the job. What would a pretty girl like her want with a guy like him anyway?

Logan flipped through the letters as he walked slowly back to his office. There were three letters from attorneys and the rest was junk mail. When he got back to his desk he threw the junk mail in the trash and tossed the other letters on his desk. He would get to them soon enough. Getting letters from the law offices of this guy or that guy was common for Logan. Most of the time he just ignored the letters until the lawyers got frustrated enough to start calling on the phone.

Logan poured himself a cup of coffee and sipped on it while he stood by the window and surveyed his lot. Two cars in two days... If business was this good all the time he wouldn't have to live in a trailer and eat bologna sandwiches or microwave pizza. Logan thought about the steak from last night. He could have one of those every week if business stayed like this. But Logan knew from experience that it wouldn't.

Once back at his desk, Logan picked up the three letters from the law offices. He recognized two of them and tossed them aside immediately. He knew what the letters were going to say, but the two people suing him had no legal recourse whatsoever. His cars were always sold "as is" with no warranty either expressed or implied. What part of "buyer beware" did these people not understand?

Logan read the return address on the third letter and almost tossed it aside out of reflex. But something in the return address caught his eye. The letter was from a law office in the town of Starlight, NC. Logan had lived in North Carolina his entire life but had never heard of a town named Starlight.

Logan held the letter up in front of his face and read the return address again. The name of the law office was Blackwell and Burns and they were located on 104 Magnolia Avenue in the town of Starlight, NC. Logan frowned as he read the complete address again. Why would a law office in a town he had never heard of be sending him a letter? All of his customers were from the Wilmington area and he didn't ever remember doing paperwork on a car with a customer from a town called Starlight. What the hell kind of name for a town was that anyway?

Logan dropped the letter on his desk and leaned back in his chair. *Just what I need*, he thought to himself. Now some out-of-town legal eagle was after him for a pound of flesh. And if it wasn't over a car, what could they be after? Maybe they wanted his shitty old trailer. Logan knew lawyers made a living by taking one-third of whatever they won in court so if they wanted one-third of his shithole trailer then they could have it. And his car lot wasn't worth much more. He was in hock for most of the cars he had for sale and by the time the bank repossessed all of them there wouldn't be enough left over to buy lunch, much less make it worth a lawyer's time to sue him. Logan ran his hands through his hair and let out a long sigh. Then he glanced at his whiskey drawer. Just one shot, he mumbled as he opened the drawer.

The shot of whiskey was good but Logan knew there was a better way to deal with this situation. He moved the envelopes and several pieces of paper aside until he found the cell phone number he was looking for. He had written it on his desk calendar. The calendar had expired several years ago but Logan knew the phone number was still good. He picked up the phone and dialed the number. A woman answered after three rings.

"Can I speak to Sarah, please?"

"Hey Logan, it's good to hear from you. How's business?" Sarah replied, cutting Logan off.

Logan smiled. He knew that Sexy Sarah knew the answer to the question. She knew he wouldn't be calling her if business was bad, which it usually was.

"Business is great, or at least it has been for the last two days. I moved two vehicles, a car and a truck. Made some coin on both. Enough to pay the rent for a month and buy myself a piece of shoe leather and a potato."

"Still eating alone?" Sarah said with a hint of playfulness in her voice.

"Well, there was Lowell, my neighbor. But he didn't eat with me. We just had a beer. He just got back from Cape something, Cape... Town or some shit like that."

Logan was stalling. He knew what he wanted, and he knew that Sexy Sarah knew what he wanted. It was her business to know what he wanted, and she was very good at her business. Finally he worked up the nerve to ask. He chided himself for being shy about it but it still bothered him that this is what his life had degenerated to. But he knew Sarah was special, and that there was a method to her madness. She had a plan and Logan knew that he was helping her with her plan while getting a little something out of it for himself.

"I'm locking up at eight tonight. Why don't you come by."

"I think I can accommodate that request, Mr. Shaw. Anything else?"

"Wear the black one. Match it to your stockings."

"Yes sir. Eight o'clock it is. See you then."

With that the phone line went dead. Logan placed the receiver on the base and leaned back in his chair and rubbed his eyes. It had been a while since he had made enough extra cash to give Sexy Sarah a call. He knew he should probably save his money because he would most likely not sell another car for the rest of the month, but it was either her or the whiskey bottle. And it didn't take a genius to figure out which one was the better choice.

The rest of the day passed slowly for Logan. Around a quarter to eight he walked over and flipped the switch on the OPEN sign in the window next to the front door, extinguishing its yellow neon glow. Then he drew the shades and turned off all of the lights except for one small lamp sitting on a table in the corner of the office. He wanted just enough light to be able to see what Sarah would be wearing. He took three one hundred dollar bills out of his desk drawer and laid them on his calendar where Sarah would see them. He knew she was worth every penny.

Right on time, Sarah drove up in the BMW he had sold her six months ago. He watched through the blinds as she stepped out of the car. She was wearing a black skirt and a white blouse and looked very business-like. Logan realized she would look right at home in any corporate boardroom. But he was not surprised. He knew Sarah was no bottom-dollar streetwalker. She was both classy and sexy, and any man that would cheat on her for another woman had to qualify and the dumbest man on the planet as far as Logan was concerned.

Logan knew Sarah would come in without knocking so he walked over and sat down in his desk chair. He knew Sarah would walk right in and lock the door behind her. She knew the routine.

"Well hey there, car man," Sarah said as she closed the door behind her. Just as Logan had suspected he heard the deadbolt click after Sarah closed the door.

"You look like a million dollars of tax-free money," Logan said as Sarah walked across the small office before finally stopping beside his desk. Logan rotated his chair to face her as a smile worked its way onto his face. Hell yes this was going to be better than a damn bottle of whiskey. A whole lot better.

Sarah didn't say a word. She walked behind Logan's chair and put her hands on his shoulders. He closed his eyes and exhaled as she slowly began to give him a massage. Then she moved her hands down his chest and began to unbutton his shirt while kissing the side of his neck. He knew that the most expensive bottle of whiskey in the world could not compare to the touch of Sexy Sarah.

When she finished unbuttoning his shirt, Sarah rotated the chair until Logan was facing her. Then she slowly descended to her knees while her hands slide down his bare chest. When her hands touched his belt buckle he felt a wave of pleasure wash over his body. To Logan there was nothing quite like the feeling of a beautiful woman unbuckling his belt.

Logan drew in a deep breath as Sarah slowly took him into her mouth. He felt the stress of an entire month of trying to sell cars and keep his head above water instantly evaporate as Sarah moved slowly up and down. Just when he thought he would explode, Sarah stopped and stood up in front of him. She reached up and released the clip in the back of her hair, letting it spill onto her shoulders. Logan watched as she slowly unbuttoned her blouse and let it fall to the floor revealing an expensive black lace bra. Then she unbuttoned her skirt and let it fall to her feet. Just has he had requested she was wearing a black garter belt that matched her stockings, and no panties.

Sarah moved over Logan and guided him into her. At first she moved slowly but then began to grind against him faster and faster. His hands moved over the lace material of her bra and then down to the garter belt. Before long he felt his climax building. He finally let go as Sarah let out a long moan while holding onto his shoulders. Then she collapsed and leaned forward onto Logan, both of them panting and out of breath.

§§§

"You know Logan, you're a good guy. You can do better than this," Sarah said as she waved her arm and motioned to his small office. She was dressed and had herself together. Logan had done the same and was still sitting in his desk chair. "You just need the right woman, that's all."

"Yeah, well my mother-in-law said I'd never amount to anything. I mean my ex-mother-in-law, that is. Maybe she was right." Logan looked down into his lap, almost ashamed of himself. Sarah just shook her head at him.

"I'm just a used car salesman," Logan said as he raised his eyes and admired Sarah. She had gotten up and walked across his office to the front window. She was peeking through the blinds at the cars out on the lot. He was once again taken aback by her beauty. He could not take his eyes off her long, slender legs.

"You can be more and you know it," Sarah said as she let go of the blind and looked over at Logan in his chair.

"I guess," he finally replied. He decided to try and change the subject.

"So how are things going for you?" he asked Sarah as she walked back over and sat down in the chair next to his desk. He could see a hint of satisfaction in her dark eyes.

"I'm almost finished with them, every last one of the partners in my husband's firm. Only one is left, and he's the top guy. Once I have him, I'm going to ruin them all."

Logan couldn't help but smile. He hated lawyers as much as Sarah did.

"I've fucked every last one of them and I've got the audio to prove it. You know lawyers and politicians rue the day the cellphone was invented. Once I get done with the last partner then I'll make sure every last one of their wives gets an email with an attachment. I made sure I screamed each of their names when I had sex with them just so their wives could hear it. The first thing the partners will do is fire my sorry ass husband and that will complete my revenge. It will serve him right for cheating on me. Since his affair he thinks I've forgiven him because I haven't left. But I haven't forgiven him. I'm just biding my time."

"So why are you here with me? I'm no lawyer. What gives?" Logan said as he leaned forward and put his elbows on his desk.

Sarah paused for a moment, got up and then walked back over to the front window of the office. She peeked through the blinds again and then turned towards Logan.

"You were nice to me, Logan, nice to me on a day that was probably the worst day of my life up until that point. I had just found out my husband was cheating on me and I was in a state of shock. I wasn't thinking clearly. I took some money out of the bank and just wanted to run. I didn't want half of what he had, half of the house, or any of that crap. I just wanted to run away. So I just started walking. It must have walked for hours before and I finally came here. I saw the cars and figured that any one of them could be my ticket out of town."

Logan was silent. Sarah had never opened up to him like this before. He knew her situation but these details were something new to him. She had never told him any of this.

"And here's what did it, Logan. I had heard stories about used car salesmen. I fully expected that I'd have to blow you in your office, or let you fuck me bent over your desk to get a good deal on a car. But you didn't try that with me. You were nice to me and I've never forgotten it. You're a good guy, Logan. You may not be rich, and I know you probably have a bottle over there in your desk, but deep down inside you're a nice guy. I like you. You give me faith that there might be a few good men left in the world."

With that Sarah reached for the knob on the deadbolt. Before Logan could say anything she pulled the door open and stepped out into the darkness. Logan stood up and called out to her but after a few seconds he heard her crank the BMW. The sound of the engine was followed by the crunch of gravel under the tires as Sarah drove off the lot.

Logan let out a long breath. He was bowled over by what Sarah had just told him. He ran his fingers through his hair and then looked down at his desk. The three one hundred dollar bills were still lying on his desk calendar.

Sarah had apparently decided that she didn't want his money.

4

Two days after his evening with Sarah, Logan was in his office watching heavy rain pelt the cars on his lot. Rain was bad for business. But then again the sun had been out yesterday and no one had walked onto his lot. He was convinced that his lucky streak was over and things were now back to normal.

Outside the thunder was getting louder as the rain hammered the roof and walls of his office. With nothing to do, Logan walked over and sat down at his desk. After a few moments he picked up the letter from the law office in Starlight.

Logan pulled his cellphone out of the clip on his belt and did a search on the name of the town. The only town by the name of Starlight came up somewhere in the middle of New Mexico. No such town was found in the state of North Carolina. Logan then searched the name of the law firm and found no firm by the name of Blackwell and Burns anywhere in the country. The closest match was a firm that contained the name Burns but it was in Kansas City.

Logan looked at the screen on his cellphone. He was glad he had sold the red Toyota and settled up with his provider over the bill. Otherwise he wouldn't even have service. Still, he wished he could find something on this law office. He knew that all he had to do was rip open the letter and read it if he wanted to find out more, but it was raining outside and he was bored. He figured the least he could do was play up the mystery of this strange letter from a town that he couldn't even find on the Internet.

With his curiosity now at its peak, Logan finally ripped open the envelope and removed the letter inside. He unfolded the single sheet of paper and began to read.

Dear Mr. Shaw,
As the attorney of record for the estate of the late Rosemary Abigail Shaw, it is my

18

duty to inform you that you have been named as the sole beneficiary in her will. Mrs. Shaw was very specific in her last will and testament that you be located and notified at the time of her death. The instructions in her will state that you are to be told in person of your inheritance, therefore please understand that I cannot convey any details to you over the phone. Please visit my office at your earliest convenience so that we may discuss this matter.

To my knowledge you are the only family member of Mrs. Shaw to survive her. I have represented Mrs. Shaw for many years and the discussions I had with her before her death led me to believe that you have been unaware of your connection to her over the years. I will provide more details when we meet in my office.

Very Truly Yours,
Harmon Blackwell III, Attorney at Law

Logan read the letter again and then dropped it on his desk calendar. Then he frowned as he looked down at the letter.

"What the fuck?" he said after staring at the letter for almost a minute.

Logan picked up the letter and read it one more time. Then he began to smile. After a few seconds, he began to laugh.

"Jeez, what kind of shit is this?" Logan said as his voice echoed through his empty office. "Somebody has way too much time on their hands. I'll bet it's that shithead Gavin over at the Post Office. He probably typed up this crap and talked my new mail girl into sticking the envelope in my mailbox."

Logan was beginning to believe his theory until his eyes caught sight of the postmark on the envelope. If Gavin had typed it up as a joke, he had actually mailed it like a normal letter. Logan knew his buddy was a cheapskate so he found it hard to believe that Gavin would waste money on a stamp just to pull off a practical joke. But maybe he did. The fact that Logan had not been able to find the town of Starlight or a law office by the name of Blackwell and Burns anywhere on the Internet only helped to convince him that the letter was a joke. If the town existed, surely he would have been able to find in online. And every business has a webpage nowadays, Logan thought as continued to try and convince himself that Gavin was having fun with him.

Logan looked at the letterhead. There was a phone number listed, along with the address of 104 Magnolia Avenue, Starlight, NC. He immediately picked up his cellphone and dialed the number on the letterhead. He was greeted by the friendly voice of a woman.

"Blackwell and Burns, may I help you?"

"Uh, yes, my name is Logan Shaw. May I speak to mister, uh," Logan fumbled for the letter. He had suddenly forgotten the name of the attorney that had signed it. When he located the name he regained his composure. "Uh, yes, Harmon Blackwell. May I speak to Harmon Blackwell, please?"

"Mr. Blackwell is in court today. May I take a message?"

Logan was suddenly at a loss of words. Apparently this wasn't a joke. Or if it was, Gavin had gone to great lengths to make it all seem real. This was apparently a bona fide law office with real attorneys.

"I'll just call him back tomorrow. Thank you."

Logan hung up the phone before the woman on the other end could say goodbye. He immediately felt embarrassed by his actions. What was wrong with him? This was apparently a real letter, written by a real attorney from a real law office. That meant there might be a real inheritance just like the letter said. But who in the hell was Rosemary Shaw? He knew of no relative by that name. Logan knew very little about his family's roots. There had been no family reunions over the years and his mother and father had never shared any details about anyone else in the family before their deaths. All they had ever told him was that they had a very small family and that the three of them were the only ones still living.

Logan stared at his phone for a few seconds and then put it back in the case on his belt. What in the world was going on? The thought of actually inheriting something was dancing around in his mind despite his best attempts to stop it. What if it was a fortune? What if some old aunt of his that was estranged from the family had died and left him a million dollars? How nice would that be? He would finally be able to give up the lousy car business and retire to the Keys. Logan liked the idea of not selling cars anymore. Maybe he'd ask Sexy Sarah to run away with him. They could spend their days with their toes in the sand and umbrella drinks in their hands, and their nights having sex under the stars.

A loud crack of thunder broke Logan free of his daydream about rich aunts and running away with Sarah. A bright flash of lightening blistered the windows of his office, followed by another clap of thunder a few seconds later. The storm was getting worse. He knew that he was wasting his time in his office on a day with such crappy weather. No one would go car shopping in this weather.

Logan decided that Gavin probably didn't have anything to do with the letter about this Rosemary Shaw lady. He would just have to call the law office back tomorrow and see if he could get the lawyer to tell him something. But then Logan remembered what the letter said about this. Maybe he wouldn't be able to get Mr. Blackwell to spill the beans about Rosemary Shaw, but Logan knew that he would at least be able to get the lawyer to confirm that he had sent the letter.

Logan thought about how he had not been able to find the town of Starlight on the Internet. Either the attorney would have to tell him where the town was located or Logan knew he would have to find it on a map himself. For all he knew it could be on the other side of the state, way up in the mountains. Or it could be less than an hour's drive away. He had no way of knowing until he found the town on a map.

§§§

Logan brought his car to a stop outside of the public library. He had spent thirty minutes digging through the drawers in his desk and then every box in the small storeroom in the back of his office. He could have sworn he had an old road atlas tucked away somewhere but he had not been able to find it. Who used those things anymore? But modern technology was failing him so he had hoped that he could find the town of Starlight on his old atlas. But he had not been able to find it. He had finally given up and decided that he was going stir crazy in his office. That's when he came up with the idea of going to the public library. At least it would give him something to do.

The library was in an old brick building that dated back to the early 1900's. It was in downtown Wilmington about halfway between Logan's car lot and his trailer by the port. He figured that even if he couldn't find the town's location in the library that at least he was halfway home. He would dig around in some old books about the state and then hit a taco drive-thru on his way to his trailer. Then he would watch whatever old movie he could find on TV and fall asleep on his couch. It would be just another typical Friday night for him, just like the last one and the one before that.

The musty smell of books brought back memories when Logan walked through the huge front doors of the public library. The last time he had been in a library was in high school, and that was only because he had not had a choice in the matter. He didn't much like to read but if the mood did came over him he usually just hit a used book store or the pawn shop that was close to his car lot. Sometimes in the winter reading a book was the only way to cure the boredom of being cooped up in his small office waiting on a customer to wander onto the lot.

"May I help you?" the librarian said as Logan approached the counter.

"Yes ma'am. I'm looking for old road maps of the state of North Carolina. I'm looking for a small town that I can't seem to find on any of the Internet maps."

"What's the name of the town?" the woman said as she peeked over the reading glasses perched on the end of her nose.

"Starlight," Logan replied.

The woman crinkled her nose and Logan watched as her reading glasses rose up closer to her eyes.

"I've never heard of it," she finally replied.

"Me neither. Can you point me to the section where I might find a book about North Carolina? Maybe one with maps in it?"

The woman told Logan to go to the second floor and then to the rear of the building. There along the back wall she told him he would find lots of books about North Carolina and that many of them would have maps of the state that went back over a hundred years. Logan thanked her and headed for the stairwell.

Once he got to the back wall he was overwhelmed with the number of books about the state of North Carolina. All he really wanted was an old map, or maybe even just a new one. But it was raining outside and he had nothing else to do so Logan decided to take his time and look at a few of the books. What could it hurt to maybe learn a little something about the state he was born and raised in?

Logan pulled a large book from the shelf that looked like it might contain a lot of pictures. He sat down at the table and began to flip through the pages. The book was a collection of black and white photographs taken all across the state starting back around the time of the First World War.

Flipping through the pages Logan saw old photos of Moonshiners and their stills way up in the Blue Ridge Mountains, along with photos of some of the larger cities in the state when they were nothing more than small towns. Logan was amazed at how many horses were in the photographs. Then he flipped to the index in the back of the book and looked for the town of Starlight. It was not listed.

Frustrated, Logan returned the book to the shelf and then began to walk down the aisle until he spotted another book. He turned his head sideways and read the title engraved on the binding.

One Hundred Years of the Golden Leaf in North Carolina, 1850 to 1950.

Logan whispered the words as he read the title, then he pulled the book from the shelf and sat back down at the table. He knew he could just go find the town on a road atlas but all that would tell him was where it was located. He wanted to see if he could learn a little more about the town before he did that.

"What the hell is a golden leaf?" Logan mumbled as he opened the book. There were only three other people on this floor of the library but he still didn't want to disturb them. One of them, a very pretty young girl wearing a college T-shirt, glanced up at him. He smiled at her and then turned his attention to the book in front of him. The first page of the book had a photo of a large plant with yellow-green leaves. Underneath the photo was a caption that read Tobacco, The Golden Leaf.

Logan read the paragraph underneath the photo of the tobacco plant and learned that it was called the golden leaf not only because of the color of the leaves but also because of the money a farmer could make from a crop of tobacco. Other crops paled in comparison to tobacco when it came to profit. The leaves might as well have actually been made out of gold.

Flipping through the pages of the book Logan didn't see the connection between money and the people working the fields in the photos. They looked extremely poor to him. They also looked like they were about to drop dead from exhaustion. Even the mules looked tired, Logan thought.

Logan read a few more paragraphs while continuing to look at the pictures. All of the people looked poor as dirt and Logan still wondered how the term "golden leaf" could be related to their lives.

When Logan got to the back of the book, to the portion which chronicled the middle of the 20th century, he noticed that things had greatly improved for the farmers. Tobacco by that time was wildly popular and farmers were making a very good living growing it. Machinery had made it easier but it was still hard work. On a page entitled "the government and the golden leaf" Logan learned that the government regulated how much tobacco could be planted, and that only farmers who had a government-issued allotment could plant it. This caused profits for farmers to be even higher since only those with a tobacco allotment could grow it and then sell it at the market. And North Carolina, Logan learned, produced more tobacco than any state in the country.

Amazed that he had been born and raised in North Carolina and that all of this tobacco stuff was news to him, Logan closed the book and frowned. He didn't smoke and neither had his parents when they had been alive. It wouldn't have mattered if they had smoked, Logan thought, because they had both died young anyway. His father had died in a car wreck and his mother had died several years after that from some sort of liver problem. Logan had only been twenty-five years old when his mother had passed leaving him to carry on all by himself.

Logan felt a pang of sorrow at the thought of this. His parents had not left him much, and once everything had been settled all that was left was enough money to buy his old trailer and a few used cars to start his business. There had been no life insurance and the bank had taken the house. It had been a struggle for Logan ever since. Over five years of hard work and he had little to show for it. His car lot had grown slightly and for right now his head was above water, but Logan never knew what tomorrow would bring so he had quit worrying about tomorrow years ago. He took life one day at a time.

Snapping out of his reverie, Logan suddenly remembered the town of Starlight. He reopened the book and flipped to the index. He ran his finger down the page and found the town listed on page 285.

Logan found the page and was greeted by several more photos of people working in the fields of tobacco. At the top of the page was an outline of the state of North Carolina, with a small red dot denoting the location of Starlight. It was on the banks of the Skeleton River in the middle of the eastern portion of the state. From the photos on the page it was easy for Logan to surmise that Starlight was nothing more than just a small tobacco town in the middle of nowhere.

The photos on the page looked like most of the other photos in the book, grainy and black and white. There were people working the fields, large carts full of tobacco leaves being pulled by mules and several photos of small barns with smoke coming out of the chimneys. Logan noticed there were lots of children in the photographs picking tobacco out in the hot summer sun. They looked tired and worn out, just like the adults did. Logan figured that back in those days the whole family had to work just to be able to survive, and the kids in the photos looked none too happy about it.

Logan read the captions of the photographs and some of the text on the page. It mainly talked about how tobacco had put Starlight on the map and that almost everyone in town was connected to it whether they actually grew it or not.

Several of the photos showed the small main street area of Starlight and two other photos showed large antebellum homes that Logan knew were probably over a hundred and fifty years old. Apparently someone in the town had some money, Logan thought as he looked at the homes. The last photo on the page, taken in the 1950's portrayed Starlight as a nice little country town with just enough people living in it to keep it going.

All of this information about Starlight now led Logan to the obvious question – what in the hell did the town have to do with him? Why had some lost relative that he had never met named him as the sole beneficiary in her will? Who was she? Had his parents known about her? If they did, they had certainly never let on to him that she existed. Why? Logan had no answers.

Logan got up and put the book back on the shelf. Then he walked over to where the maps were located. He pulled a road atlas off the shelf and it didn't take him long to find the town of Starlight on the page containing the state of North Carolina. The atlas was dated 1963.

Just as the other book had indicated, Starlight was nestled on the banks of the Skeleton River, a river that Logan had never heard of. To Logan's relief Starlight looked like it would be less than a few hours' drive from Wilmington. None of the major highways were close to the town, so he knew that he would have to travel along the back roads to get there.

Logan took the atlas to the desk and checked it out after filling out the short form to get a library card.

5

William Sparks moved quickly through the tobacco field, a cane pole in one hand and a small bucket full of chicken livers in the other. He was young, in his late teens, and even though he was tired from picking tobacco all day with his family he still wanted to do a little catfishing before he turned in for the night. The rest of his brothers had already gone to bed, and he had promised his mother that he would only be gone for an hour or two. She had fussed at him, reminding him that he needed his sleep so that he could work the fields tomorrow, but had then reluctantly agreed that maybe a little catfishing would be the best way for him to take the edge off of another long day in the hot sun. William was her oldest and as such she often let him do things that his younger brothers were not allowed to do. And after all, what kind of life was it for young man like him to just work the fields from dawn to dusk?

William's mother knew that the world was a dark place and getting worse by the day. She had seen the newsreels about what was going on in Europe and she feared that all of her boys would be called to service if the United States got involved in the war. This wore heavy on her heart as she stood at the window of the sharecropper house and watched William as he moved down the edge of the field towards the river. The harvest moon gave off enough light that she could see him, as well as the bank of the Skeleton River in the distance.

William knew better than venture into the field on his way to the river. He smiled when he looked up at the moon, remembering how his dad had always told him that catfish bite better under a harvest moon. He shrugged off the stories he had heard after moving to town with his family about what sometimes happens in the tobacco fields around Starlight under the light of a harvest moon. Tonight he kept his mind on the catfish and the big five pounder that he knew was waiting on him in the river. Maybe his bucket of chicken livers would do the trick. He knew that catfish loved chicken livers the way he loved his mama's chicken pot pie.

His father had planted the tobacco almost right up to the edge of the riverbank. Once William reached the river, he stepped onto the small clearing that ran from the tobacco down to the water not more than twenty feet away. He was pleasantly surprised to find the soil of the riverbank solid instead of the muddy mess he had encountered several weeks ago when he had last gone fishing. That trip had yielded no catfish but William had a plan tonight to make sure that didn't happen again. Tonight he was going to try a new fishing hole. This one was just a ways down the river bank where an old tree had fallen over into the water. He figured that it wouldn't hurt if he walked down the riverbank until he got to that fishing hole. What difference would it make as long as he stayed out of the tobacco field?

William walked quietly down the riverbank, his cane pole by his side along with his pale of chicken livers. They were beginning to stink, and he knew this was like ringing the dinner bell for a big catfish. The worse the bait smelled the better, and William just knew that tonight would be the night and that he would catch a catfish large enough to feed his entire family.

The light of the harvest moon reflected off of the mirror-like surface of the Skeleton River as William walked down the riverbank. The light was bright enough that his body cast a shadow on the ground in front of him. The night was beginning to cool and William felt a shiver run down his back and he chided himself for not bringing his matches. A small fire on the riverbank would be just the ticket on a crisp September night like tonight.

William tried to force himself to look out over the river as he walked down the bank. But he couldn't help but glance over at the tobacco plants bathed in the light of the harvest moon. Most of them were almost bare, save for the few leaves near the top of the plants. The harvest was almost complete.

William stopped when he got to the large oak tree that had fallen over into the river. The tree marked the fishing hole that he was looking for. He knew the big cats liked to lie on the bottom near the submerged tree limbs. All he had to do was bait his hook and get one of those smelly, bloody chicken livers into the water and he was bound to catch something in no time at all.

William sat down on a small log someone had cut and left on the bank. It made the perfect seat. The light from the moon was bright enough that he could easily see to bait his hook. He reached into his bucket and removed two chicken livers. He speared each of them with his hook and then lifted his cane pole in the air. He gave the bait a gentle toss and watched as it splashed about twenty feet from the shore. Perfect, he thought to himself. Now all he had to do was be patient.

About fifteen minutes passed before William felt a bite on the end of his line. He knew better than to yank his pole right away. The trick was to let the catfish take the bait into its mouth first. William knew that once the catfish did this that it would lie there for sometimes as much as thirty minutes just sucking on the bait. When the catfish decided to move off to another spot, that was when William knew would be the best time to pull his rod and hook the fish.

A cool breeze sifted through the tobacco plants in the field behind William. He turned his head and looked at the plants bathed in the yellow light of the harvest moon. Just then he thought he heard a voice, just a whisper as the wind slid across the river and into the fields behind him. The breeze caused him to shiver but he shook it off. He was a young man, he thought to himself, and a young man didn't need a coat until it got cold enough to snow. He turned his attention back to his pole, sure that his big catfish would run with his bait at any moment.

William heard another whisper from the field behind him. He turned his head quickly to try and see where it was coming from. Maybe it was his brother playing a joke on him, he thought. That would be just like him. He had done that last month and nearly scared William out of his skin after sneaking up behind him when he was fishing on the riverbank late one night. William remembered how embarrassed he had been after he screamed like a girl when his brother grabbed him from behind.

The only thing William could see were the tobacco plants, their remaining leaves gently swaying in the light breeze. Then he heard it again. It was definitely a human voice, and William knew immediately that his brother had to be up to his old tricks again.

"I'll teach Jimmy a damn lesson this time. Trying to sneak up on me through the fields, I'll show him."

William laid his cane pole down on the riverbank and propped the end of it on a large rock near the water's edge. Then he stood and looked at the tobacco field. He knew that his brother was crazy to try to sneak up on him through that field, but William knew his brother was not known for being very smart. It would be just like him to ignore the warnings about the field. Everyone in town knew better than to go into that tobacco field during the night of the harvest moon. The talk around town was that two people had already been murdered in the fields over the years.

William walked to the edge of the plants. His sudden desire to whip his brother's ass for trying to sneak up on him was suddenly tempered by the voice of his mother warning him, as she had all her boys, about the field. But William knew that he had to teach his brother a lesson. And William realized that if his brother really was in the field then it was his responsibility to get him out as fast as he could, ass whipping or not.

Against his better judgment William stepped into the row of tobacco plants directly in front of him. He would find his brother and then they would get the hell out of the field and back to the fishing hole. William looked back at his pole one more time and then began to walk across the rows of tobacco plants towards the middle of the field, stepping between the plants as he went.

"Jimmy, come on out. I know it's you. We need to get out of this field. Mom will tan our hides if she finds out about this. Come on out!"

William tried to keep his voice low but strong enough so that his brother could hear him. The tobacco plants were only about waist high so William knew his brother was probably crouched down just a few rows over and would pounce on him at any moment. As soon as he did that, William planned on dragging his brother out of the field and back down to the riverbank. Maybe by then the big catfish would be ready to run and they could pull him in and go home.

"Jimmy! Come on… Joke's over."

A strong breeze suddenly rolled through the field causing all of the tobacco plants to sway in unison. William waited for his brother to stand up and try to scare him, but Jimmy did not appear. William began to worry. Perhaps his brother was not in the field after all. And if he wasn't, then William knew he had made a terrible mistake.

William stopped in the row and stood completely still. He scanned the sea of yellow-gold leaves glowing softly in the moonlight. As the breeze died down the leaves of the tobacco plants stopped dancing and became eerily still. William felt Goosebumps rise across his arms.

Fear washed through William's abdomen as he realized that his brother was not in the field. What had he been thinking? William knew it had been hard enough for him to convince his mother to let him go fishing tonight much less let his younger brother out of the house. His mother would have never allowed that, and William knew that his brother Jimmy would not have dared sneak out of the house without asking. He knew that Jimmy would get their father's belt for doing something like that.

William knew he needed to get out of the field and back to the riverbank. That was the shortest route to safety. He began to move down the row as quickly as he could, trying to watch his step in the dark shadows between the plants. Then he turned and cut through a row of plants and headed straight for the point where he had entered the field. Suddenly it seemed that the moon was not nearly as bright as it had been just a few minutes before, but William knew this was just his imagination. Terror was clawing at his insides and he knew he wasn't thinking clearly.

Suddenly William lost his balance when he stepped in a low spot in a row, causing him to fall face first into the dirt between the plants. He cursed to himself as he got up on his hands and knees while spitting the sandy soil out of his mouth. He knew better than to run so fast down the row.

William felt a little safer now that he was hidden in the shadows down between the tobacco plants. He took a moment to catch his breath and then he began to feel sick to his stomach. He wiped his face with his hand and then sat back on his heels. He did not hear the rustling of the tobacco leaves as the dark figure moved down the row towards him.

The blade of the tobacco axe cut through the chilled air and buried itself into William's back, just between his shoulder blades. He screamed out in agony as his head jerked to the rear. Then he fell forward before rolling onto his back. It was then that he saw the killer silhouetted against the moonlit sky.

Before William could raise his arms, the sharp blade flashed in the moonlight as it descended towards his face, cutting into the bridge of his nose and splitting his head like a melon. Death came instantly. The blade continued to rise and fall violently until William's body was chopped into a bloody mass of flesh. Just as with the previous victims, the killer was not satisfied with merely taking a life. Full of rage, and with an insatiable desire for revenge, the killer always chopped and hacked the victims with the tobacco axe until not even the family could recognize the body.

It was over as quickly as it started. The killer moved away from William's lifeless body as another strong breeze rolled across the field. Down by the riverbank, the tip of William's pole began to twitch and jerk. Suddenly the entire pole was dragged into the river as the big catfish took off with the bait, leaving only the bucket of chicken livers to mark the spot where William Sparks had fished for the last time in his life.

6

2014

When Logan left the library the rain had stopped. The sky above was dark but the distant horizon burned a fiery orange. The storm had cleared and the air was scented with the smell of hot asphalt and rainwater. Logan thought that maybe tonight he would use his grill again. He remembered that he had half a pack of hot dogs in his refrigerator and that a couple of them cooked on his grill would be a nice supper. It wasn't sirloin, but it was the next best thing as far as he was concerned. He was just too tired to stop at the grocery store.

Once back at the trailer park Logan was dismayed to see the lights out in Lowell's trailer. He knew Lowell made good money when he was at sea and Logan figured that Lowell had probably decided to take his wife out on the town to celebrate his return home. Logan chuckled when he thought about Lowell's wife opening the door to their trailer to call for her husband. With that business taken care of Logan figured that now Lowell and his wife were probably at one of the seafood pubs down by the beach eating steamed shrimp and drinking beer. Logan felt a pang of loneliness when he thought of Lowell and his wife out on the town for the night. He envied Lowell for having someone.

Logan removed the hot dogs from the crisper and laid them on the counter. He went out to start his grill and then realized he had left the bag of charcoal outside last night and the bag was now soaked from the rain. He cursed and went back in the house. He would just have to settle for boiling the hot dogs on the stove.

Logan put the hot dogs in a pot of water and turned on the stove, then went and took a quick shower. After his shower, he put a few dogs in buns and grabbed a paper plate out of the cabinet. Before long he was parked in front of his television eating his supper and watching one of the more popular shows where cheating husbands were confronted by their wives.

Logan ate one of his hot dogs while a pretty young woman had to be pulled off of her husband kicking and screaming after his mistress was brought on the stage.

"It's not always the husband doing the cheating," Logan said to the television as he chewed his hot dog. Despite his problems, particularly with alcohol, Logan knew that he would never be a cheating man and that if he ever was lucky enough to have another woman that the last place he would find himself would be on the stage of a TV show being slapped by his wife for cheating on her.

Sarah... Logan suddenly thought about Sarah. Her husband had cheated on her and she was gorgeous, much prettier than the women he was watching on the television show. Logan just shook his head. Maybe it was just in the blood of some men to cheat on their wives.

Logan finished his supper and watched a few hours of television until he finally fell asleep on the couch. He awoke sometime after midnight and went and crawled into his bed. He was proud of himself for not stopping at a convenience store to buy beer for the evening. A beer or two would have certainly made his hot dogs taste better, but he knew that it was time to get off the bottle and he knew that it would take every ounce of willpower he had to do it.

Once in his bed Logan laid awake for almost an hour while thinking about the letter from the attorney, the town of Starlight, and all the images he had seen in the books in the library. In the morning he would pack an overnight bag and drive to the town. Whatever his inheritance was it was his for the taking according to the letter. Apparently this long lost relative of his wanted him to have something and Logan knew he had little to lose by spending a day or two on a roadtrip to Starlight to find out what it was. Maybe she was rich and had left him her old Bentley or maybe a Rolls Royce. The thought of this caused Logan to smile. How would that look, him driving onto his old used car lot driving a car like that? Logan chuckled lightly at this idea and then finally drifted off to sleep.

§§§

The next morning Logan awoke just after sunrise. He went into the kitchen and made a pot of coffee and then took a quick shower. Breakfast was a couple of eggs and toast, washed down with several more cups of coffee.

"A man with a pot of coffee can do anything," Logan announced to his empty trailer, as if it could understand him. He turned up his cup and took the last swallow of coffee. Then he went into his bedroom and packed his overnight bag with two pairs of jeans and a few of his favorite shirts. He made sure one of his shirts had a collar on it. He planned to change into it before he met the attorney so that he would look presentable. It was obvious that this long lost relative of his had been wealthy and Logan didn't want to show up for his inheritance looking like he didn't have a penny to his name.

Once he was finished packing Logan took his overnight bag and sat it on the couch. Then he suddenly had a bright idea. Before he could talk himself out of it he grabbed his cellphone and dialed Sarah's number.

"Logan?" Sarah sounded half asleep when she answered her phone.

"Hey," Logan said, suddenly ashamed of himself for calling Sarah so early in the morning. He hadn't even thought about it before dialing her number.

"Logan, what's up? Is something wrong? You've never called me this early in the morning."

"I'm sorry," Logan said. "And I just realized you must be at home. I hope I didn't wake your husband."

"He's in Myrtle Beach for a big golf tournament. She's with him." Logan could hear the edge in Sarah's voice at the mention of her husband's mistress. Logan knew that Sarah planned to leave her husband when she was finished with her plan and that she knew he was still cheating on her, but it didn't ease the pain of knowing he was out of town and holed up in a fancy hotel with another woman.

"So you're alone?" Logan said as a flicker of hope danced in his chest.

"I'm alone," Sarah answered.

Logan decided to just ask her what he wanted to ask her. He figured he had little to lose.

"Say, I just got a letter from an attorney in the town of Starlight. It's some little one-horse town a few hours north of here. Apparently some long lost estranged aunt or whatever she is has left me something in her will. The letter said the will stipulated that I be told in person of the inheritance so I have to ride up there to see what it is. I was wondering if you, well, I was wondering if you wanted to ride up there with me. You know, just for the hell of it."

Sarah was silent for a few seconds. It seemed like minutes to Logan.

"Oh Logan, I'd love to. But I've got plans tonight. You know that partner I was telling you about? He's coming over to my house tonight to help me with an insurance policy. At least that's what he thinks he's coming over to do. And he knows my husband is out of town. You remember my plan, right?"

Logan closed his eyes and winced. Yes, he remembered Sarah's plan to have sex with every married attorney in her husband's firm and then ruin their marriages by emailing the proof to their wives. Logan couldn't understand why he was so disappointed and he felt a flash of jealously at the thought of Sarah having sex with another man. What was wrong with him? It wasn't like they were dating. Why did he care?

"Hey, don't worry about it. I thought you might like to go on a road trip. You know, through the countryside, eating gas station food, listening to the radio, that sort of thing. But it's cool. No worries. I wish you the best of luck tonight, Sarah. Like I've always said, your husband is the biggest fool on the planet."

Logan chided himself for rambling. The last thing he wanted to do was sound pitiful to Sarah. There was an uncomfortable pause in their conversation but then Sarah finally spoke.

"You'll have to tell me all about this long lost relative of yours when you get back," Sarah said. Logan could sense that she wanted to get off the phone. *Who am I kidding?* he thought to himself. He knew Sarah had better things to do than to waste her time on the phone with a man who moved used cars for a living.

7

Logan tossed his overnight bag in the backseat of his car and then got behind the wheel. The atlas from the library was lying on the passenger's seat. He would have much rather had Sarah's perfect ass in the seat instead of the atlas but he knew that it had been a foolish thing to hope for. Today it would just be him and the forty year old atlas.

The sky above was clear and the air carried the industrial scent of the nearby shipping port. He knew he should probably go tell Lowell where he was going and ask him to watch his trailer while he was gone, but Logan knew that Lowell and his wife were probably still asleep recovering from their night on the town.

Logan already felt bad about waking Sarah up this morning and asking her, like a stupid teenage boy, if she wanted to go on a road trip with him. Logan didn't want to compound his guilt by waking up Lowell and his wife to tell them he was going on some damn fool snipe hunt to a little tobacco town that he was sure Lowell and his wife had never heard of. Besides, he had already told Sarah so at least one person knew where he would be if something happened to him. Logan grinned and shook his head. What could happen to him? About the only thing he could think of would be him dosing behind the wheel and driving off the road into a tree or a bridge abutment. Logan knew that few people, if anyone, would even care if that actually happened to him.

Logan flipped open the atlas and found the page he was looking for. He traced a few lines on the map to figure out where to go and then tossed the atlas back onto the seat. He flipped open his cellphone and called the Harmon Blackwell's office in Starlight. He was greeted by the same friendly voice that had greeted him the last time he called. He informed the lady that he would be in Starlight by that afternoon. She told him Mr. Blackwell was free after 1 p.m. and that he could come by any time after that.

He cranked his car and rolled down the windows. In a few minutes he was headed up the coast highway on his way to a town that he was still not convinced would actually be there once he got to the point on the map. He couldn't figure out why he had to find an old atlas to locate the town of Starlight, and seriously had no idea why he wasn't able to find the town on the Internet. Everything was on the Internet, he thought to himself as he began to fumble with the dial on the radio.

Logan hit a drive-thru window of a fast food joint and got himself one more cup of coffee and a sausage biscuit to go with it since he was still hungry. Then he got back onto the coastal highway and headed north. As the salt air circulated around the interior of his car, he took a sip of his coffee and realized that he had seen worse days than this. He knew that as long as he just took one day at a time that he would be okay. And for today at least he had a nice cup of coffee in his hand, gas in his tank and the smell of the ocean around him. He was alone, but he was used to the feeling. A few more months of it and he knew he would get to the point where he wouldn't even care.

§§§

Thirty minutes north of Wilmington, Logan left the coastal highway and turned northwest onto Highway 6. According to his atlas he needed to follow this road for about fifty miles. Then he would turn north onto State Road 7 that would lead, at least according to his forty year old atlas, right into Starlight.

Logan sipped his coffee and finished his biscuit as he watched the countryside glide by. An occasional farmhouse and barn sitting in the middle of a huge field were the only signs of civilization. Logan tried to figure out what was growing in each field as he drove by but had no idea. He had been born and raised in the city and as far as he was concerned things like vegetables came from the supermarket, not a farm. But Logan knew one thing, and it was that the fields he was driving through were not growing tobacco. And they were not growing corn. Even a city boy knows what cornstalks look like. And after looking through the books in the library, Logan now knew what a tobacco plant looked like as well. He knew that the short, bushy plants that were in the fields on each side of the road were definitely not tobacco plants or cornstalks.

It wasn't until he turned onto State Road 7 that Logan saw his first field of tobacco. He was awed at the sight of it. Waist-high plants with large, broad green leaves spread from the side of the road to the distant tree line. A farmhouse sat in the middle of the field and along the tree line Logan could see a row of what looked like to him to be barns, and these barns had chimneys like the ones in the books from the library.

Suddenly Logan heard the sound of a loud air horn. He had been so intent on studying the field of tobacco to his right that his car had wandered across the yellow line in the middle of the two-lane road. A large farm tractor was coming from the opposite direction and the driver was laying on his horn in an effort to warn Logan.

Logan jerked the wheel to his right and narrowly avoided the slow moving tractor coming at him on the opposite side of the road. He overcompensated and the wheels on the right side of his car left the pavement. He jerked the wheel again and managed to get all four wheels back onto the road. He felt a rush of panic flood his bowels.

"Fuck!" he yelled as he clamped down tightly on the steering wheel. "Pay attention shithead!" He always called himself a shithead when he screwed up. After a few seconds, he settled back into his seat and looked into his rearview mirror. He could see the huge tractor turning onto a dirt road to leave the highway.

"They just let them drive those fucking things on the roads with the cars? Holy shit!"

Logan was in new territory. He was surrounded by tobacco plants and was sharing the road with huge green and yellow tractors, the likes of which he never seen before. He checked his rearview mirror again and saw that the tractor had disappeared in a cloud of dust down the dirt road, apparently headed to some field to do whatever it was big tractors did. Despite almost hitting the tractor head-on, Logan found himself enjoying this newfound rural world. He had definitely never seen anything like it. When he was younger the only traveling he did was with his parents, and all they had ever done was drive to Carolina Beach in the summer. And that was not even twenty miles from their house. And since their deaths he had barely had enough money to live much less take vacation trips out of town.

A thought suddenly entered Logan's mind. He checked his rearview mirror again and there was no sign of a car behind him nor was anything coming towards him from the other direction. Not even another big green and yellow tractor. He let off the gas and began to slow down. Then he pulled off the side of the road next to a row of tobacco plants on the edge of the field to his right. Even though he was a grown man he suddenly felt as mischievous as a teenager.

Logan brought his car to a stop and checked once again for cars coming from either direction. Nothing. There was a lonely farmhouse standing vigil to his left, across a huge field of tobacco. Apparently the field to his right also belonged to this house as well. Several more of those strange barns with the chimneys sat near the far edge of the field.

It was midmorning and the warm air was crisp and clean. As he got out of the car, Logan thought about how much better the air smelled out here in the country as opposed to the industrial, diesel fuel-laced salt air in his trailer park. He raised his arms over his head and stretched, and then walked around to the other side of the car so that it was between him and any prying eyes that might be looking out of the windows of the farmhouse across the road. Once there he unzipped his fly and took a leak. He could not ever remember pissing by the side of the road way out in the middle of nowhere. He was amazed at how liberating it felt.

Once finished, Logan looked over his shoulder at the farmhouse and then back at the row of tobacco plants not ten feet away. Full of curiosity, he couldn't help but feel the urge to touch one of the plants. Keeping the car between him and the farmhouse as best he could, he walked over to the closest tobacco plant. He had no idea what a farmer would have to say about someone messing around in his field, but Logan figured that it would be anything but friendly.

Logan looked down at the strange plant and wondered why he had never started smoking. Lots of people did, but it had just never appealed to him. And now he was staring down at the plant that made it possible for people to smoke. Logan looked at the strange plant as its leaves hung motionless in the still air. The leaves were large, about a foot across, and were green near the top of the plant and yellow near the bottom. Logan frowned when he saw the stubs near the bottom of the stalk where the leaves had apparently been pulled from the plant. He had no idea why anyone would pull the leaves from the bottom of the plant.

Logan reached over and touched a broad leaf near the top of the plant. The surface had a moist, waxy feel to it. He wondered what it would be like to just tear the leaf off the plant, roll it up into a cigar and light it up using his car's cigarette lighter. A homemade cigar, he thought as he rubbed the edge of the leaf between his thumb and forefinger. Then he thought about just ripping the leaf from the plant and tossing it in his car as a souvenir. This seemed a little more appealing. Logan didn't smoke and he knew now was not the time to start.

Just as Logan was about to tear the leaf from the stalk of the plant, he glanced over his shoulder at the farmhouse. Apparently someone had taken notice of him because there was a man standing on the porch looking directly over at Logan's car. Logan immediately let go of the leaf and walked back to his car. Once he got around to the driver's side he brought one hand up to shield his eyes from the sun and used his other hand to wave at the farmer. This gesture was not so much an act of friendliness on Logan's part as it was a way to show the farmer that both of his hands were empty and that he had not taken a leaf from the tobacco plant. Logan remembered how the library book had called tobacco the *golden leaf* because of its value, so he understood why the farmer would be leery of anyone in his fields.

Once back in the car Logan wasted no time in getting back on the road. Maybe he could get himself a souvenir tobacco leaf some other time. Logan figured it would be a nice thing to show Lowell since Lowell liked to smoke, and would give them something to talk about during their late evening patio shoot-the-shits by the grill.

Logan pulled his car back onto the road and waved once again at the farmer standing on the porch. To Logan's surprise, the farmer waved back. Logan was relieved the farmer did not appear to be upset. The last thing Logan wanted was a run-in with the local sheriff, who probably knew the farmer or was even related to him. Logan brought his car up to speed as the farmhouse receded in his mirror.

The fields continued on each side of the road. The scenery didn't change much as Logan made his way up the road to Starlight. He knew he couldn't be more than an hour or so away. The sun was high in the morning sky and the warm air circulating through the car was beginning to make Logan drowsy. He decided to stop and get a soda at the first place he came to.

After thirty minutes Logan had all but given up hope on finding a store when ahead to his right he finally saw a sign that advertised gasoline. He pulled into the small gravel parking lot and came to a stop near the front entrance to the store, which looked like it was at least fifty years old and badly in need of a paint job. Once inside he found the cold sodas, grabbed a candy bar and then took both to the front counter to pay. Behind the counter sat a gray haired woman who looked to Logan to be in her late sixties. A cigarette was pinched between her lips and one of her eyes was squinted shut. Logan paid for his soda and candy bar and then decided to ask the woman a question.

"Can you tell me how to get to the town of Starlight? Is this the road that goes to it?" Logan then waved his hand at the road in front of the store. "Am I going in the right direction?"

The woman smiled at Logan and removed her cigarette from her mouth. She turned her head slightly to her right and exhaled a large blue cloud of smoke.

"Starlight? Why do you want to go there?" Her eyes then walked down Logan's body from his face to his belt buckle before returning his eyes. "Not much left of that town, if you can even call it a town now."

Logan frowned. "Really? It's that small?"

"Used to be a damn sight bigger. Fifty years ago that town put out more of the leaf than any other town in these parts."

Logan knew she had to be talking about tobacco when she said *the leaf.* He quickly surmised that she had probably lived around tobacco for most of her life. And if she didn't grow it, she obviously used it. He fought the urge to cough as she exhaled another cloud of blue smoke. This one hung above the counter directly over his soda and candy bar.

The woman handed Logan his change and then put his things in a small paper bag.

"Yep, used to be a damn sight bigger. That road out there goes right through what's left of it. But I'd stay away from it if I were you. There's something bad in that town. Always has been. And they don't even put it on the map anymore."

Logan frowned at the woman and looked out of the window of the store at the road. He was trying to figure out if the woman was just messing with him because he obviously wasn't a local. The last thing he wanted to do was to get drawn into some sort of weird conversation even though he could tell that the woman wanted to talk. Logan knew he was probably her first customer of the day and might be her last. He had not seen a lot of traffic on the road before getting to her store. The big green and yellow tractor had been the only other vehicle he had seen in over an hour. But he couldn't resist asking the obvious question.

"So what's bad about the town of Starlight?"

Logan had apparently read the woman wrong. She wasn't nearly as chatty as he had thought. Instead of launching into a long story about Starlight, she merely smiled at him and gave him a wink through the blue smoke floating in front of her face.

"Just bad, that's all. If you're hell bent on going there you'll find out soon enough."

Logan knew the woman wasn't going to say much more. And he was suddenly glad of it. He wanted to get back on the road and have his soda and candy bar. He thanked the woman for her time and was about to walk out of the door when he realized that he should probably hit the restroom again. The coffee he had earlier was still working on his bowels.

"Say, do you have a restroom?"

"Out back, behind the building," the old woman said before taking a long pull of her cigarette.

"Is it locked?" Logan replied. The woman chuckled when Logan asked her this.

"No," she said, trying not to laugh. "It's not locked."

Logan smiled and thanked the woman and then went outside and put his bag in the passenger's seat. Then he walked around to the back of the store to use the restroom. Once he saw it he realized why the woman had tried not to laugh when he had asked if it was locked. The restroom was nothing more than a wooden outhouse sitting on the edge of the field that bordered the store's parking lot. Just like most of the fields he had seen earlier, the field beyond the outhouse was full of row after row of tobacco plants.

Logan used the restroom and was dismayed that he could not wash his hands. Then he returned to his car, screwed the lid off of his soda and took a long drink. As he pulled onto the road he tore the wrapper open on his candy bar while thinking about what the woman had said about Starlight. Now his curiosity was really going into overdrive.

As he brought the car up to speed he began to roll the question around in his head.

What in the world could possibly be wrong with the town of Starlight?

8

After leaving the gas station, Logan drove at least ten miles before he noticed an approaching sign up ahead by the side of the road. The sign was covered by Kudzu preventing him from reading it as he drove past. After he passed the sign a thought hit him causing him to put on the brakes. He stopped his car and then began to back up before maneuvering his car onto the shoulder of the road in front of the sign.

Logan got out and walked up to the foot of the post holding the road sign. He reached up and pulled at the vines of the Kudzu until he could finally see the words printed across the green metal sign. In faded white letters was the word *Starlight* and underneath it *Population 356*. Logan frowned. He expected Starlight to be small but not that small.

"There's only three hundred and fifty six fucking people in this town?" Logan's own voice almost startled him. Just then the loud air horn of a tractor trailer sounded and almost scared Logan out of his pants as the truck drove by coming from the direction of the town. It was the first vehicle he had seen since the green and yellow farm tractor. He cursed the truck as the wind created by its passing rearranged his hair and lifted sand into his eyes.

Logan got back in his car and pulled out onto the road and headed towards town. The first thing he saw was an abandoned factory on the outskirts of town with a large water tower sitting in between the factory and the road. The water tower at one time had been painted silver but was now mostly covered with rust. Logan could just make out the faded word Starlight painted across the large tank. Across the street sat a small building with a plate glass window and a sign above the door that read "Video Rentals". But the store had long since closed down.

Up ahead Logan could see a few small houses on each side of the road. The houses looked like someone lived in them, and then again Logan thought that they could also easily pass for abandoned as well. The windows were boarded up on one of them but two of the other houses had cars in their driveways.

Before long Logan came to the intersection with Main Street. Every little town had a Main Street, he thought to himself and he leaned forward and read the words on the sign. He brought the car to a stop at the intersection and quickly pulled the envelope from his console that had come from the law office. Then he read the return address.

"Magnolia Avenue…" he whispered as he looked both ways down Main Street. Then he took a gamble and turned right.

Only a few stores were open for business along Main Street. The rest were closed up and vacant. Logan saw a pawn shop, a consignment store, a small Karate studio and an old 1950's-era movie theater that had probably once looked like something out of Norman Rockwell painting. The large marquee over the front entrance sported the words "Jesus is Lord" in the place where the names of the movies playing had once been placed. Now apparently the movie theater had been converted into a church.

Logan didn't see anyone coming or going on the sidewalks on each side of the road. After he traveled a few more blocks he noticed a diner on the corner and decided that it was time for lunch. Maybe he would be able to ask someone inside if they knew where Magnolia Avenue was and the law office of Harmon Blackwell.

Across the street from the diner sat a small Post Office. The word Starlight was engraved in stone above the front door. Just like the movie theater, Logan realized that the Post Office building had seen better days.

Logan parked his car in the small lot next to the diner and checked his look in the rearview mirror. He had a case of road buzz from driving all morning and felt groggy. The heat was oppressive and the air conditioner on his car had stopped working months ago. Plus, he was coming down from the sugar high that he had gotten from eating the candy bar and drinking the soda. His stomach was beginning to rumble and he knew that he should probably eat before going to see this Harmon Blackwell fellow. Logan knew there was no telling how long he would be in the lawyer's office. His past experience with lawyers had taught him that they loved the sound of their own voice so this Blackwell guy would probably want to talk all afternoon, billing by the hour as he went. Who was paying him was anyone's guess, Logan thought, but he imagined that it was probably being drawn from the estate of the Rosemary Shaw lady.

§§§

Sheriff Tom Patterson sat in his cruiser on the edge of the parking lot of Starlight's only remaining feed and grain store, just a block away from the diner. He watched Logan Shaw get out of his car, adjust his shirt and pants and then walk to the front door of the diner.

"Now who the hell could that be?" he whispered as he took a sip of his stale coffee. Then he typed in Logan's license tag number and waited for the report. When it appeared, it was short and showed no record of Logan's vehicle being in the system. The sheriff was relieved at this. The last thing he needed was trouble.

Sheriff Patterson watched Logan disappear into the diner. Then he looked back at Logan's car, an old, dilapidated Chevy sedan.

"Doesn't look like he has a pot to piss in," Patterson said as he took one more sip of his coffee. Then he opened the door and poured it onto the sidewalk. It was time for a fresh cup, and this would make the perfect excuse to go into the diner and perhaps say hello to the newest visitor to Starlight. Being an old-school Southern sheriff, Tom Patterson knew it was his job to keep watch over the town, and just like any smart sheriff he was leery of new people in his town no matter how small it was.

Just then Sheriff Patterson looked back at the screen of his computer. Then it hit him – Logan's last name was Shaw. Could it be possible that this was the kid he had heard about? Everyone in town knew that old lady Shaw had passed away. Could this be the member of the family that Harmon Blackwell had been looking for? Sheriff Patterson grinned at the thought of how much Sandy, Blackwell's secretary, liked to gossip. He knew all about what was going on with the estate of the late Rosemary Abigail Shaw. So did just about everyone else in town.

Sheriff Patterson cranked his cruiser and drove a block up the street, pulled into the diner's small parking lot and then parked right next to Logan's car. Then he got out and walked into the diner.

Logan was sitting at the counter talking to Colby. Sheriff Patterson smiled at her and tipped his hat. It was no secret to anyone that he had been sweet on Colby since high school, but he had never been able to get her to return the affection. But it didn't mean he had stopped trying, and it also didn't mean that he liked the sight of her talking to some stranger that had just blew into town in an old beater.

"Hey Colby," Patterson said as he closed the door behind him. Colby forced a smile and nodded at him. Then Patterson walked over to the bar and sat down next to Logan, leaving just one stool in between them.

"Coffee please, to go," Patterson said as he looked at Colby. She was just as beautiful as ever and this caused him to wonder why she had never left Starlight. Why would a beautiful girl like her stay in Starlight to work in the diner? I just made no sense to him, but then again, it wasn't like he wanted her to leave. That's the last thing he wanted to happen. Patterson knew that one day she would give in to his advances. Then they could ditch this little town together and run off into the sunset, or something like that.

Logan turned his head to Sheriff Patterson and nodded. He read the patch on Patterson's sleeve and then said, "Afternoon, Sheriff."

"So you're Logan Shaw. Welcome to my town."

Logan frowned. How did this sheriff know his name? Patterson picked up on Logan's apprehension and answered before Logan could ask the question he knew was coming.

"Ran your plates when I saw you park at the diner. Just wanted to make sure the Feds weren't looking for you or anything like that." Sheriff Patterson then chuckled at his joke just as Colby sat a large Styrofoam cup full of coffee in front of him. She was glad he had ordered a to-go cup. Maybe he wouldn't stay long.

"Cream and sugar?" Colby asked as she slid a small bowl of creamers toward the sheriff. She already knew what his answer would be.

"You know better than that, girl. Real men drink it black."

Logan looked down into his coffee cup. He had put more cream and sugar in the cup than coffee.

"You must be in town to see old Harmon Blackwell. I hear he's handling Rosemary Shaw's estate. You must be what, her nephew maybe? Or grandson?"

Logan didn't like the sheriff asking so many questions. What business was it of his? And besides, Logan had no answers for the sheriff. He had no idea what his relation was to Rosemary Shaw.

"Gosh, Tom, why are you giving him the third degree? The poor guy just wants some lunch," Colby said as she smiled at Logan. Then the smile disappeared as she turned and looked at Sheriff Patterson again.

"I'm just looking out for you, Colby. It's my job."

"I don't need you looking out for me, Tom. Go look out for the rest of the town. Go see if you can find Jimmy Hoffa's body or something." Colby then turned to look at Logan again. "Your BLT will be right out." Then she winked at Logan and walked out from behind the counter to a table in the middle of the diner where a new customer had just sat down. When Patterson saw her wink at Logan, he felt a little flash of anger heat his face. He knew right then that he didn't like Logan Shaw.

"Uh, look sheriff, I'm just having some lunch and I really don't know much about Rosemary Shaw. I got a letter saying to come to town to meet Mr. Blackwell and that's about all I know. I'm not a troublemaker so you don't have anything to worry about."

"Let's keep it that way, Mr. Shaw. By the way, welcome to Starlight."

With that, Sheriff Patterson tipped his hat again, pulled a five dollar bill out of his wallet and left it in place of his coffee cup. He always tipped Colby a lot more than he did the other waitresses. Then he turned and walked out of the diner. Just then, Colby returned with Logan's sandwich.

"He's such a dickhead." Colby said this before she could catch herself. She quickly put her hand over her mouth and apologized. At that moment Logan looked at Colby and realized she was one of the prettiest girls he had ever seen. And here she was working in some run-down diner in a backwater town he had never heard of until just a few days ago.

"I mean, he likes to give strangers a hard time, that's all. Forgive my language."

"It's okay," Logan said. "I've been known to cuss like a longshoreman every now and then. You're in good company."

Logan had suddenly lost interest in his sandwich. Here was a woman standing in front of him with an attractiveness that was almost disarming. He could barely keep a thought in his head. She had sandy blonde hair tied in a ponytail and pale blue eyes full of kindness. Logan looked into those eyes and then tried to regain his composure by focusing on his sandwich.

"Thanks for the sandwich. It looks well. I mean, it looks good." Logan felt his spirits suddenly drop. Why did he have such a hard time talking to women?

"You're welcome," replied Colby. She thought it was sweet to see Logan fumbling with his words like a shy teenager. "So is it true? I mean, I don't want to be nosey, but is it true?"

"Is what true?" Logan said as he took a bite of his sandwich.

"That you're the long lost relative of Rosemary Shaw that they've been looking for? It's all over town."

"It seems that way. But I don't know anything else. I just got a letter saying come to Starlight and that I would be told everything once I got here. The letter said they couldn't tell me anything over the phone and that I had to come to the office in person. I live in Wilmington so I just decided to drive up here and find out what the deal is."

Logan had already surmised that Colby, as well as the sheriff, obviously knew more about Rosemary Shaw than he did. Maybe he could get Colby to tell him more. Just when he was about to ask, Colby looked down to the end of counter at a customer who apparently wanted their coffee cup refilled. He was a young man wearing a dirty bib hat and old overalls. His hair was the color of dishwater and his dark eyes were studying Logan intently from under the bib of his hat. Colby exhaled as if irritated, then smiled at Logan and said she would be right back. Then she walked down the counter and tended to the customer before returning to Logan.

Logan couldn't help but ask about the young guy at the end of the counter.

"Who's Mr. Bib Hat?" Logan said just as Colby returned.

"Oh, he's the town…" Colby then looked over each of her shoulders before leaning towards Logan. "He's the town asshole. Comes from a long line of assholes. His family has lived in this town for generations. Their land borders Rosemary Shaw's. His name is Chip McPhale."

"The town ass…" Logan then lowered his voice as well. "The town asshole?" he whispered. "What's his beef with me? He hasn't taken his eyes off of me since I came in here."

"Well," Colby said, "you're new in town for one thing. And you're talking to me for another. Both of those things are probably pissing him off."

"You seem to be pretty popular," Logan said as he grinned and took another bite of his sandwich. When he finished chewing he said, "The sheriff is after you and so is Mr. Bib Hat."

"Lucky me," Colby said as she gave Logan a crooked grin. "What more could a girl ask for?"

Logan suddenly realized this was the first conversation he had had with a woman in a long time that lasted more than a minute or two. It felt good. Logan thought about Sarah but knew that when he was with her that they didn't do as much talking.

Chip McPhale continued to stare at Logan from the end of the bar. Logan tried to ignore him and concentrate instead on Colby. He still could not get over how sweet she was. If this was what a typical country girl was like he was suddenly sorry he had grown up in the city. Then Logan decided to change the subject. He didn't want Colby to get bored with him and walk off to other customers.

"Can you tell me about her?" Logan asked as Colby began to refill his glass of water.

Colby smiled. "Rosemary? Sure. Everybody knows about Rosemary Shaw," Then Logan noticed a strange look in Colby's eyes, but only for a brief second.

"She's a fixture in town. The house she lives in has been around since the town was founded way back before the Civil War. She lives out on the edge of town. Her land runs right up to the Skeleton River."

Colby, embarrassed, paused for a moment. "I mean, she *lived* on the edge of town. God rest her soul."

Logan watched as the troubled look in Colby's eyes returned. Logan knew there was something she wasn't telling him.

"So she was a tobacco farmer?" Logan didn't know what else to ask.

"Oh Lord no," Colby said as she smiled at Logan. He noticed that the strange look in her eyes had disappeared.

"She hired people for that. She liked to rent out the fields as she got older and then take a cut of the profit. At one time sharecroppers worked her land. But that was a long, long time ago."

"What happened to Rosemary's husband? I assume she is, uh, *was* married. Where is he?"

Colby paused when Logan asked this question. Logan could tell he had hit on something.

"He's been dead for years," she finally replied. Then she topped off Logan's coffee. He watched as the black coffee turned his coffee from a light creamy color to dark brown.

"Could I have a Coke, please?" Colby seemed to brighten up when Logan asked for the soda. It was a chance to break the line of the conversation. She really didn't want to tell Logan about Rosemary Shaw's husband.

When Colby returned with his Coke, Logan decided to let it go about Rosemary's husband. He didn't want to make Colby uncomfortable. He couldn't remember the last time that he had enjoyed talking to woman as much as he had enjoyed the last fifteen minutes he had spent talking to her.

"You wouldn't by chance know where I can find Harmon Blackwell would you?" Logan then wiped his mouth with his napkin and pushed his plate away from him. Then he began sipping at his Coke.

"Harmon? Sure. Everybody knows him. We call him the town legal eagle. His firm is the last one left in Starlight. I'm not sure what he does to stay in business but he manages somehow. Old Harmon has been seeing to Rosemary Shaw for the past forty years, I guess. Maybe longer. Other than the occasional land spat or stolen mule, Harmon doesn't have much to do other than to see to Rosemary Shaw's business. Now that she's gone there's no telling what he'll do with his time. Starlight isn't exactly a hotbed of legal work if you know what I mean."

Colby then smiled at Logan causing him to completely lose his train of thought. It took a moment for him to recover.

"The letter said Magnolia Avenue. That's where his office is at. I would imagine it's got to be close by."

"Yep, just go back out there to Main Street and take a left. Magnolia is a few blocks down, almost right at the old town square. His office is on the corner of Magnolia and Main."

Logan wanted to stay and talk to Colby but he knew he had to locate Harmon Blackwell and find out what was going on with Rosemary Shaw's will. Logan had so many questions and he could feel the excitement building in his stomach. What could his inheritance be?

Colby smiled as Logan pulled his wallet out of his back pocket. He handed Colby enough to pay for his meal plus an extra five dollars for a tip. Colby smiled as she took the money.

"Good luck with that old coot," she said as she took a few steps to her right to get to the cash register. "You'll think you've wandered into the office of some big time New York City lawyer when you meet him. But remember, it's all just a show," Colby said as she winked at Logan.

From the far end of the bar, Chip McPhale felt the temperature of the blood in his veins rise ten degrees. Who in the hell was this guy talking to his woman? Maybe he and his brother would have to teach this stranger that he shouldn't come into town and mess with a woman that was spoken for. Chip McPhale knew he had a hard enough time with the sheriff thinking that he had a chance with Colby, now some guy from out of town was obviously interested in her. This was more than Chip could take. He pushed his plate of food away and got up and walked down to the cash register where Colby was standing. She waved at Logan just as he stepped through the door and out of the diner.

"Who's your new boyfriend?" Chip asked as he stepped in front of the cash register.

"Shut up, Chip. He's not my boyfriend for God's sake. Is there something I can help you with? Ready to pay your bill and leave?"

Chip pulled a few bills from his wallet and handed them to Colby.

"You know I don't like anyone messing with my girl," he said as he adjusted his hat. His cold, dark eyes gave Colby the creeps.

Colby put the bills in the register drawer and then pushed it shut so hard that the sound caused a few of the other patrons to look in her direction.

"I'm not your girl, Chip," she said as she turned and walked away towards the kitchen.

Chip McPhale watched as Colby walked away, trying to imagine what her naked body looked like under her waitress uniform. A thin smile then crossed his face.

"We'll see about that," he whispered as he pulled a toothpick from the dispenser. Then he looked out of the diner's front window just as he saw Logan's car turn left onto Main Street.

9

Logan had no trouble finding Harmon Blackwell's office. It was right where Colby had said it would be. The building looked to Logan to be very old, like most of the other buildings he had seen so far in town, with ornate stonework along the cornice above the second floor and a large wooden front door with a glass pane engraved with the law firm's name. The law office was on the first floor but Logan couldn't tell who or what business occupied the second floor of the building. The window shades up there were all pulled down.

Next to the building was a clothing shop called the Velvet Horseshoe. The front window contained several mannequins dressed in gaudy outfits that looked like something from the Roaring Twenties. Logan chuckled to himself and wondered how a big time legal eagle, as Colby had called Harmon, felt about having his office next to a second-hand clothing store called the Velvet Horseshoe.

Logan followed a sign on the front corner of the building that directed visitors to a small parking lot in the rear. He drove his car down the narrow alley between Harmon's office and the Velvet Horseshoe and parked in the small lot.

Grass was growing up through the cracks in the asphalt of the old parking lot. The sun was high and the temperature bordered on a hundred degrees as Logan walked back through the alley to get to the front door of Harmon's office. He ran his fingers along the old, weathered bricks of the wall of Harmon's building as he walked while thinking about how old everything was in Starlight. Logan had not seen a new building since coming to town. Everything looked to be at least fifty to a hundred years old. Harmon's building was no exception.

A small bell tinkled when Logan opened the front door to Harmon's office. An elderly woman with gray hair in a bun on top of her head was sitting behind a desk in the far corner of the waiting room trying to look busy. She smiled at Logan as he closed the door behind him.

"Good afternoon, may I help you?"

"Yes, ma'am, I'm Logan Shaw. I believe we spoke on the phone. I have an appointment to see Mr. Blackwell this afternoon."

The woman smiled and began to flip through her appointment book. It was another reminder to Logan that he was in a small town that seemed stranded in a bygone era. Normally a receptionist would be pecking on a computer to verify his appointment.

"Yes, Mr. Shaw. I see you in my book now. We really didn't set a specific time; we just agreed that you would come by this afternoon. If you'll have a seat, I'll find out when Mr. Blackwell will be able to see you. My name is Sandy, by the way. It's nice to meet you."

"Nice to meet you too," Logan replied. He was not used to being treated so cordially by someone in a law office. Usually he was being sued over a car and the law offices that contacted him were anything but cordial. Logan smiled again at Sandy and sat down in one of the leather chairs in the waiting room. Next to the chair was a small round table holding several magazines. Logan began to pick through them, noticing that all of the magazines were either about golf or saltwater fishing. He had no interest in golf so he chose one of the fishing magazines.

Sandy disappeared down the hallway near her desk and stopped in front of one of the doors on the far end. Logan watched as she tapped on the door with the back of her hand and then opened the door and stepped into the room.

Logan began to flip through the saltwater fishing magazine in his lap. The pages were graced with tanned people holding large fishing rods and even larger fish. Logan recognized the Marlins and Sailfish but had no idea what some of the other fish were in the photos. His father had not been much of a fisherman when Logan was young, and the only memory of fishing that Logan had was the one trip his father had taken him on to a small pond near their home. The fish they had caught using worms were no bigger than his hand. Logan remembered how he had enjoyed the trip not so much because of the fishing but because of the time he got to spend with his father. But they had certainly never gone on any sort of fishing trip to catch the kinds of fish he was now looking at in the magazine.

Logan flipped through a few more pages of the magazine and then grew tired of it. The boats and the kinds of rods and reels the people were holding looked expensive, very expensive, and Logan knew he would probably never get to go out on a boat like the ones in the magazine. He knew that kind of fishing was reserved for wealthy people, not used car salesmen that lived in trailers and ate hot dogs and TV dinners every night.

The walls of the waiting room were wooden and stained a deep walnut color. Several framed photographs of men standing on docks holding some of the same kinds of fish he had just seen in the magazine adorned the walls. There were several other photos of these same men with rifles in their hands posing with large deer and elk. Logan figured that one of the men in the photos had to be Harmon Blackwell, although he didn't know for sure. Logan then looked over at the large Marlin mounted above a fireplace located on the far wall of the waiting room, its eye staring blankly back at him. Logan figured Harmon had to have caught it.

Just then Sandy reappeared in the hallway and then sat back down at her desk.

"Mr. Blackwell will see you shortly. He asked me to convey to you how glad he is that you were able to make it in today. He's very busy and he asked that you please be patient. Help yourself to coffee while you wait."

Sandy then nodded at the small table in the corner of the waiting room. On top of it sat a small coffeemaker and an assortment of sugar and creamer packets spread out in small boxes.

"Thank you very much. I'm fine for now."

An hour later Logan found himself making a cup of coffee, wondering if he had ever had a cup of coffee this late in the afternoon. But he had started to get drowsy while waiting for Harmon to call for him and he knew he needed a shot of caffeine or he would fall asleep right in the leather chair he had been sitting in since arriving. Sandy could tell that he was getting impatient.

"I'm so sorry, Mr. Shaw. It shouldn't be much longer. Mr. Blackwell is so busy but he will see you soon."

Logan remembered that there were only two other cars in the parking lot behind the building. One of them had to be Sandy's based on the age of the car, and the other had to be Mr. Blackwell's. Perhaps Mr. Blackwell was on the phone with someone, Logan thought to himself as he remembered what Colby had told him. What if all of this was just an act to make him think Mr. Blackwell was in high demand? Logan thought about this while he stirred his coffee. Then he sat back down and started thumbing through one of the golf magazines. He had already exhausted the supply of saltwater fishing magazines. Apparently golfing was Mr. Blackwell's other passion.

§§§

Logan was gently kissing Colby's neck as his hands moved slowly down to her hips. The faded denim jeans and the curves of her body felt nice under his hands. Her breathing was heated as she pulled him closer to her. Then their lips met, and he could not ever remember feeling anything as soft and passionate as her kiss.

"Mr. Shaw..."

Logan was fast asleep with a golf magazine covering his lap.

"Mr. Shaw..." Sandy reached out and put her hand on Logan's shoulder. Just then he bolted awake.

Logan sat up in the chair, disoriented and unsure of where he was at. Then he looked around the waiting room, at the big Marlin staring at him from over the fireplace, and then at Sandy. She was trying to suppress a grin. Normally she would consider it rude for a client to fall asleep in the waiting room, but she knew Logan had been waiting for hours. It was almost three o'clock in the afternoon.

"I'm sorry. I guess I dosed off. I didn't mean to," Logan said as he regained his composure. I guess I should have had a second cup of coffee." He quickly brought his hand up to his face to wipe away the small amount of drool that he could feel tickling his chin.

"It's quite alright, dear," Sandy said as she gave Logan a compassionate smile. Then she patted him on the shoulder. "Mr. Blackwell will see you now."

Logan stood up and adjusted his shirt. He had meant to change into something a little more business-like but he had not had a chance to. Then he figured that it probably didn't make much difference. It wasn't like he was going to court to stand in front of a judge. This was just a meeting between him and the attorney that was handling the estate of his late whatever-she-was. Logan smiled at Sandy and then followed her as she led him down the hall to the door of Harmon's office. Before opening the door, she looked at Logan and winked.

"Good luck," she whispered.

Logan didn't know what to make of Sandy's comment so he just smiled. Then he stepped through the door into the office of Harmon Blackwell the third, attorney at law. Sandy quickly closed the door behind him and went back to her desk.

Harmon was sitting in his leather desk chair swiveled around so that his back was to the door. He did not turn around as Logan entered the room. All Logan could see was the gray hair on the back of Harmon's head underneath a large cloud of blue smoke. Logan could tell that it wasn't cigarette smoke but rather pipe smoke. Harmon was smoking a pipe and the sweet, aromatic smell of the pipe tobacco filled the room. Logan immediately thought about how no one would be smoking inside of an office building in Wilmington but then realized that maybe out in the country the rules weren't so strict. Especially if you were a big time legal eagle like Harmon Blackwell the third.

Harmon slowly rotated his chair until his eyes met Logan's. Then he reached up and removed his pipe with his left hand. He stood as he did so, extending his right hand to Logan.

"Logan Shaw... Well I'll be damned," Harmon said as the two men shook hands. "I can't tell you how happy I am to meet the only living relative of my dear friend and client, Rosemary Abigail Shaw. God rest her soul. It truly is an honor. Please have a seat. We have much to discuss."

Harmon then returned his pipe to his mouth, biting down on the mouthpiece to hold it firm as he sat back down in his chair. As Logan sat down he noticed the law degree hanging on the wall behind Harmon's desk.

"It's a pleasure to meet you too, Mr. Blackwell."

"I'll have none of that. Call me Harmon. Formalities like "mister" are for big city law firms and have no place in our firm here in Starlight."

"And please call me Logan," Logan replied, feeling somewhat relaxed. Harmon Blackwell the third didn't seem like such a bad guy so far.

"I'll just bet you have a million questions," Harmon said has he removed a folder from his desk drawer. He placed it on the desk in front of him and then folded his arms across it. He leaned in towards Logan and studied him intently for a few seconds.

"The resemblance is remarkable," Harmon said, his voice barely above a whisper as he studied Logan. Then he leaned back in his chair and regained his demeanor.

"Um, yes, about that," Logan said. "I have no idea who Ms. Shaw was or how I'm related to her. Can we start with that?"

"Of course we can. First things first, however. I apologize for not being able to tell you more in my letter or over the phone. But Rosemary's will was very specific about how you were to be told of your relation to her, and of your inheritance."

Logan felt another tingle of anticipation when Harmon said the word *inheritance*.

Harmon then took another long draw from his pipe, his lips popping in quick succession. Logan thought it was eccentric, if not comical. Logan didn't smoke, and hated the smell of cigarettes but Harmon's pipe tobacco had a different aroma, one that was a little easier to tolerate. But still, Harmon could sense that Logan was bothered by the smoke.

"Please excuse my manners," Logan. I keep forgetting that not everyone knows the pleasures of the leaf. Let me just put this out."

Harmon then took a small wooden plug from his ashtray and pushed it down into the bowl of his pipe, extinguishing the smoldering tobacco. Then he placed the pipe in the ashtray and pushed it to the edge of his desk.

"So, Mr. Black... I mean, Harmon, how exactly am I related to Ms. Shaw?"

"Why you are her great-grandson, of course. The only one she has. Your father was her grandson."

At the mention of Logan's father, Harmon's demeanor changed slightly. Logan almost didn't pick up on it but he knew he saw the ghost of a frown momentarily cross Harmon's face.

"My father never mentioned her," Logan replied. "In fact, neither of my parents ever talked much about the family. I was always led to believe that everyone had died off and it was just me, my mother and my father."

Harmon leaned back in his chair and looked at Logan. He exhaled and then looked towards the window on the far wall of his office just as a car passed on the street outside. Then he returned his eyes to Logan.

"I guess I've known Rosemary Shaw for the better part of half a century, Logan. She was a kind woman, a bit aloof sometimes, but kind and gentle. But she had a falling out with her daughter, a woman by the name of Elizabeth Shaw. That's your grandmother, Logan."

Logan thought for a few moments about what Harmon had just said about Elizabeth Shaw.

"Her last name was Shaw? Did she not take her husband's name when she married?"

"Therein lies the rub, Logan. Your grandmother, well…" Harmon cleared his throat and looked at Logan. He desperately wanted his pipe or maybe a shot of bourbon. Either one would make this conversation easier for him.

"Your grandmother was not married, Logan. She got pregnant out of wedlock by a laborer that was working the Shaw land during one of the harvests. Rosemary was furious and threw her daughter out of the house. Or so the story goes. But they never spoke after that. You're grandmother raised her child, your father, estranged from the family. She left town and no one ever saw them again. Rosemary never forgave herself for it. But she was a traditional woman and in her world, keep in mind this was a long time ago, a woman was supposed to have a husband when they were pregnant and the child was supposed to belong to that husband. But it just didn't work out that way for Elizabeth."

Logan was dumbfounded. In the span of just a few minutes he had learned more about his family than he ever had while growing up. Now all of a sudden it made sense to him why his father had never wanted to talk to him about the family.

"Are you alright, Logan?" Harmon's question broke Logan free from his trance. He had been pondering how it must have been for his father growing up.

"I'm fine. So tell me more, Harmon. What about Rosemary's husband? I assume I have a great-grandfather as well? Can you tell me about him?"

The same look as before flashed across Harmon's face. Logan knew he had hit on something again. He waited for Harmon to answer his question.

"His name was Carson Shaw. He passed away in 1965." Logan watched as a Harmon's eyes grew dark. "Yes, he died in 1965. The leaf got him, Logan. His lungs, I mean. The leaf got him just like it got Wilfred."

"Wilfred?" Logan asked.

"Wilfred Burns, my former partner. I just didn't have the heart to take his name off the firm. The leaf got him as well about five years ago."

Harmon knew he was only telling Logan half of the truth about his great-grandfather, but he knew Logan didn't need to know the real circumstances of Carson's death. At least not right now.

Logan leaned back in his chair and tried to absorb everything he had just learned about his family. It seemed straightforward enough. A baby out of wedlock had broken the family ties, resulting in his father and grandmother growing up outside of the town of Starlight. But despite his belief that Harmon was a good man and was telling him the whole story, Logan still had a feeling that there was more to it. But he was certain that at this point Harmon probably wouldn't tell him what it was. So Logan decided to ask the next question that was on his mind. He decided to ask about his inheritance.

Harmon could sense what Logan was about to ask. He silently admired Logan for first asking about his relation to Rosemary before demanding to know what his inheritance was. Still, Logan was human and obviously of limited financial means, so Harmon couldn't exactly blame him for wanting to know what he had inherited from a great-grandmother that he had never met.

"So, uh, what have I inherited, Harmon? I mean, what has my great-grandmother left me?"

Harmon leaned forward and placed his arms on his desk.

"Well, everything Logan. She left you everything she had. You are, like I said, her only living relative. So it's all yours now – the land, the house and everything inside of it. And a trust fund to take care of all the taxes and expenses for as long as you live."

What Harmon said suddenly registered with Logan. Not about the inheritance, but about him being Rosemary's only living relative.

"With all due respect, Harmon, how do you know I'm the only living relative?"

Harmon smiled. He had expected this question and was ready for it.

"Logan, I'm a lawyer. We often hire people to gather information for us. Like I said before, I have been Rosemary's attorney for quite some time now. Many, many years in fact. We were... very close, Logan."

Logan watched as Harmon seemed to drift away. After a few seconds he snapped out of it.

"I was instructed by her years ago to find her daughter and grandson and to keep up with them over the years. We have always known they were in Wilmington. But mind you, I was under strict instructions from Rosemary to never have any contact with them. Your father and grandmother, that is. Don't ask me why because Rosemary never told me why. I simply did as I was instructed. I did what I was paid to do. For some reason, Rosemary decided that upon her death you were to have everything she owned. She may have planned to leave everything to your father, but then you were born.

"Well he's..." Logan said.

"He's dead. I know, Logan. So is Elizabeth. She died before you were born. Like I said, we have people that gather information for us. That's how I knew where to mail the letter that I sent to you. How's the car business by the way?"

Logan frowned. "It sucks, to be quite honest." It was all he could think of to say. Harmon's question had caught him completely off guard.

Logan thought about what Harmon had just told him, that he had inherited a house, some land and a trust fund. He didn't know how excited he should be, and it still seemed inappropriate to be happy about it. His great-grandmother was dead, after all, and he had never even had a chance to meet her. And now everything she owned belonged to him. But what did that mean? She obviously lived alone. What kind of house had he inherited? He decided to ask Harmon.

"So I have a house now. That's certainly a step up for me. I currently live in a..."

"A trailer? I know. I told Rosemary that about six months ago. For what it's worth Logan, it seemed to make her very happy that she would be leaving you something nicer to live in than a trailer by an industrial shipping port."

Logan wanted to be offended but he knew Harmon had pegged it. Yes, he lived in a trailer by an industrial shipping port, and yes it was a dump.

"So may I ask about the house? Is it close by? I mean, can we go see it?"

Harmon tried his best to hold his composure when Logan asked about seeing the house. He got up out of his chair and walked over to the window. Outside the clouds were growing dark and angry from an approaching thunderstorm. Harmon mused that the same clouds seemed to roll through the area every day of the summer at almost the same time in the afternoon. Then he turned and looked at Logan sitting sheepishly in the chair.

"Logan, have you talked to anyone in town besides me?"

"Well, yes. I talked to a nice girl at the diner."

"Colby?" Harmon asked as he raised an eyebrow.

Logan was at first surprised that Harmon knew Colby's name. But then he remembered how small Starlight was and it wasn't hard to figure out that in a town this small everyone knew everyone.

"Yes, Colby. She was very nice to me. She even asked if I was the long lost relative of Rosemary Shaw. I guess everyone in town knows about me. This is such a change from Wilmington. There I could lay dead in my trailer for a week and no one would even notice. Here in Starlight it's almost like everyone already knows my name."

"We do all know each other, Logan. Welcome to small-town life." Harmon chuckled but his amusement was just for show. He was trying to hide the uneasiness percolating in his stomach.

"That's why I'm asking who you might have talked to before coming to my office."

"Just Colby, and like I said, all she did was ask me if I was the relative that they were looking for. By *they* I guess she meant you."

Harmon looked out the window again at the approaching clouds. Then he heard the distant rumble of thunder. After a few seconds he walked back over and sat down at his desk. Then he leaned in towards Logan.

"First of all, Logan, let me say that when I tell you that you have inherited a house I don't mean just any house. Same with the land. Rosemary's house is one of the largest, if not *the* largest antebellum mansion in Starlight. The house was built before the Civil War and has been in her, well, *your* family ever since. It's quite beautiful, Logan. And the land has some of the best soil in the county for growing the leaf. Tobacco, Logan. Tobacco made your family very wealthy."

Logan suddenly thought about eating TV dinners every night and driving around with little more than fumes in his gas tank. He certainly didn't feel like he came from money.

"So you're telling me I'm rich now, Harmon?"

Harmon leaned back in his chair. "We'll discuss the financials later, Logan. Right now just understand that you are now the owner of a large antebellum mansion and over three hundred acres of prime tobacco land and the government allotment that allows the tobacco produced on the land to be sold at market. They call the land the Shaw Fields, and buyers from across the state damn near fight over the tobacco that is grown in those fields. Like I said, the soil is as close to perfect as it can get. It's weak and thin and grows perfect Brightleaf tobacco. Why, I've even seen the Shaw Fields produce a crop when the rest of the tobacco in the county was killed off by tobacco worms. No one knows why or how, but it just happens."

Logan wanted to be happy with what he was hearing. But he couldn't get past the look on Harmon's face. Something was up, and he was tired of waiting to find out what it was. It was time to ask Harmon to spill the beans and tell him the whole story.

"Harmon, I don't mean to sound rude but it just seems that there is something you're not telling me. Why are you concerned about whether or not I've talked to anyone else in town?"

Harmon's face clouded over. It was a few moments before he spoke again.

"Because of the stories you might hear, Logan. It's important that you hear this from me. I was just concerned that someone else in town might have filled your head with wild stories about the Shaw mansion and the land. Most of it is just bunk. But there is a story to tell. And you have a right to know what it is."

Harmon looked longingly at his pipe in the ashtray. Logan could tell the man needed a smoke."

"Harmon, please, light up if you want to. It doesn't bother me. Pipe tobacco smells a lot better than cigarette smoke. I don't mind it."

Harmon's face lit up. "Don't mind if I do, Logan. Thank you for your compassion towards and old chap like me. I do love my pipe."

Harmon relit his pipe and Logan watched as a look of pure pleasure crossed Harmon's face as he took a few deep puffs. Now maybe the man would be able to relax and tell him the whole story about the house and land.

"That's much better," Harmon said as he puffed on his pipe. "It'll probably kill me but I do love it so. Now then, where were we?"

"The house, the land... There's a story behind them."

Harmon's face darkened again. Despite having his pipe it was still going to be difficult to tell Logan the story behind the Shaw land.

"Keep in mind Logan, some of this happened before my time, before I was even born mind you. And I'm not sure I believe some of it. There are people in town that believe one thing, and there are others that believe something else. I suppose I should tell you both versions of the story and let you decide which one sounds more plausible."

"Fair enough," replied Logan. He wished Harmon would just get on with it and stop stalling.

Harmon took a long draw on his pipe and tilted his head back. Then he exhaled a cloud of blue smoke that hung in the air above him. He stared into the cloud of smoke for a few moments and then leveled his eyes on Logan.

"Some people say it's the McPhale family. Generations of McPhales have lived next to the Shaw land for at least a hundred years. Not a damn one of them has ever been worth a pound of dry shit, pardon my French. One school of thought is that they have been behind it all. Maybe they thought over the years that if they could drive the value of the land down to the point where it was worthless then they would be able to buy it on the cheap. And it's no secret that they've been waiting on Rosemary to die for years. Now that she has passed I do have to say that I don't envy you, Logan. You will probably have to deal with them at some point. The current bunch is led by Chip McPhale and his brother Ethan. They're the only two remaining other than their father, but he's in a nursing home near Raleigh and can't even remember his own name. Very sad. Their mother is gone. But Chip and Ethan are alive and well. Together those two don't have enough brain wattage to light a two dollar string of Christmas tree lights. But they're mean, Logan. Beware of them both."

"They're behind what? You said some people think they're behind it all.

Behind what, Harmon?"

Harmon cleared his throat.

"The murders."

"Excuse me?" Logan said. "The what?"

Harmon took a draw on his pipe and then sat it in the ashtray.

"The murders, Logan. There is a reason Starlight is not what it once was. Every so often there is a murder in this town. And not just a simple murder like what you might read about on any given day in Wilmington. This is not a case of a mugging or a home invasion gone wrong. The murders I'm talking about are always a most gruesome event, Logan. Often the victim is unrecognizable once the killer is finished with the body."

Logan was dumbfounded. He had no idea how to handle what he was hearing. All he could do was ask the obvious question.

"And what makes you think the McPhales are behind these murders?"

"I didn't say that's what I think, Logan. I said some people think that. Some people in town think the McPhale family has been behind the murders through the years and that they pass on the killing duties from generation to generation. About fifty years ago one of the McPhales was actually caught and convicted of a murder but it turned out to be the result of someone owing the wrong person money."

"Damn..." Logan said. "So it's not beyond them to commit murder."

"No it's not, Logan. But like I said before, their aim is to get the Shaw Fields as well as the house. Either by driving down the value or by just scaring people into doing what they want. But Rosemary refused to leave the house and the land. The McPhales never could get through to her. She was a tough old bird, my good friend Rosemary. She was indeed. God have mercy on her soul."

Harmon then leaned back in his chair again. At first Logan didn't think he was going to continue. But then Harmon reached for his pipe, took another long draw and then sat it back down in the ashtray. Then he continued.

"The other theory is that the land is cursed, Logan. I'm an old man and I've seen a lot of things in this world. Can I tell you that I don't believe the land is cursed? Honestly, I can't tell you that. I'm ashamed to say that if I had to pick a story behind the murders, I don't think I'd pick the McPhale story."

"Why?" replied Logan.

Harmon suddenly became very frank. "Because that entire family has always been as dumb as a box of hammers, Logan. I refuse to believe that they would be able to carry out those murders and never get caught. Our sheriff would have caught them by now. Or the sheriffs that came before him would have caught them. The McPhales would have tripped up sooner or later and left a clue, or something that pointed to them. You've got to be pretty smart to get away with that many murders over such a long period. And like I said, the McPhales are anything but smart."

What Harmon had just said suddenly registered with Logan. He frowned and looked at Harmon sitting underneath his cloud of pipe smoke. "Over such a long period?" Logan repeated.

Harmon paused and looked away while the words gathered in his mind. Then his eyes returned to Logan.

"The first murder occurred in 1931, Logan. And there have been more killings since then. They've become known as the 'tobacco killings'. They always occur around the same time of the year, right near the end of the tobacco harvest. And always under a harvest moon. Sometimes there is a murder every few years, sometimes longer. We once went almost twenty years without one, and then one night when the harvest moon rose..."

Logan's mouth dropped open. He slowly inhaled a long breath.

"Excuse me, Harmon? 1931? That's over eighty years ago."

"Exactly," replied Harmon as he reached for his pipe. "And I'd say we're due for another one."

Logan sat quietly for a minute while digesting what Harmon had told him. Then it hit him.

"Harmon, where...?"

"Where do the murders take place? I knew you were going to ask that question, Logan." Harmon puffed his pipe and then removed it from his mouth. He looked Logan directly in the eyes before answering his question.

"Every single murder has taken place in the Shaw Fields."

10

Sandy knocked gently and then opened the door to Harmon's office. She peeked around the door until she saw Harmon and Logan sitting at the desk.

"Excuse me Harmon, but I think I'll be going for the day. It's past five thirty."

"Yes Sandy, by all means. I'll lock up. We're going out to the house shortly. Have a nice night, dear."

Logan thought that calling his secretary "dear" would land Harmon in hot water if he worked at a large law firm in the city. Harmon seemed to be stuck in another era but Sandy didn't seem offended at all. She was from the same era as Harmon.

Harmon looked at Logan. "It is getting late," he said as Sandy closed the door.

They had been talking about the Shaw house and land for over two hours. Logan could not believe that just a week ago he was nothing more than a broken-down used car salesman barely getting by and now was the owner of one of the largest mansions in the town of Starlight, a mansion that had murder mystery tied to it. Logan thought about the McPhale story, and the story about the land being cursed. This caused one final question to come to his mind.

"Harmon, you said that some people think the Shaw land is cursed. Why would they think that?"

Harmon looked at Logan and then crossed his hands in his lap. He looked down as he began to rub his thumbs together.

"To tell you the truth, Logan, I have no idea."

Logan looked at Harmon's face. He could tell the old man was lying. But Logan was tired and he had been in Harmon's office too long. He wanted to leave, go see the house and then find somewhere to stay for the night so he let the question go.

"I guess we're about done for today," Logan said. "Can you tell me where I can find a motel for the night? I can stay there after we see the house."

Harmon chuckled and then reached for the plug to extinguish his pipe. "A motel?"

"Well, I assume we still have business to take care of and I'm in no hurry to get back to Wilmington. My staff is watching my car lot, so I have no need to hurry back." Logan instantly regretted the remark. He remembered what Harmon had said about how lawyers hire people to find out things for them. Harmon knew he didn't have a staff of people. But Harmon let the remark go without challenging it. After a few seconds of uncomfortable silence, Logan said, "After we see the house I figured I'd find a place to stay and come back in the morning."

"You have no need for a motel, Logan. I've got the keys to your new home right here in my desk. You can stay there tonight, and tomorrow night or for as long as you want. I assume you'll need to go back to Wilmington to take care of things at some point but if I were a betting man I'd say that your car selling days are over. At any rate, the house is yours now so you won't need a motel. And that's a good thing, by the way. The few motels we have left in town are not exactly the best places to stay. Some of them even rent their rooms by the hour, if you know what I mean." Harmon winked at Logan and smiled.

Logan was relieved at the sound of this. He was hoping that Harmon would say that he could stay in the house. Motels were expensive, even cheap ones. He knew he didn't have enough money to stay in a motel all week while he settled his great-grandmother's estate.

"That's sounds great, Harmon. Anything beats a roach motel."

Harmon smiled as he opened the drawer to his desk. He removed a key ring containing two keys.

"Those days are over for you, Logan. It wouldn't be right for the great-grandson of the late Rosemary Abigail Shaw to be staying in a roach motel." Harmon then closed his desk drawer and Logan watched as he locked it with a small key on his own key chain.

"Now, shall we take a drive out to your new house?"

"That would be great, Harmon. And when we get there the first thing I'd like to see is maybe a photo of my great-grandmother."

"I believe I can accommodate that request," Harmon said as he rose from his chair.

11

September, 1965

Carson Shaw walked slowly towards the row of tobacco barns situated at the edge of his field. The night was cool and the fields of bare tobacco stalks were bathed in the yellow light of the harvest moon. He could see the smoke from the first chimney rising into the night sky like a ghostly finger pointing towards the heavens.

The harvest had been good and Carson smiled to himself when he thought of the amount of money hanging in the barns, money in the form of tobacco leaves. He needed to check the fires before turning in for the night to make sure everything was okay. Soon Shepard, one of his hired hands, would arrive to tend to the fires for the rest of the night. But Carson always liked to check things for himself before calling it a day.

Carson thought about his wife Rosemary and how she was still distraught over their daughter. But he knew Rosemary would be okay. Surely their daughter would return home with her child and things would get back to normal. But Carson knew that there was also a very good chance that she would not, and that he and Rosemary would never see their daughter, or their grandson again. But the leaf waits for no one, Carson thought as he walked towards the tobacco barn. He knew that he had work to do and that he could worry about his daughter once the tobacco was sold at the market.

Times were good for Carson and his family. His fields had produced another harvest for them. And times were reasonably good for the country. Things had recovered from the assassination of President Kennedy and the only dark cloud on the horizon was what was going on in Vietnam. But Carson knew that he and Rosemary only had a daughter, so they didn't need to worry about a son being drafted into the Army. Carson knew he had seen enough fighting during his time in the Army during World War II to know that he never wanted to see his son, or anyone's son have to go through what he had gone through in Europe. But people in the country were worried about what was going on in Vietnam and as much as Carson didn't want to admit it, this worrying was good for business. People tended to smoke more when they were worried about something.

Carson walked around to the rear of the first barn and stoked the fire in the firebox. The heat and smoke from the fire traveled up into a flue that led into the barn, thus heating the interior of the barn and drying the tobacco leaves without directly exposing them to the smoke. Then he walked around to the door of the barn to have a look inside. Hung from the rafters were dozens of tobacco spears, each strung with hundreds of leaves of Brightleaf tobacco. Carson knew those leaves were as good as gold.

Carson checked the rest of the barns spaced in a row down the edge of his field. When he finished tending to the firebox on the last barn, he walked inside to check the leaves.

Carson did not see the lone figure standing in the corner of the barn when he opened the door and stepped inside. He removed his hat just as he walked underneath the first row of tobacco leaves hanging above him. The heat in the barn was stifling, and just as he brought the back of his hand across his forehead to wipe away the sweat, he caught movement out of the corner of his eye.

Carson Shaw feared no man. His experiences during the war coupled with two decades of hard tobacco farming had made him a strong and willful man. But when he saw the figure move in the shadows of the corner of his barn he felt fear rush through his body.

"It's true..." Carson said as he looked at the killer, his voice nothing more than a whisper. His eyes grew wide as the killer stepped out of the shadows into the yellow moonlight pouring in through the open door. In one hand the killer held a tobacco spear and in the other what looked like a small hatchet. Carson knew the small hatchet was a tobacco axe. He had used one for many years to cut the stalks of the tobacco plants when that was still done by hand.

Before Carson could move, the killer dropped the tobacco axe, put both hands on the spear and lunged towards him. The tobacco spear pierced Carson's throat and traveled upwards into his skull. His limp body fell forward, snapping the wooden tobacco spear in half as he fell. But as with all of the victims, death was not the end of the ritual. The death of the victim was never enough. It was only the mutilation, one borne out of anger and rage that could satiate the killer.

The killer walked slowly back to where the tobacco axe lay on the dirt floor of the barn, its blade glinting in the yellow moonlight. The killer picked up the axe and walked back to Carson's body, which was still twitching in the last throes of death. The killer raised the tobacco axe high in the air and then brought it down violently so that it sliced into the side of

Carson's skull. Blood splattered against the side of the barn and the tips of the tobacco leaves hanging overhead. This blow from the axe extinguished what life was left in Carson Shaw and caused his body to go limp. Then the axe was raised and brought down again and again in an act of fury until Carson's entire body, face and head included, was hacked into nothing more than a bloody mound of unrecognizable flesh and bone. Then as quickly as it had started, the mutilation ended. The killer stepped out of the barn into the moonlight and disappeared into the tobacco field.

It would be more than an hour before Shepard would find Carson's mutilated corpse in the barn, or what he thought was Carson's corpse. He could not be sure at first. In the days that followed it was said that Rosemary's wails of agony could be heard wafting through the tobacco fields every night as she mourned the loss of her beloved Carson. Those that believed the McPhales were behind the killing would cast yet another suspicious eye on the members of that family as they walked the streets of the town in the days following the murder. The others that believed the land was cursed would cast a wary eye on the Shaw Fields as they drove past them, wondering when the ghost of tobacco road would return under a harvest moon to kill once again.

12

2014

Chip McPhale sat in his dilapidated pickup truck under the shade of an oak tree just down the road from the long driveway that led to the Shaw house. In his mind he could see himself turning into the driveway in a brand-new truck and parking in front of the stately house. It just wasn't right that old Rosemary had sat in that house for decades, nothing more than a recluse waiting on the Reaper to show up and escort her to Hell. Well, Chip thought, now the Reaper had done his work and the old woman was gone. Word around town was that now the house belonged to some long-lost relative of hers. But that wasn't going to be a problem, Chip thought as he watched Harmon's Mercedes followed by another car turn into the driveway. This new guy would leave. Yes, Chip thought, this new guy will leave in a hurry if he knows what's best for him. Chip knew that this new relative of Rosemary's wouldn't last a week in the Shaw house.

As the second car disappeared down the driveway, Chip put his old truck in gear and slowly pulled out and onto the road. It was time to introduce himself to the new owner and say hello to that damn highfalutin Harmon Blackwell. After all, Chip reasoned, he and the new guy were going to be neighbors and it wouldn't be right for them not to have a proper introduction.

§§§

Logan's mouth dropped open as he brought his car to a stop next to Harmon's Mercedes. Their cars were parked in the circle in front of the house, a house the likes of which Logan had never seen before. It wasn't that the house was all that large, but it had a stately appearance that Logan found overwhelming.

The house had four large white columns and a front porch that ran the length of the house. Eight large windows, four above and four on the first floor covered the front of the house. The dormers on the roof told Logan that the house either had either a third floor or a large attic. The paint was peeling and most of the shrubbery was overgrown and it was evident to Logan that the house needed some maintenance. There were two chimneys, one on each side of the house, which gave the house a balanced look and feel. Simple yet stately, Logan thought as he turned off his car and opened the door. Before getting out of his car, Logan tucked his keys under the edge of the visor. Harmon had already gotten out of his car and was waiting for Logan to join him.

Logan shut his car door and walked over to Harmon who was standing by the front steps that led up to the porch. Harmon was studying the large statue in the middle of the driveway circle in front of the house.

"She had the water turned off to that statue years ago," Harmon said as he nodded towards the statue sitting in the middle of the dry fountain pool. "She said the noise kept her up at night." Harmon was trying to downplay the house and grounds in an effort to calm Logan. He could tell by looking at Logan that he was overwhelmed by the sight of the house.

Logan stopped halfway between his car and where Harmon was standing. He tilted his head back and ran his eyes across the roofline of the house before settling on the dark windows of the dormers poking out of the roof above the second floor of the house.

"Me?" The word was more of a statement of doubt than a question.

"I beg your pardon?" Harmon said.

"Me. You're telling me that I own this? This house?"

Harmon smiled.

"Yes Logan, you own it and the land. Like I said, it was Rosemary's wish for you to have it. This is your home now, that is, if you want it to be."

Harmon's last statement was more than Logan could process. Of course he wanted the house. That was easy enough. Only a fool would choose an old mobile home in an industrial park over a stately Southern manor like the one sitting before him. Still, Logan was having a hard time believing that all of this was really happening and that the house he was looking at was going to be his new home.

"That's some driveway," Logan said as he looked back down the long narrow road that tunneled through the trees between the main road and the house. The trees were live oaks with beards hanging from the limbs. At least that's what Logan had called them when he was young. His father had always told him the trees with beards were called Grandfather Oaks.

"Yes it is," replied Harmon. "Rosemary liked her privacy." Harmon then patted his forehead with his handkerchief before returning it to his pocket. "Sorry for the condition of the house, Logan. Rosemary kind of let it go in her later years. But it's all just on the surface. The house is sound and you won't have any problems. It just needs to be painted."

Logan nodded and looked at the statue again. Then his eyes wandered over to a strange contraption sticking out of the ground near the front porch steps. It was about five feet tall and made out of what looked like wrought iron rods. One large wrought iron rod came out of the ground and fanned out into a dozen smaller rods that were welded to the center rod near the top. Each small rod had a colorful bottle stuck on the end of it.

"It's a bottle tree," Harmon replied as he once again removed his handkerchief and patted his forehead. Logan figured it had to be the heat, but part of him had the funny feeling that Harmon was nervous.

"A what?" Logan replied as he returned his eyes to the colorful bottles.

"A bottle tree," Harmon repeated. "Lots of people around here have them. Some people believe they trap evil spirits. They date back hundreds of years." Harmon let this hang in the air to see what Logan would say.

"You're shitting me," Harmon. "Evil spirits… Yeah, right."

Logan looked at the bottles and even though he knew it had to be a bunch of baloney, he couldn't help but wonder if it might be true. People in the old days were a lot smarter than people were nowadays, he thought as he looked at the bottle tree.

Logan started to ask Harmon another question but he was interrupted by the sound of Chip McPhale's approaching pickup truck. He brought it to a stop directly behind Logan's car, so close in fact that Logan thought for a moment that the truck was going to nudge his rear bumper. Logan recognized the hat on Chip's head and remembered seeing him in the diner earlier in the day. Then he remembered what Colby had said, and also what Harmon had said about the entire McPhale family.

"Harmon," Chip said as he shut the door of his truck and tipped the bib of his hat. Harmon didn't reply. He only narrowed his eyes as he watched Chip approach.

Chip walked between Logan's car and Harmon's Mercedes before stopping near the front of both cars. He looked down at Logan's car and then turned around and leaned up against it. It was his way of telling Logan that he wasn't afraid of him.

"Chip," Harmon finally said, forcing as much cordiality into his voice as he could. He knew Chip was a troublemaker who had no regard for anything, least of all the law.

"So you must be the new owner," Chip said as he looked at Logan.

"That's what they tell me," Logan said as he looked at Chip and then at Harmon.

"Welcome," said Chip as he adjusted the bib of his hat. Then he looked at Harmon.

"Have you told him?"

Harmon paused for a second and then cleared his throat.

"Yes, Chip, I have. He knows about the land."

"We're due for one. Did you tell him that too?"

"I believe I mentioned that to Mr. Shaw in my office. I told him that if history is our guide there will be a murder in the Shaw Fields soon."

"You did mention it, Harmon. You were very thorough." And then Logan turned to Chip and mustered what courage he could find. While he spoke to Harmon he kept his eyes on Chip.

"You told me all about the murders, the McPhale family and the curse on the land. And I like I told Mr. Blackwell, Chip, I don't believe in ghosts and goblins rattling chains in the attic."

Chip looked at Logan and felt his blood begin to simmer. Who the hell was this new city kid and who did he think he was talking to?

Logan had figured that Chip would be in his face by now trying to pick a fight. The fact that Logan had said what he did and Chip was still leaning against the car gave Logan a small bolt of self-confidence. But then it was gone as quickly as it had arrived when Logan saw Chip push himself off of the car's fender and adjust his hat. Logan swallowed hard as he watched Chip began to walk directly towards him and Harmon.

Chip stopped less than a foot away from Logan, close enough that Logan could smell the whiskey on Chip's breath. Logan had demons of his own and knew that whiskey smell better than most men.

"If you know about the land and that old lady that lived in this house then I imagine you won't be staying around here very long. I give you a week. You'll leave, and my brother and I will take this land once and for all. You can count on it." Chip then took another step towards Logan and was close enough that the bib of his hat almost touched Logan's forehead. Logan knew he had to do something to respond to what Chip had said. If Chip wanted to measure dicks, then so be it, Logan thought to himself before finally speaking.

"According to my attorney, this house and land now belongs to me. So you're trespassing. I suggest you get back in that piece of shit 1978 Chevy of yours and get off my land." Logan's experience with cars allowed him to accurately nail the year of Chip's truck. For a second he saw a flicker of doubt in Chip's eyes but it was quickly replaced with anger.

Chip looked at Logan and then at Harmon. He then turned his head and ejected a stream of red tobacco juice from his mouth. It hit the ground near the front bumper of Logan's car. He wiped his chin with the back of his hand and then looked into Logan's eyes.

"If that's the way you want to play it then suit yourself, city boy."

With this Chip got back in his truck, cranked the engine and put the transmission in reverse. He back around the circle and then drove down the driveway and out onto the main road. Logan and Harmon both watched as Chip's truck slowly disappeared down the road.

"Logan," Harmon said quickly, "I should have told you that he'd probably show up today."

"Don't worry about it," Logan said, interrupting Harmon. Then he nodded in the direction of the road. "Should I worry about him?"

Harmon paused and then reached for his handkerchief. He patted his forehead and then put it back in his pocket.

"I won't lie to you, Logan. If I were you, I'd be worried. Like I said before, that family has wanted this land for generations. I don't know what Rosemary did to keep them at bay but now that she's gone I wouldn't underestimate them if I were you."

Logan squinted as he looked into the distance at the point on the road where Chip's truck had disappeared from sight. Then he turned to Harmon.

"Can we see the inside of the house?" he said. Harmon responded immediately.

"It would be my pleasure, Logan."

§§§

Logan stood in the large foyer of the house unable to hold a thought in his head. He had never seen anything like the entry foyer to the Shaw house. He was standing at the base of a large staircase that led to the second floor and it reminded him of the old movies he had seen about Southern plantation homes. The staircase ran up the side of the foyer, which to Logan was large enough to be a room on its own. The foyer was open and well lit by a large chandelier hanging above them. The floor was very old hardwood covered by a large, intricately woven rug. Off to his right was a huge dining room and to his left was what appeared to be the main living room for the house. A large fireplace sat against the wall and above it was a portrait of a woman. Harmon noticed Logan looking at the portrait.

"Logan, I present to you your great-grandmother, Mrs. Rosemary Abigail Shaw."

Logan looked over at Harmon and then back at the portrait. He could not find any words so he simply nodded at Harmon and then walked slowly into the living room. He moved around the furniture, which consisted of an antique couch with matching high-back chairs gathered around an oval-shaped table with a marble top, until he was standing within a few feet of the portrait.

Rosemary was a tall and slender woman. The portrait had obviously been made in her later years. Her hair was gray and her dress was long and hung almost to the floor. She was wearing a necklace, earrings and a wedding band on her finger but she was alone in the portrait. Everything about her appearance reflected affluence and wealth to Logan, and he could not believe that he was her great-grandson, nothing more than a used-car salesman from Wilmington.

"That portrait was made long after her husband Carson passed away." When Harmon mentioned Carson's name he again removed his handkerchief and patted his brow. Then he returned it to his pocket. "If you would like to see her in her younger years, there is a portrait of her and Carson in the dining room."

Both men walked out of the living room, across the foyer and into the dining room. There in the center of the far wall was another large portrait. A man was standing beside Rosemary, who was seated in a chair. Her hair was a light shade of brown and Logan could tell she was much younger than she was in the portrait in the living room.

"Your great-grandfather, Logan. His name was Carson Wentworth Shaw. He was a good man."

Logan had no words to describe how it felt to see the man and woman in the portrait. For so many years he had wondered what his relatives looked like and where they had lived. All those years of not knowing, and now here he was standing in a stately manor looking at a portrait of Carson and Rosemary Shaw, his paternal great-grandparents.

"The resemblance is striking," Harmon finally said, breaking the silence in the room.

Logan looked over at him and then back at the portrait. He knew Harmon was talking about Rosemary because he could see the resemblance himself. He did look like her, and the realization of this caused a small pang of pride to flutter in his chest.

They stood for another minute while Logan studied the portrait of Rosemary and Carson. Then Harmon spoke.

"It's getting late, Logan. I'll take you around the house and then I'm going to call it a day. My wife will have supper ready soon." Logan was getting hungry too, but he didn't mention this to Harmon. Logan didn't want Harmon to think he was trying to invite himself to dinner. Logan was sure there had to be something to eat in the house and he would find it as soon as Harmon left.

"Sounds good, Harmon. Let's have a look around."

The two men left the dining room and moved into the kitchen. To Logan it was like stepping back in time. The kitchen was large and expansive, with a black and white checkered tile floor. The stove was a pastel yellow color and sat on four legs. The refrigerator looked about as old, but was extremely well maintained. The countertops were some sort of stone, and there was a large island in the middle of the kitchen. Above the island hung a large metal rack that held an assortment of pots and pans.

"Wow..." Logan said as he looked around the room. Off to his left he could see into the pantry, and he immediately realized that it was larger than his entire kitchen back in his mobile home. He could see canned food and boxes of dry goods lining the shelves.

"You'll find plenty to eat in there, Logan. I'm sorry that you'll have to eat all by yourself on your first night in the house but you'll enjoy it. It will give you some time to think about things."

"I don't mind at all, Harmon. This is still so unbelievable to me," Logan said as he waved an arm at the kitchen. "And don't let me keep you from your wife. We can take up where we left off tomorrow if you'd like."

"Nonsense, Logan. Let's finish the tour and then I'll be on my way."

13

Harmon shook Logan's hand on the front porch. They had finished the tour of the house, including the upstairs bedrooms. They had not gone up into the attic but Harmon had taken Logan on a brief walk around the backyard and had showed him one of the closest tobacco barns. As they had walked around the backyard, Harmon's rumbling stomach and the thought of his supper waiting on him at home had caused him to finally tell Logan that it was time for him to go home and that they could take up their business again in his office at ten o'clock tomorrow morning. They chatted for a few more minutes on the front porch before Harmon handed Logan the keys to the house and told him to be sure and lock it up if he went anywhere.

Logan waved at Harmon's Mercedes as it moved slowly down the long driveway towards the road. Then he took a look across his expansive front yard before his eyes settled on the old statue sitting in the middle of the dry fountain. Maybe he would find a way to turn the water back on to the old fountain. But right now it was time to find something to eat.

The pantry held an assortment of canned vegetables, soups and even an assortment of home-canned jams and jellies. Logan then walked over to the refrigerator but was dismayed to find it completely empty. He figured this was a good thing, and that anything that had been in it on the day his great-grandmother died would have been spoiled by now anyway. Someone had obviously cleaned out the refrigerator. Perhaps he would ask Harmon about that tomorrow. It didn't matter anyway. Logan doubted that his great-grandmother would have had any TV dinners in her freezer, or hot dogs in the refrigerator, and he wasn't used to eating anything else.

Logan remembered that he had spotted a large tin of coffee in the pantry so at least in the morning he would be able to brew a pot and maybe enjoy a cup while sitting on the back porch. He smiled to himself at the idea of having coffee on the back porch while trying to figure out what he was going to do.

Logan ambled around the kitchen for a few more minutes and noticed that the sun was almost ready to slip over the horizon. As he looked out across the field behind his house he wondered what in the hell he was going to do with all of those tobacco plants. He would have to ask Harmon about that in the morning.

Suddenly Logan heard a pecking sound from somewhere near the front of the house. He walked across the kitchen to the entrance to the foyer and paused. The house was still and silent. Then the pecking noise resumed and Logan felt his heart begin to thump in his chest. Then he realized where the noise was coming from and breathed a sigh of relief.

Someone was knocking on the door.

Whoever was at the door was pecking at it with their knuckles instead of ringing the doorbell. Who would be knocking on his door at this time of the evening? Perhaps Harmon had forgotten something and had returned for it.

Logan walked uneasily down the foyer to the front door. He was almost certain that it wasn't Harmon but who else could it be? He knew Harmon had been ready to go home to his supper and wouldn't have come back for anything. But still, it had to be him.

Logan suddenly thought about Chip McPhale. Maybe Chip had returned and wanted to discuss the ownership of the land in a more personal way, one that involved fists and elbows to the chin. Logan knew he had to stand up to Chip and that he couldn't let him push him around. But it was obvious to Logan of what side of the tracks Chip came from, and that the last thing he wanted to do was to fight with him.

Logan put his hand on the doorknob and swallowed the rock in his throat. He was just going to have to face Chip man to man. There was no other way. Logan hoped that the playground mentality of standing up to a bully to make him back down would work in this situation.

Logan turned the doorknob and then opened the large wooden door. He was greeted by the smiling face of Colby. And she was holding a large dish covered in a red and white checkered cloth.

Logan felt his spirits lift at the sight of Colby's pretty face. Her blue eyes and sandy blonde hair were just as gentle and kind as they had been at the diner. She was wearing faded blue jeans and a pale yellow shirt that accented her summer tan.

"Hey there," Colby said, "thought I'd bring you a little housewarming gift, courtesy of the diner. I'm sorry for dropping by unannounced. It's so rude." Colby then smiled again causing Logan's mind to go completely blank. Colby's pretty face, along with the smell of whatever was in the dish had completely disarmed him.

"Oh no no, it's fine," Logan stammered. "Please come in."

Colby stepped through the door and walked by Logan. She didn't make any attempt to put distance between him and her, and as she moved close to him Logan caught a gentle hint of perfume. But then the smell of the dish in her hands reclaimed his senses. It smelled good, and he could feel his stomach starting to rumble.

"What's in the dish?" Logan said as he closed the front door.

"Chicken and dumplings," Colby replied. "It's one of our specialties at the diner. I make it myself."

"I don't think I've ever smelled anything better," replied Logan. He was having a hard time hiding his astonishment. Here he was standing in the foyer of a large Southern manor talking to a pretty girl holding a dish full of chicken and dumplings that smelled absolutely heavenly. What a difference a day makes, he thought to himself.

"Hold this for a moment. I brought some tea but I left it in my car. I'll be right back."

Colby handed Logan the dish and then opened the front door. She left it standing open as she went to her car and retrieved a half-gallon jug of sweet tea. The she returned to find Logan sniffing the dish of chicken and dumplings, his eyes wide with wonder. Colby couldn't help but grin at him.

"You know, in a little town like Starlight no one can keep a secret. So when Sandy stopped by the diner and said you and Harmon were going out to the house tonight I knew you would need something for supper. Sandy was friends with Rosemary and her and a couple of Rosemary's other friends kind of got the house in order after Rosemary died. I remember Sandy saying that they cleaned out all of the food in the refrigerator so it wouldn't spoil."

"Yep, it's empty. But the pantry is full of stuff. I was just in there looking around trying to figure out what I was going to eat for dinner."

"That problem has been solved. Let's get busy," Colby said with a wink. "I haven't had supper either. I'm starving."

Logan and Colby walked to the kitchen where he sat the chicken and dumplings down on the table. Colby sat the sweet tea down beside the dish and began looking through the cabinets for the drinking glasses. When she found them she picked two and sat them on the table. Logan had already put two bowls on the table and was in the process of getting the silverware. Once they had everything they sat down at the table and Colby spooned their bowls full of chicken and dumplings while Logan poured the tea.

"The icemaker is empty too," Logan said, unable to think of anything else to say. He was still overwhelmed at his turn of luck. If someone had told him last week that he would be sitting in a house like this having dinner with a girl that looked like Colby he would have certainly told them they needed to check into rehab to kick their drug addiction. How in the world could he have such a turn of luck?

Logan ate a spoonful of the hot chicken and dumplings and felt a wave of pleasure course through his body. It was by far the best thing he had tasted in years. Colby could tell by the look on his face that he was enjoying the food. When Logan's eyes met hers, he suddenly felt embarrassed. He had eaten four or five spoonfuls of the chicken and dumplings without even saying a word.

"Sorry," Logan said sheepishly. "I'm being a slob. It's just that my supper usually comes in one of those plastic trays that go in the microwave. I haven't tasted food like this in, well, I don't know how long. You said you made this? It's delicious. In fact, delicious isn't a big enough word." Logan realized he was rambling again. He couldn't believe that Colby was having this effect on him. He felt like a teenager on his first date.

"Oh, it's easy. You just boil chicken on the bone in a pot of water. Add some salt and pepper and a few more other spices, a bay leaf or two, maybe. The chicken has to have bones in it so that it will make a good broth. But I don't make the dumplings. We buy the frozen kind. Some people make their dumplings out of biscuit dough but I can't for the life of me figure out how to make good homemade biscuits. My grandmother tried to teach me once but I just couldn't get it. Biscuit making is turning into a lost art in the South. Imagine that," Colby said as she smiled at Logan and then went back to eating her chicken and dumplings.

Logan and Colby finished their meal while talking about Starlight. Colby told Logan a little about growing up around the tobacco fields when Starlight was more prosperous and he told her about growing up in Wilmington. When Logan finished his second bowl of chicken and dumplings, he leaned back in his chair and smiled.

"That's the best meal I think I've ever had. Thank you for making it. How about I repay you with a tour of this big old house that they tell me now belongs to me. And to think, my mother-in-law said I'd never amount to anything." Logan was immediately sorry for the remark.

"Oh? I didn't know, um, I didn't know you were married," Colby said as she pulled her hands off the table and dropped them into her lap.

"No, I uh, well, I used to be. I'm divorced," Logan said as he looked down into his empty bowl. Then he took his hand and began to push his half-full glass of tea around in small circles on the table. "And I guess my mother-in-law, I mean, my ex-mother-in-law was right. I'm just a used-car salesman. But no, I'm not married anymore. She left me for a..."

Colby spoke up before Logan could finish his sentence. "Well, that's a good thing," Colby said as she grinned at Logan. "I mean, it's a good thing that you're not married anymore. In this town people would talk if we were sitting here having dinner together and one of us was married to someone else." Colby winked at Logan and then took a sip of her tea. "Gossip travels pretty fast in a small town like Starlight. Don't let the slow pace of life around here fool you. This town has its fair share of busybodies, let me tell you."

Logan smiled at Colby. Her Southern charm was intoxicating. She was a far cry from any woman he had ever met in the city.

"So how about that tour?" Logan said as he patted the table with both of his hands. He was relieved that Colby obviously didn't want to hear all the details of his divorce. "We can put the chicken and dumplings in the refrigerator. I'll have the leftovers for breakfast in the morning." Colby crinkled her nose at the sound of this.

"I'd love a tour. I've never been in this house, even though I've known Rosemary for most of my life. Then again, everyone in town knew Rosemary. She was a sweet lady. She didn't socialize much, but everyone still knew her."

14

Logan and Colby walked down the long hallway on the second floor of the house. They had just finished looking at all of the bedrooms full of antique furniture. Each bedroom had a four-post bed, a dresser and a nightstand on each side of the bed. The furniture was elegant yet modest and fit the antebellum character of the house to a tee.

At the end of the hallway was a door that Logan assumed led to another bedroom. When he opened it he saw that it was a narrow staircase that led to the third floor of the house.

"Must go to the attic," Colby said as she moved close to Logan and peeked up the staircase to the dark attic above. Logan caught a hint of her perfume again as she stood close to him and in his mind he wanted to believe she had moved close to him on purpose, but in reality he figured that she just wanted to see up the staircase out of curiosity. But when she turned and looked into his eyes he got the feeling that his first inkling had been correct.

"Wanna go up there and have a peek?" Colby said as she grinned at Logan.

"Absolutely," Logan said as he stepped into the doorway. He knew he would gladly fumble around in any dark room, basement or attic if it meant getting to spend a few more minutes with Colby. She was magnetic and he knew he had never been so attracted to a girl in his entire life.

Logan fumbled around for a light switch but was unable to find one on the wall. With Colby following close behind, he slowly crept up the creaking stairs through the darkness until he could poke his head up above the attic floor at the top of the stairs.

The fading twilight coming in through the dormers cast long, soft shadows across the floor of the attic. In one corner Logan could see several old pieces of furniture and a large wooden trunk. Then he scanned the rest of the attic until his eyes came to rest on what appeared to be a large pile of dolls. As Logan studied the pile of dolls he suddenly realized that it was just a pile of doll heads and that none of the heads had bodies attached to them. Just then Colby squeezed beside him in the narrow staircase so that she could see into the attic. She took in a short gasp of air when she saw the pile of doll heads.

"Oh how creepy," she said as she put her hand on Logan's shoulder. "I wonder where those came from."

"I dunno," Logan replied. I wish we had a light. Maybe tomorrow we can check this out in the daylight. It's getting late outside and there's not much light coming in through the dormers. It'll be pitch dark up here pretty soon. I can't believe there's not even a lamp or something up here." *I'm babbling again,* Logan thought to himself.

"I think I'd rather see it in the daylight. Besides, it is getting kind of late. I should probably be going," Colby said. Just then Logan spied a string hanging in the center of the attic. It led to a small light attached to one of the rafters.

"There's the light," Logan said. Wait here and I'll turn it on.

Logan walked across the dim attic and pulled the string. There was a resounding *click* and then the attic was bathed in the dim yellow light of the solitary incandescent bulb.

Colby climbed the last few steps and then joined Logan in the middle of the attic. Through one of the dormers Logan could see the long, tree-lined driveway that led from the house to the main road. But the light was fading fast. Logan knew it would be dark soon.

Colby walked over to a small chest of drawers and pulled open the top drawer. Then she did the same to the remaining drawers before remarking to Logan that every drawer was just full of clothes. While she was doing that, Logan had begun to examine the old cedar trunk. But the padlock on the trunk prevented him from opening it.

"I wonder what's in this trunk," he said as Colby walked up beside him.

"Whatever it is it must be important," she said. "Look at the size of that lock. We're not getting into that thing tonight unless you have the key."

"I don't," replied Logan. "Does Starlight have a hardware store?"

"Yep," Colby replied.

"Tomorrow I'll buy a set of bolt cutters and we'll make short work of that lock. I don't want to tear up the trunk. It looks like an antique."

Colby then walked over to the corner where there was something covered in old sheets. She had to crouch down to avoid hitting her head on the angled rafters. She pulled up the edge of one of the sheets until she could see that they were covering several large, framed photographs. Logan joined her and they pulled the blankets gently off of the photographs, careful not to knock them over.

"Wow, must be old." Logan said as they sat down beside each other.

"Looks like your house and land," Colby replied as she gently poked Logan in the ribs. Her touch sent an electric shock through his body.

Several of the large, black and white photographs were of the house and the surrounding fields. The house looked the same, just in better condition and the fields were full of tobacco plants. Logan pulled the largest framed photo onto his lap and examined it closely.

"Hard to believe it all belongs to me now," he said as he gingerly touched the house in the old photo.

While he was staring at the large photo of the house, Colby picked up one of the smaller framed photographs leaning against the attic wall. This one was of was of a man and a woman standing beside a little girl. None of them had a smile on their face. Colby was quick to notice this and point it out to Logan.

"They look unhappy," she said.

"Pissed off is more like it," Logan countered as he looked over at the photo Colby was holding. "I guess life was hard back then. From the looks of their clothes these photos have to be a hundred years old at least."

"They could be some of your long lost relatives."

"Maybe," Logan replied. "Right now I'm just getting used to the idea of Rosemary being a long lost relative. But you could be right. Why else would photos of these people be in the attic?"

"They could be tenant farmers or sharecroppers that worked the land way back then. But I don't know why someone would have taken their pictures and put them in the attic," Colby replied. "Most tenant farmers had lots of children. It's strange to see just one child in the photo."

"What kind of farmer?" Logan said, ignoring the last part of what Colby had said about children.

Colby chuckled at Logan. She had forgotten that he was from Wilmington.

"You don't know much about farming, do you city boy?" she said as she poked Logan in the ribs again. It made him flinch with pleasure.

"Nope. But I'll have you know that I now own the biggest tobacco farm in town. Go figure. I'm the kind of guy that if you asked me where eggs come from I'd tell you the supermarket, not a chicken. So no, I don't know much about farming but I can sell you a used Chevy and make you feel like you just stole it from me." Logan was trying to make fun of himself. Colby picked up on it immediately.

"Well where would we be without car salesmen? No one would have cars." Colby winked and once again poked Logan in the ribs. He wanted to grab her and kiss her and make love to her on the attic floor but he knew he didn't have the nerve for such a bold move.

"Tenant farmers paid rent to live on the land. They did all the work and the owner got a cut of the crop price when it was sold at market.

Sharecroppers did about the same thing but they didn't get as much money. They worked their fingers to the bone for a share of the crop, hence the name sharecropper. It was way before my time, but this land was once worked by sharecroppers and tenant farmers. Rosemary has had someone else plant and harvest her tobacco for as long as I can remember. They say that after her husband was killed that she never so much as stepped foot in the fields again. She's been renting out the land over the years. There are no sharecroppers or tenant farmers anymore, but farmers still rent land out when they can't farm it. That's what Rosemary has been doing all these years. I would imagine whoever she hired to plant that crop out there in her fields, I mean, your fields, will be harvesting it soon. It's that time of the year."

"How did you get to know all this?" Logan said as he raised an eyebrow at Colby. She was getting more interesting by the minute. He had never met a girl like her.

"My great-granddaddy was a sharecropper. At one time he even worked the Shaw land. Poor as dirt, let me tell you. I've seen pictures of him and my great-grandmother and they looked like they didn't have a pot to pee in. But they were just like everyone else back in those days. The tobacco farming was all done by hand and it was almost a death sentence because the work was so hard. Or that's what I've been told. I've never worked the fields myself. My parents owned a small tobacco farm at one time, but they managed to get out of tobacco farming right after I was born."

Logan thought about what Colby had said about Rosemary's husband. He suddenly realized it didn't jibe with what Harmon had told him.

"You said Rosemary's husband was killed? Harmon told me my great-grandfather died years ago but he didn't say he was killed. What happened to him?"

"Harmon didn't tell you?"

"No. He just said he died years ago. Carson was his name, right?"

"I think so. Carson Shaw," Colby said.

"But Harmon did tell me the story behind the land and the murders. He told me all about the McPhale family and how they want the land. And he told me about how lots of people believe there is some sort of silly curse on the land. Or something like that."

Colby paused for a moment. She felt her skin begin to crawl. She thought about Harmon, and understood why he wouldn't have told Logan about the murder of Carson Shaw. After all, Carson was Logan's great-grandfather.

"Carson was killed right out there in one of those tobacco barns back in the Sixties," Colby finally said. "Everyone in town knows the story. Someone used an axe and hacked him into little pieces. They never caught the killer and in my opinion they never will. There have been other murders like Carson's and our sheriff hasn't been able to solve them. And he never will, if you ask me. No sheriff has ever been able to find even a single clue as to who is doing all the killing."

As he listened to Colby talk, Logan knew that he was about to learn a lot more than what Harmon had told him about the land. Colby seemed to know the history.

"Harmon said that most people think it's the McPhale family."

"Harmon always says that," Colby said. "It's his standard story. But he doesn't believe it."

"That's true. He did tell me that much, that he didn't think it was the McPhales. He seems like a straight up kind of guy."

"He's a good man. And I'm sure he figured that your great-grandmother dying and you inheriting her house was enough for you to deal with right now. But there's more to the story of this land than he told you."

"I'm all ears. I mean, I do own the place now," Logan said as he winked at Colby. He wanted to hear all about the land and the murders, and he wanted to be close to Colby. He knew the more she talked, the longer he would get to be with her.

Colby exhaled and pulled her legs underneath her until she was sitting cross-legged next to Logan.

"They call the killer "the ghost of tobacco road". Tobacco road is a nickname for this part of the state due to all the tobacco farms."

"A ghost…" Logan furrowed his brow. "How can a ghost kill someone? Where I come from ghosts just make noise at night and scare people. They can't actually hurt you."

"Well around here they can hack you into little pieces with an axe. Every murder victim in the Shaw Fields has been chopped up beyond recognition. And it's been a while so lots of people think we're due for another murder."

"I know, Harmon and Chip McPhale brought that up when Chip dropped by for a friendly visit right after we got to the house," Logan said. "He was a one-man welcoming committee."

"He's just a pure asshole. Stay away from Chip McPhale. But as for the people that believe the McPhales are behind the killings, well, they're all just crazy. There's no way the McPhale family has been killing people for almost a hundred years. That's just bunk. The first murder was in 1931."

"Harmon said as much. He said the McPhales are pretty stupid and that he didn't believe they were behind the killings. But you never know. It's easier to believe that story than some story about a ghost wandering the fields."

Colby said, "Some people think it's the ghost of a slave. Slaves worked the fields until the Civil War."

"I can't say as I could blame the ghost of a slave for wandering the fields and hacking people to pieces," Logan said as he looked up at a dormer. The light from outside was almost gone. "I would imagine this isn't the only field haunted by those kinds of ghosts. The South is probably full of fields like that. Lots of restless souls…"

"And the murders only happen under a harvest moon," Colby replied.

"Harmon mentioned that. I'm ashamed to say I have no idea what a harvest moon is," Logan said. "Where I come from we don't pay any attention to the moon. It's all streetlights and neon signs."

"It's a full moon so bright that you can harvest a crop by the light from it," replied Colby. "Usually comes in September."

"Makes sense," Logan said, ashamed that he hadn't known that.

"And every murder has taken place in the Shaw Fields. Carson was murdered in one of those tobacco barns out there, but at one time the fields came up past where those barns are located. Every victim was hacked to pieces by a killer that no one has ever seen. Only the victims know what the killer looks like and they're not talking." Colby smiled at Logan, hoping that it would lighten the mood. Logan picked up on it immediately.

"Enough of all this talk about slave ghosts and spirits," he said. "Let's check out the rest of the attic." Logan then patted Colby on the knee and was about to stand up. But she put her hand on top of his and held it against her knee.

"Logan, I…" Colby then looked down into her lap for a few seconds. When she finally lifted her face he could see that the twilight coming in from the outside had turned her eyes a dusty shade of gray. Her beauty momentarily threw him off balance.

"What is it?" he finally said.

"Well, I just hope you're going to be okay. I mean, here in this house all by yourself." Logan watched as Colby's eyes scanned the attic rafters above them. She appeared to shiver just a bit as her eyes moved from the rafters to the attic space around them.

"Hey, I'll be alright." Logan was thrilled that Colby cared about his welfare, but she was obviously upset and he didn't like that. He was overcome with as strong desire to protect her.

"I know you will, but it's just that I've lived in this town my entire life and no matter which story you want to believe about the murders, one thing is for sure – there have been murders in those fields out there since 1931. And it has been years since the last one. I'm just, well I'm just a little worried about you. Promise me…"

"Promise you what?"

"Promise me you won't go in those fields at night, moon or no moon. Just stay out of them after the sun goes down. That's the safest way to do it."

Logan gently squeezed Colby's knee. The denim felt nice against his hand.

Then Colby continued. "And it's not just the fields, Logan. This house… Well, it's just that this house has a past too. Everyone in town knows about it. It wouldn't surprise me if it were full of more ghosts that those fields out there. I know I could never spend the night in this house by myself. I don't know how you're going to do it."

"Hey, I'll be alright. Really. Besides, what ghost would waste its time on an old car salesman like me? Or what McPhale kid would risk a jail sentence by coming after me? My legal staff would make short work of him."

"Harmon?" Colby said, trying not to laugh.

"Yep, Harmon. He's the best legal eagle in the state. I'll be just fine. Now let's check out the rest of the attic."

Colby and Logan got up and stacked the photos back in the corner before covering them with the sheet again. Then they walked over to the pile of doll heads.

"What do you make of this?" she asked Logan.

"Beats me. Just a pile of old doll heads. They look like they're hand painted. Ceramic, or porcelain or something like that." Logan frowned at the doll heads and scratched his chin. He stared at some of the blank expressions on the faces of the heads and after a few seconds Colby reached up and put her hand on his upper arm. Suddenly everything seemed to catch up with her – the story about the murders, the old photos and now the doll heads. As she looked around the attic she felt a sense of dread wash over her as she noticed the old trunk sitting in the corner. Suddenly she didn't like the idea of being in the attic.

"I think I better go."

Logan felt his spirits sink.

"Are you sure? We can go back downstairs. We don't have to rummage around in this spooky attic." Logan wanted to reach out and put his arm around Colby but was afraid to.

"I really need to get home. Maybe I can drop by tomorrow and we can finish the tour. I've always wanted to see inside those tobacco barns out back. Maybe we can walk down to the Skeleton River."

"It's a deal. Harmon and I have to do some stuff at his office in the morning but I'll probably be done around lunch time."

"Drop by the diner when you're through," Colby said. "I get off at two."

Logan and Colby then turned and went back down the attic stairs. The hallway at the bottom of the stairs was dark and Logan silently chided himself for not leaving the hall lights on. He knew the dark hallway scared Colby.

"Hold on a second," he said as he let go of Colby's hand and walked several feet over to the wall to turn on the lights. He hit the switch and the hallway was suddenly bathed in the buttery glow of incandescent light.

"Much better," Colby said as she walked over and joined Logan.

Once back in the kitchen Colby put the leftover chicken and dumplings along with the sweet tea in the refrigerator. Then Logan walked her to the front door. Once out on the porch, she turned and smiled at him. He didn't want her to go but he knew that a girl like Colby wasn't going to spend the night with a guy she had just met. He felt stupid for even considering the idea.

"Thanks for stopping by. And thanks again for the chicken and dumplings." Then Logan forced himself to stop talking. The last thing he wanted to do was start babbling again.

"You're welcome," replied Colby. An awkward moment of silence followed. Logan's mind began to race as he tried to think of something to say. But Colby spoke before he could think of anything.

"Good night," she said as she turned and began to walk down the stairs. Just when she was at the edge of the circle of light being thrown off by the porch lamp, she turned at looked back up at Logan standing on the porch.

"By the way, don't mess with those bottles. You'll set them free."

Logan paused for a second and then it dawned on him what Colby was talking about. Already upset with himself for not walking her to her car, he quickly walked down the stairs until he was standing beside her. Then he looked over at the bottle tree next to the porch steps.

"I know, I know. Harmon told me all about it. They're full of evil spirits or something."

Colby gave Logan a "bless your heart" smile while reminding herself once again that he was from the city and didn't know much about Southern folklore.

"The story goes that evil spirits roaming in the night are attracted to the bottles. They get trapped inside the bottles and then burn up when the morning sun hits them. They say when the wind blows through the bottle tree you can hear the spirits moaning. It's just an old Southern wives' tale."

"Well as old as this house is I'm sure every one of those bottles has a spook inside of it. There's no telling how many evil spirits have been through here over the years."

"Don't be a butthead," Colby said as she grinned at Logan. He slowly turned his head towards her.

"A what?"

"You heard me, city boy."

Logan then walked Colby to her car. Before he let himself overthink it, he put his hands on her cheeks and gave her a gentle kiss on the lips. Then he opened her car door for her. At first it seemed like she didn't want to get in the car but then she stepped around the door and sat down in the seat. Then she looked up at Logan and smiled.

"I'll see you tomorrow," she said as Logan closed the door.

Logan waved as Colby's car circled the statue in the driveway. Then he watched as the taillights were swallowed up in the tunnel of trees that led to the main road. He was happy that he had not fumbled the kiss with Colby and was even happier that she had kissed him back. In fact, he was pretty satisfied with the entire evening.

§§§

With nothing else to do, Logan washed the dishes he and Colby had used, dried them and put them in a rack next to the sink. What was he going to do now? About the only thing he could think of was to go back upstairs and choose a bedroom for the night. There were no televisions in the house so he figured that the only thing left to do was to lock up and turn in. Outside the sun had set and the surrounding fields were dark. The thought of sitting on the back porch for a while crossed his mind but he decided against it. It had been a long day and he needed some rest. He figured he could turn in for the night and think about how nice it would be to see Colby tomorrow at the diner.

Logan's thoughts were interrupted by a knock on the door. It was just a slight, gentle peck and he almost didn't hear it. But when he realized what it was his heart skipped in his chest.

Colby had returned, and she was knocking at the front door.

Logan walked quickly through the foyer, grabbed the doorknob and pulled the door open. Colby was nowhere to be seen. Instead, standing on the porch in the dim glow of the porch light was a little girl in an old, tattered dress. She was holding a small yellow flower in her hand.

Logan was dumbfounded. What was a little girl doing standing on his porch at this hour of the night? And where did she come from?

"Um, well hello there," Logan said as he looked down at the little girl. Then his eyes scanned the driveway circle in front of the house. There were no cars in the circle other than his. Logan then looked back down at the little girl. Her hair was long and sandy blonde and looked like it had not been combed or washed in several days. Her dress looked homemade and very old. Logan reminded himself that he was not in the city and that country people often made their own clothes, or so he had always heard. After a few seconds he spoke to the little girl again.

"My name is Logan. What's your name? And where is your mom?"

The little girl didn't respond. She only looked at Logan while holding the yellow flower in her hand.

Logan had no idea what to do. He knew not to invite the little girl into his house but he also didn't want to just shut the door in her face. How did she manage to end up on his porch at this hour of the night? Even in broad daylight it would be strange for a child of her age to show up on his porch without a parent.

"Can I help you, sweetie? Are you selling cookies or something? It's kind of late to be doing that. You can come back tomorrow if you want to…"

Suddenly the little girl raised her hand towards Logan like she was trying to hand him the flower. He looked down at the flower but before he could reach out to take it, the little girl dropped it onto the porch floor. She giggled slightly, then turned and ran down the porch stairs. At the bottom of the stairs, she turned and ran past the bottle tree and around the corner of the house towards the backyard.

"Hey! Wait a minute! Don't go back there!" Logan yelled at the little girl but she ignored him and disappeared into the darkness. Logan quickly ran down the porch stairs and followed the route the little girl had taken. When he reached the corner of the house he stopped and looked out into the moonlit tobacco field.

"Hey! Come back! You can't be out there in my fields!" Logan knew the little girl couldn't hear him and even if she could it was obvious she wasn't going to obey his commands. Flustered, he ran down the side of the house until he was standing in the backyard. He could see the looming hulks of the tobacco barns lined up in a row down the edge of the field.

In the distance, Logan could barely make out the little girl as she continued on through the fields between the rows of tobacco plants. If it weren't for the rising moon he would not have been able to see her at all.

"What the fuck?" Logan said, exasperated. He reached up and ran his fingers through his hair.

"Where the fuck is she going?"

Logan moved down to the edge of the tobacco field. He scanned down the rows to the far tree line but could no longer see the little girl. In the distance he could see the a small opening in the tree line revealing the bank of the Skeleton River, the still water glowing silver in the moonlight. Unable to figure out what to do, he put his hands on his hips and exhaled sharply.

The little girl was gone.

"The McPhales…" Logan whispered to himself. Maybe she was a McPhale and they had put her up to coming over to his house. If so, they really were as stupid as Harmon said they were. Logan tried to force his mind to accept this theory, but the more he thought about it the less likely it seemed that anyone, even a crazy family like the McPhales would send a child over to a stranger's house after dark. Then he remembered that Harmon had said there were only the two McPhale brothers. He hadn't mentioned any younger children.

"Whatever…" Logan said has he scanned the field one more time. He knew there was no way he was going out into the fields to look for the little girl. Whoever she was, she was gone and he knew it would be a waste of time to look for her.

Logan turned and walked through his backyard and around the house to the front porch. When he walked up the steps he saw that the flower the little girl had dropped was gone. He paused under the porch light and looked around him but there was no sign of the flower. Then he looked over at the bottle tree sitting still in the moonlight. After a few more seconds he walked back into the house and locked the door behind him. Then he checked the back door. He turned and began to walk through the kitchen but stopped after a few steps. He returned the backdoor, unlocked it and walked out onto the large back porch. He moved slowly in the darkness until he was at the handrail that bordered the porch. One more time he let his eyes scan the expansive tobacco field stretching to the far tree line. There was no sign of the little girl.

"That's it. I give up, little girl. I don't know who you are or where you came from but you're on your own."

Logan then returned to the kitchen and locked the backdoor as he went. Then he climbed the stairs to find a bedroom for the night.

He had retrieved his bags from his car earlier and had everything he needed to settle in for the night. He was ready for the day to be over and he wanted nothing more than to crawl into a bed and go to sleep.

Logan wanted to fall asleep quickly, dream about Colby, and wake up refreshed and ready for another day. But little did he know the night ahead of him would be one of the longest nights of his life.

15

Logan chose the largest bedroom on the second floor of the house. The room contained a four post bed, a large dresser and a nightstand. A very ornate crystal lamp sat on the nightstand. The bedroom even had a fireplace and above it hung another very large portrait of Rosemary.

On the dresser sat a large doll with a porcelain head. The head looked just like the ones Logan and Colby had seen earlier. But the doll was still intact and had not suffered the same fate as the ones whose heads were now in a pile on the attic floor. Logan thought this was amusing, even though the sight of the doll sitting on the dresser unnerved him more than he wanted to admit to himself. He shook it off and put the thought out of his mind as he walked across the bedroom while the doll sat motionless on the dresser, its colorful dress contrasting against the dark walnut finish of the wood.

Logan placed his bags on the bed and removed his shaving kit from one of them. He couldn't help but look over his shoulder once again at the doll and quickly chided himself for letting something so harmless get to him. The thought of walking over and putting the doll in one of the drawers suddenly felt like a good idea, but Logan knew he was just being childish. Finally he put the doll out of his mind while trying to concentrate on his bags.

Logan took his shaving kit into the adjoining bathroom. It had been a long day and when he saw the large shower in the corner of the bathroom he immediately decided that a hot shower would be the perfect thing to help him relax for the night.

He grabbed his soap from his shaving kit and sat it on the edge of the sink. The shower was large and appeared to be more modern than the rest of the bathroom. Logan figured it had been added later, most likely after Rosemary had gotten tired of climbing in and out of the claw-footed tub that was sitting in the opposite corner of the bathroom. The only thing

Logan didn't like about the shower was the large curtain pulled across it. He hated closed shower curtains. It was just a childhood fear that he had never been able to shake.

The hot water brought welcome relief as it ran down his back. After a few minutes, the steam in the bathroom began to fog the mirror over the sink. Logan was almost in a trance enjoying the hot water when he heard something crash to the floor outside of the shower.

Logan quickly pulled the shower curtain to the side and looked out through the steam in the bathroom. His shaving kit was lying on the floor in front of the sink. He felt a wave of relief wash over him. He closed his eyes and pulled the shower curtain closed and resumed his shower. After about ten minutes he finished up and then grabbed a towel from the small shelf on the wall next to the shower above the toilet.

Wrapped in his towel, Logan walked through the steamy bathroom until he was in front of the sink. Through the haze he looked into the mirror fogged up from the steam.

The words *I'm sorry* were scribbled into the film of water vapor covering the mirror.

Logan quickly turned and looked behind him. The bathroom was filled with water vapor but he could see through it into the bedroom. He put his hand on the towel to keep it from falling and walked quickly to the door that led to the bedroom. Then he stepped through the door into the bedroom and felt an instant chill from the difference in temperature. He looked around the bedroom and then walked back into the bathroom. He looked at the mirror again but the words were gone.

"So this is how it's gonna be," Logan said as he bowed his head and looked down into the sink. Then he looked back up at the mirror before wiping it clean with his hand. "Next it will be a real ghost and not just words on the mirror."

Logan tried to calm his nerves and then began to doubt whether he had actually seen the words on the mirror or if it had just been his imagination. He removed his toothbrush and toothpaste and then brushed his teeth. When he was finished he looked into the mirror one more time and realized from his reflection how tired he was from the long day.

Wrapped in his towel, Logan walked into the bedroom and pulled out an old T-shirt and a pair of boxer shorts from his bag. Then he climbed into bed and turned out the lamp on the nightstand. He didn't have a book to read so he decided to just try and go to sleep.

Logan wanted to think about Colby and the time he had spent with her earlier in the evening. He wanted to envision his hands on her body as they made slow and passionate love. But images of the things in the attic kept coming to his mind. The old portraits, the doll heads, the antique trunk. It was all right above him in the attic. Every time tried to conjure an image of

Colby and fantasize about making love to her, the people in the old portraits would flash through his mind. Who were they? Was he related to them? Had they lived in the house, or perhaps worked in the Shaw Fields?

Then Logan thought about the little girl on the porch. What had that been all about? Who was she, and what was she doing on his porch at such an hour? Where were her parents?

And then the words in the mirror… Had he actually seen them or not?

Despite all the questions and images marching through his mind, it wasn't long before exhaustion overtook Logan and he finally drifted off to sleep.

§§§

Sometime after midnight Logan woke up to go to the bathroom. The house was still and quiet and the creaking of the floorboards under his feet as he walked to the bathroom seemed louder than normal. After he finished he returned to the bed and crawled back under the sheets. He rolled over onto his side with his back to the door of the bedroom. Once again the house fell silent. There wasn't even any noise coming from outside. No wind, no approaching storm, nothing to make any noise. Logan could not remember ever hearing a night as quiet as this. Back in his trailer the constant drone of noise from the shipping port made the nights anything but quiet and peaceful. But now he was experiencing his first night in the country, and the silence was disturbing.

Logan wasn't sure how long he had been lying there when he heard the first hint of a sound. It seemed to be coming from the other end of the hallway, near the door that led to the attic. Slowly, Logan rolled over until he could see the door of the bedroom. Was he hearing things? Or was the sound real.

Time seemed to stand still. Logan knew that what he was hearing was real. It was the sound of someone walking down the hall. Slow, deliberate steps one after the other. They were gentle steps, to the point where it made it seem as if whoever it was coming down the hall was trying to do it in the quietest manner possible.

Logan wanted to bolt out of the bed, turn on the light and find something to defend himself with. Anything would do. Perhaps he could use one of the andirons by the fireplace. He knew he could certainly use one of them to teach someone a lesson about breaking into his house. But instead of jumping out of the bed, Logan stayed still under the blankets, as if they afforded him some sort of protection from the approaching intruder.

Just when it seemed that whoever was out in the hall was about to arrive at his bedroom door, the sounds stopped. For several seconds, seconds that seemed to last for an eternity, there was no sound at all coming from the hallway.

The moonlight streaming in from a crack in the window drapes was just bright enough to cast a line of silvery light through the middle of the bedroom. Logan kept his eyes glued to the black rectangle that led out into the hallway. Just as he was about to resign himself to the fact that he had probably just been hearing things, he heard another slight sound come from the hallway. It was the sound of a floorboard creaking under the weight of someone standing just outside of bedroom door.

Logan felt the blood flare in his veins. Then a cold shiver rocketed up his spine as the intruder stepped into the doorway.

Standing in the doorway was the little girl that had been on his porch earlier in the evening. In the dim glow of the moonlight coming in from the window, Logan could once again see the small flower in her hand.

A wave of terror washed over Logan as he looked into the little girl's face. The fight or flight mechanism was raging inside his body. Just then he threw back the covers and reached for the lamp on the nightstand, almost knocking it over in the process. He managed to grasp the small knob under the shade and fumble with it until he finally twisted it in the right direction to turn on the light.

Logan squinted under the glare of the lamp as he tried to adjust his eyes and focus on the doorway. When his eyes finally adjusted he saw that the little girl was gone.

Gasping for breath and trying to calm his pounding heart, Logan buried his face in his hands. After a few seconds, he realized that something felt wrong about the room. He kept his hands over his face but spread his fingers enough to be able to see through them to the dresser across the room. He felt every nerve ending in his body ignite as he focused on the doll sitting on the dresser. The doll's head was turned in his direction.

Logan closed his fingers over his face and took another deep breath. Then he opened his fingers again and looked at the doll. This time its head was facing forward like it had been when he had first climbed into bed.

"Any damn day you wanna wake up, Logan. Enough of this fucking nightmare. That's what it is… A fucking nightmare. I must be asleep. I *have* to be asleep."

After a few minutes, Logan slowly turned his body until his feet came out from underneath the blanket. He slowly lowered his feet until they touched the cool wood of the floor. Then he got out of bed and slowly crept over to the bedroom door. He had to have a look down the hallway. He knew there was no way he was going back to bed until he looked down the hallway and proved to himself that it was empty, and that the sight of the little girl had been just what he thought it had been – a nightmare.

Logan swallowed hard as he put his hand on the doorframe. Then he slowly moved until his head was close to his hand. In one quick move he stuck his head into the hallway and looked towards the attic door on the other end. The hallway was dark, but he could make out the lines of the attic door as it sat closed on the opposite end of the hallway from his bedroom.

A quick exhale brought relief, but then Logan thought about the porcelain doll. He quickly turned his head in the direction of the dresser but the doll was just as it was the last time he had looked at it. It was still staring blankly across the room in the direction of the bathroom.

Logan felt his nerves beginning to calm. Maybe he was sleepwalking, maybe he was dreaming, he had no idea. Surrendering to his earlier impulse, he walked over to the dresser, opened the top drawer and then dropped the doll into the drawer. Then he slammed the drawer shut.

Once back in bed, it was over an hour before Logan fell back asleep and when he did it was a shallow and fitful sleep laced with dreams about working in the tobacco fields in the blazing sun. In the dreams he was a laborer using primitive hand tools to cut the tobacco stalks. In another dream he was between two rows of tobacco plants and as he looked down one of the rows he could see children pulling worms from the tobacco leaves before depositing them in cans hung by strings looped around their necks.

By the time dawn came, Logan was awake once again. He felt like he had not slept at all. The first thought that came to mind was the talk he planned to have with Harmon about this house. After one night in the house, Logan knew that Harmon had not told him everything about his great-grandmother Rosemary Abigail Shaw, or about the house she had willed to him.

As Logan climbed out of the bed, he noticed something lying on the floor near the bedroom door. He walked slowly to the object until he was standing over it. Everything that had happened the night before, and the idea that it had all been a dream was suddenly cast into doubt in Logan's mind as he stared down at the small yellow flower lying on the floor at his feet. Then he slowly raised his head and turned to look at the dresser and the porcelain doll sitting on top of it. He knew he had put the doll in the drawer the night before. Or had that been a dream? At this point, Logan had no idea.

Logan exhaled a hot breath and then reached down to pick up the flower. He then laid it on the nightstand next to the bed. The next thing he did was open all the drapes covering the bedroom windows. The early morning sunlight brought comfort to his soul as he sat back down on the edge of the bed.

"Maybe it was all a dream," Logan said under his breath. "The flower was stuck to my shoe and that's how it made its way to the bedroom floor. Makes perfect sense…"

Logan knew his theory was weak but he didn't know what else to think. All he could do now was get dressed and maybe go eat breakfast. He needed to get out of the house and the thought of the diner and Colby was the first thing that came to his mind.

Logan washed his face, brushed his teeth and then got dressed. On his way out of the bedroom he picked up the small flower from the nightstand and stuck it in his shirt pocket. Maybe Colby could tell him what kind of flower it was. He knew he would have to invent some story as to how he got it, because if he told Colby the truth he was sure that she would think he was crazy and would never want to see him again.

And that was the one thing that Logan was sure that he didn't want to happen.

16

Logan locked the front door to the house and walked briskly to his car. The air was fresh and laced with the earthy smell of the tobacco fields. He had never smelled anything like it and he thought about how it was a far cry from the diesel fuel scented air outside of his trailer back in Wilmington. Despite what happened to him last night, Logan was beginning to like the country.

As Logan drove to the diner he surveyed the land around him. The fields on each side of the road alternated from corn, cotton and tobacco, mostly tobacco. Logan chuckled to himself as he looked at the plants in the fields.

"Corn for eating, cotton for making clothes and tobacco for smoking. These people have everything they need…"

Logan was trying to get his mind into a normal frame before he met Colby at the diner. But talking to himself about the farms around him wasn't helping. What was he going to tell Colby? How could he tell her about the doll and the little girl with the flower? He knew he would have to come up with something. She was probably the only person he knew that would tell him the truth. Harmon had obviously withheld things from him about the house, but Logan knew he would see Harmon soon enough and would insist that he open up about Rosemary, the house and the land.

Colby was happy to see Logan when he walked into the diner. He ambled up to the counter and sat down on a stool just as she put an empty coffee cup in front of him. Then she took the pot and filled Logan's cup almost to the top but left him room for his cream and sugar.

"Hey, stranger. I wasn't expecting you until around noon. How was your first night in your new house?"

"Awful. I think it's haunted," Logan said as he smiled and began to shake a packet of sugar. He tore off the end and poured it into his cup and then followed it with two small containers of half and half before stirring the mixture with his spoon.

"Oh yeah? Well that's no surprise. All old Southern homes are haunted. If you weren't such a city boy you'd know that."

"I'm serious. There's a porcelain doll that can turn its head and a little girl in old clothes that wanders the upstairs hallway. That is when she's not running around the yard and out through the tobacco fields behind the house." Logan winked at Colby and took a sip of his coffee. "And that bottle tree doesn't seem to be working. The little girl ran right passed it and didn't get sucked into one of the bottles."

"You're being a butthead," Colby said as she sat the coffee pot down on the counter.

"Just saying the bottle tree isn't working, that's all."

"Maybe it was full for the night," Colby said. "Like I said, the spirits trapped in the bottles burn off when the sun comes up. That makes room for the new ones that come around after the sun goes down the next night."

"Now there's a thought," replied Logan as he took a sip of his coffee.

Colby tilted her head and smiled at Logan. His attempt to make a joke out of what had happened to him the night before seemed to be working because judging from the look on her face it seemed Colby had decided that he was just pulling her leg. Logan knew that later on in the day that he could tell her that he wasn't joking.

"Two eggs over easy, home fries and toast. And keep the coffee coming and I won't make a scene." Logan said.

"Yes sir," Colby replied as she scribbled on her order pad.

After Logan finished his food he had another cup of coffee while trying to chat with Colby. The diner was somewhat busy and this made it hard for him to talk to her for more than a half a minute at a time. Finally he glanced at his watch and decided it was time to go meet Harmon.

"I get off after lunch. Are you up for an adventure?" Colby said as she picked up Logan's empty breakfast plate.

"Sure," Logan replied. He knew what kind of adventure he wanted to have with Colby but he was certain that she probably had something else in mind at this point in their relationship.

"Since you live in a haunted house and all, you might like to take a tour of some of Starlight's other spooky places. We can go this afternoon. I'll ride out to your house when I get off work."

"I should be done conferring with my legal team by then."

"I dunno," Colby said. "Harmon loves to chew the fat. He might talk for hours. Just tell him you have a hot date with a waitress at the diner if he starts rambling too much." Colby then turned and walked off with Logan's empty breakfast plate. She looked over her shoulder as she went and smiled at Logan. Then she disappeared into the kitchen.

A hot date... I like the sound of that, Logan thought to himself.

Logan left his money and tip and got up and left the diner. Once outside he took a long breath of the fresh country air, savoring it as he walked to his car. Just as he reached the small parking lot behind the diner, Chip McPhale nearly ran him over with his pickup truck.

Chip brought the truck to a stop directly behind Logan's car to prevent Logan from getting in his car and leaving. Then he got out and walked up to Logan standing on the sidewalk. His brother Ethan got out of the passenger's side of the truck.

"I thought I told you to keep your fucking ass away from my girl. You city fucks don't seem to know how to listen." While Chip talked, his brother Ethan walked over and positioned himself behind Logan effectively blocking Logan from walking back to the diner.

Logan felt the fight of flight mechanism gin up inside of him again just as it had last night. Somehow he knew that choosing to fight right now would lead to bodily harm on his part. But he also knew that if he tried to run off that it would get back to Colby and that might change the way she felt about him. Logan knew that no girl likes a coward and that he was going to have to stand up to Chip, even if it meant getting his ass kicked.

"I don't remember seeing your name written across her forehead. What makes you think that she'd be interested in a grubby loser like you, Chip?"

As soon as the word *loser* left Logan's mouth, Chip McPhale's fist landed in the middle of Logan's stomach. Logan immediately gasped and fell to one knee. Chip then placed his hand on Logan's shoulder and bent down so that he was close to Logan's ear.

"Like I said, city boy, Colby belongs to me."

Chip then got back in his truck and pulled it into an empty space next to the Dumpster sitting close to the back door of the diner. Then he got out and walked past Logan again, who was still down on one knee trying to catch his breath while at the same time trying to keep his breakfast from rushing up his throat. The last thing he wanted to do was vomit right there on the sidewalk. Chip patted Logan's shoulder as he walked by.

"Have a nice day, city boy. And tell that idiot Harmon that my family owns the Shaw land no matter what his fucking papers say."

Chip and Ethan then disappeared into the diner. After a few more minutes, Logan managed to get up and make it to his car. The last thing he wanted was for Colby to see him like this. There was no telling what Chip was telling her inside the diner right now but Logan knew there was nothing he could do about it for the time being. He knew the best thing for him to do was to just drive to Harmon's office.

§§§

Sandy was alternating between drinking coffee and filing her nails when Logan walked into Harmon's law office. She straightened up in her chair and put down her nail file when Logan came through the door.

"Good morning, Mr. Shaw," she said as Logan approached her desk.

"Well good morning to you too, Sandy. I'm a little early. Can Harmon see me or should I wait?"

"Mr. Blackwell is on an important phone call right now. I'll go stick my head in the door and tell him you're here. It shouldn't be long." Sandy took a sip of her coffee and then motioned to the small coffee station in the corner of the office.

"Help yourself," by the way. "I'll be right back."

With this Sandy disappeared down the hall. She returned moments later.

"Mr. Blackwell is almost finished. He's so busy this morning. He was in here at 6 a.m."

Logan smiled and then walked over to one of the chairs by the window. Then he had an idea so he returned to Sandy's desk. He had already figured out that everyone knows everyone in Starlight, so he thought he could make good use of this with Sandy.

"Say Sandy, can I ask you a question?"

"Well of course, Mr. Shaw." Sandy seemed to perk up at the idea of actually getting to answer a question that didn't involve finding out when Harmon would get off the phone.

"My great-grandmother, Rosemary Shaw, did you know her?"

The expression that suddenly clouded Sandy's face told Logan the answer to his question was yes, no matter what it was that Sandy was about to say.

"Well, yes Mr. Shaw. I did know her. Everyone knew Rosemary."

"Please call me Logan."

"Very well, Logan. I knew your great-grandmother. She was a little older than me but when we were younger we used to be good friends. In her later years she, well, she kind of withdrew. I hadn't talked much to her over the past twenty years. It's the strangest thing because just over the past few months I started to have the idea that I should drive out to see her. And then she…"

"She passed away?" Logan said.

Sandy shifted in her chair and suddenly seemed very uncomfortable.

"Yes, she… She passed away before I could make the time to go see her. I'm still angry at myself over that. If only I had been able to talk to her. Then…"

Logan raised an eyebrow. "Then what?"

Sandy reached for her coffee and took a long sip. Logan noticed that her hand was shaking slightly. She seemed nervous.

"I, I just meant it would have been nice to see her that's all." Sandy turned and looked into her computer screen. Logan could tell that she was getting uncomfortable with the conversation. This confirmed his theory that there was more to the story than what Harmon had told him.

"And that house, Sandy. It's very old. Do you know much about it?"

Sandy turned her eyes up to meet Logan's eyes. It suddenly seemed like she wanted to unload something off her conscience but was afraid to.

"It's been there since before the Civil War. I supposed that Harmon has already told you about the murders."

"Yes, I know all about them."

"Harmon told me that you've taken a shine to that pretty waitress at the diner. Colby is such a sweet girl. But her..."

"Yes?" Logan knew that Sandy was about to tell him something that he didn't know.

Sandy shifted in her chair and began to run her finger around the handle of her coffee mug. After a few seconds she spoke.

"Her great-grandfather was killed in the Shaw Fields in the 1930's. I wasn't even born but the story has been passed down over the years. I believe his name was Franklin. Her family got past it and got out of tobacco farming by the time Colby was born. You could do worse than dating that Colby, let me tell you. She's such a sweet young girl."

Logan could tell that Sandy had told him more than she had wanted to tell him about the land he had inherited. But now that he knew more about Colby's great-grandfather he could ask her about that later. For now, Harmon would just have to come clean about the house. Sandy was obviously not going to say much more about it.

"Thanks for the info, Sandy. That's sad about Colby's great-grandfather. She told me her family farmed the Shaw land way back when but she didn't tell me what happened to her great-grandfather."

Logan tried to hide how horrified he was that Colby's great-grandfather had been killed in the Shaw Fields. How in the world could he ever ask her about something like that? He knew he was going to have to wait until they knew each other a little better.

Sandy's face carried an expression that was a mix of confusion and fear. She hoped that Colby wouldn't be upset with her for telling Logan about her great-grandfather's murder. But then her face seemed to relax. Apparently she had decided that Logan would have found out sooner or later anyway.

Just then Harmon appeared in the opening of the hallway.

"Logan! Good morning. Why don't you come on back to my office so we can get started."

Logan smiled at Sandy as he stepped away from her desk. Then he followed Harmon down the hallway. Moments later they were sitting alone in Harmon's office.

§§§

"Just what is the deal with the house, Harmon?" Logan wanted to get right to the heart of the matter.

"The deal?" It was early in the morning but Harmon suddenly had an urge to light up his pipe. He knew where the conversation was headed.

"The deal is that you own it, Logan."

"I know that. I meant what's wrong with it?"

"Wrong with it? I don't know what you mean. Why would you ask that?"

"Let's just say I had a less than restful first night in my new home."

"Less than restful?" Harmon was stalling. He knew it and Logan knew it. Harmon had fully expected this line of questioning from Logan. He knew more about the house than he had originally let on and he knew that after one night in the house that Logan would call him on it.

"Logan, I've told you about the land and the murders. I've told you about the McPhales. Like I said, most people believe the land is cursed. Most people don't think the McPhales are behind the killings. But even though I don't believe it, there is a very good chance that they are, regardless of what I've told you in the past. They want that land and they believe it already belongs to them. They always site some sort of legal foul-up with a land survey conducted decades ago but I've looked into it and everything is fine. The survey boundaries are correct. But the McPhales don't believe it."

Harmon took a sip of his coffee and then continued.

"Just this morning I was reminded of that by Chip McPhale as I was unlocking the door to this firm. He stopped by to have one of his friendly chats about the legalities of the deed to the Shaw land."

"I know. I had a nice little chat with him myself at the diner. He has ways of getting his point across." Logan could still feel Chip's fist in his stomach. "But you said you don't believe they are behind the killings. You said you believed the ghost story."

"Yes, for the lack of better words, I believe the ghost story. That land was worked by slaves before the Civil War. Just horrible. The legend has always been that the ghost of one of those slaves wanders the Shaw Fields and takes the life of anyone unlucky enough to be out in the fields during a harvest moon."

"Slaves…" Logan leaned back in his chair and looked at Harmon.

"Yes, slaves. That's the way things were done back then, Logan. It was terrible and I'm glad it ended. Based on how things were back then it's not hard to believe that the soul of one of those slaves is carrying a grudge."

This was not the story Logan had expected to hear.

"Harmon, the things that happened in my house last night didn't seem to have anything to do with slaves, or the ghosts of slaves I should say. I'm not one to believe in ghosts, but after last night I'm starting to have a change of mind."

Harmon raised an eyebrow. He reached over to his ashtray and picked up his pipe. It didn't take him long to get it lit and soon he felt the soothing power of the nicotine snaking through his veins.

"What exactly happened? Can you describe it to me?" Harmon then took a few puffs of his pipe again.

Logan proceeded to tell Harmon all about the little girl on the porch, the porcelain doll and then the little girl's return later in the night. He left out the part about him and Colby having dinner and rummaging through the attic.

Harmon's face turned an ashen color. For a moment Logan thought the old man was going to faint.

"I see," was all Harmon could manage to say after Logan finished with his story. There was a long pause before either of them spoke.

"So what does it all mean, Harmon?"

"Logan, I wish I knew. I would tell you if I did. Honestly I would. The legend of a slave's soul haunting the fields is the only, uh, ghost story, as you called it, that I know about the land."

Logan sat still in his chair and studied Harmon's eyes. The old man seemed to be telling the truth. "Well, okay Harmon. Maybe then you can answer another question for me. I know I could probably ask someone else in town, maybe someone down at the diner, but I'd rather hear it from you."

Harmon lifted his pipe and took a long draw. He knew what question was coming and he knew he was going to need a shot of nicotine to be able to answer it truthfully.

"Ask me anything you like, Logan."

Logan shifted in his seat and leaned forward towards Harmon's desk.

"Can you tell me how my great-grandmother died? Did she... Did she die in the fields?"

"Heavens no, Logan," Harmon said sharply. "She did not die in the fields."

"Then how did she die?"

Logan watched as Harmon took the longest pull from his pipe that he had seen him take during their conversation. Clearly the old man was rattled.

"She..." Harmon then paused before he spoke again. Finally he said, "Logan this is very difficult for me."

"Please, Harmon. She was my great-grandmother. I might not have known her but that was not my fault. But I still have a right to know. Don't make me ask someone at the diner."

Harmon looked at Logan for a few seconds before speaking.

"She killed herself, Logan. You're great-grandmother Rosemary Abigail

Shaw killed herself. She took her own life."

Logan pushed away from the desk and leaned back into his chair.

"Killed herself? How?"

Another long silence followed. Finally Harmon spoke.

"She hung herself in the attic."

Logan took a long breath. He had just explored the attic with Colby last night. When he looked at Harmon, Logan could see that it seemed that the old man still had something to say.

"Harmon?"

Harmon put his pipe down in the ashtray and then turned to look across his office at the road outside of the windows. Then he slowly turned his head back to Logan.

"I was the one that found her, Logan."

Logan drew in a sharp breath.

"You found her, Harmon?"

"I found her, Logan. Swinging from a rope hung from one of the rafters. A chair was lying on its side under her feet. My dear friend Rosemary… She had become a bit of a recluse these past years, and I was one of the few people that went out to see her. You're great-grandmother was quite wealthy Logan, as you can probably tell from the house, and I was trying to help her with her last will and testament. It was just easier to go out and see her than it was to bring her to the office. She stopped driving over a decade ago and pretty much just stayed in her house. She would call her doctor when necessary, and she had accounts at some of the stores in town and they would deliver the things she needed. There was really no need for her to leave the house."

Logan didn't know what to say. He had never met his great-grandmother and felt it was inappropriate to try and offer an explanation as to why she became a recluse in her final years. But he wanted to say something, anything.

"Old people get like that, I guess. I mean, really old people like my great-grandmother. Maybe she just didn't feel comfortable in public." Logan knew it was a feeble theory but it was the best he could do.

"I think something else was bothering her, Logan. Something from her past. Maybe something in the house, I don't know."

"Something in the house?" Logan replied.

Harmon took a few puffs of his pipe and then leaned back in his chair and stared at the ceiling above his desk.

"Something in the house or on the land. Like I've told you Logan, there are some people, including me, that believe that land harbors a dark secret. Something evil has staked a claim in those tobacco fields. I must say, I don't envy you."

Logan felt a brief flash of anger.

"You're mood sure has changed from our first meeting, Harmon. You didn't tell me all of this yesterday. You talked about how those fields produce the best tobacco in the state, and you did talk about the land being cursed or something but not like you are now."

"I'm sorry, Logan. I was afraid you wouldn't even want to see the house if I told you everything about it right up front. You are the sole heir and if you don't take the house then it will sit vacant. And then it will be even harder to keep it out of the hands of the McPhales. I couldn't bear to see that bunch get their hands on Rosemary's house and land. If it's the last thing I do, I will make sure that band of hooligans never lives in Rosemary's house or plants one single tobacco seedling on her land."

Logan exhaled and then rubbed his temples with his fingertips. Then he looked at Harmon.

"It's okay, Harmon. I can see where you're coming from. It is a nice house but it needs some work. I have no plans to let it sit vacant no matter who is rattling chains in the attic or wandering around in the fields."

Harmon smiled at Logan. "Good man. You're great-grandmother would be proud of you."

Logan gave Harmon an appreciative look and then looked over just as a truck passed by the window. The town of Starlight was coming to life for the day.

"Word around town is that Colby at the diner is sweet on you." Harmon folded his hands across his chest and grinned. He desperately wanted to change the subject.

Logan turned his head back and looked at Harmon. He had to remind himself again that he was in Starlight and not Wilmington. He knew it was impossible to keep anything a secret in this town.

"Does everyone in town know?"

"Yes, they do Logan. Word travels fast around here, especially among the women. My guess is that Sandy spread the word. I love her to death but she loves gossip like she loves a nip of bourbon at lunchtime. She thinks I don't know." Harmon then gave Logan a wink that conveyed to him that the bourbon thing was to remain just between them.

"I could only hope that a girl like Colby would be sweet on me. Fat chance. I'm just an old used car salesman who can barely pay his rent. I live in a trailer park with a bunch of merchant mariners and I live off of hot dogs and TV dinners."

Harmon smiled. "That was the old Logan Shaw. The new Logan Shaw owns an antebellum home, several hundred acres of land and a bank account with five million dollars in it."

Logan felt his heart stop in his chest. It seemed like several minutes passed before he felt it start beating again.

"Excuse me, Harmon?"

"Five million dollars, Logan. That is the amount of your great-grandmother's liquid assets. It belongs to you now, and like I've already said so does the house and the land."

Logan was feeling a new range of emotions flash through his body. According to Harmon he was now a rich man. And not just on paper. He had hard cash in the bank.

"See Logan, everything is not all bad. Yes, the house and the land have their demons and my guess is that they are now stepping forward to introduce themselves. I would imagine Rosemary finally made her peace with them and that is why I found her hanging in the attic. But at least you won't have to eat hot dogs and TV dinners while you're dealing with it."

"Harmon, if you think I'm going to end up…"

"No no, Logan. I know you will not end up like Rosemary. She was old and weak. You're a strong young man. You'll be fine."

Harmon looked at his watch. "I'm sorry, Logan, I have another appointment in just a few minutes. We can continue this later. Stop by tomorrow and we'll draw up the papers so that you can access the money. Rosemary did leave stipulations on the account but nothing too severe. Some of the money is reserved for taxes and maintenance on the house and land, that sort of thing. But most of it is free for you to have."

Logan pushed himself away from the desk and stood up. Then both men shook hands. Just as Logan was turning to leave, Harmon spoke.

"Oh, Logan, by the way."

"Yes?"

"Just in case you're wondering, I mean I'm sure you're not but just in case you are, I can promise you that no one knows about Rosemary's wealth. Of course everyone knows she wasn't exactly poor just because of her house and land, but, well, no one knows about her liquid assets. The money, I mean."

"So?" replied Logan.

"So if someone is friendly to you, then…"

"I get it, Harmon. What you're trying to tell me is that Colby isn't a gold digger."

"Exactly," replied Harmon. Logan could see the wave of relief wash over the old man's face.

Logan smiled and shook his head. Harmon Blackwell the third was a character indeed, he thought to himself as he turned to leave Harmon's office.

"Thanks, Harmon. I'll see you tomorrow," Logan said as he walked into the hallway.

Once Harmon heard Logan say goodbye to Sandy and leave the office, he put down his pipe and reached into his desk drawer. He then retrieved a small bottle of whiskey and poured a shot into his empty coffee cup. He quickly downed the shot and poured himself another. Then he put the bottle back in the drawer.

"God help that poor boy," he said as the whiskey burned in his throat.

17

Logan was sitting on the steps of the front porch of his house enjoying the hot sun when he saw Colby's car emerge from underneath the canopy of tree limbs covering the driveway to the house. She pulled up slowly and then parked her car. When she got out of the car she squinted in the bright sun as she looked at Logan.

"Hey there, city boy. You look lonesome." Logan smiled and watched as she walked around the front of her car and then towards him. She was wearing a pair of white denim shorts and a pale pink T-shirt. Logan could not remember the last time he had ever seen a more attractive woman.

"City boy? I'll have you know that I am now officially a country boy, and not only that, I'm a tobacco kingpin. Just look at my fields. I feel like I should be sitting here smoking a pipe and wearing straw hat."

"Smoking a pipe is the last thing you want to do," Colby said as she walked up to Logan and sat down on the steps next to him, so close that the sides of their legs touched.

"Why? Harmon seems to enjoy it. And besides, look at my supply of tobacco. I'd never have to buy any. It's all out there just waiting to be smoked." Logan then waved his arm towards the fields behind the house.

"Oh, so you'll just go out there and tear off a leaf, chop it up, put it in your pipe and smoke it? That's funny, city boy. I'd love to see you do that."

"What's the big deal?" Logan knew he had once again ventured into a topic he knew nothing about. He had no intention of taking up smoking; he was just trying to be funny.

"I've heard stories about people that try that," Colby said. "I've even seen a few people do it. Watching someone do that is more fun than free circus tickets," Colby said as she laughed.

"Okay, I admit it. I have no idea what I'm talking about." Logan then looked into Colby's eyes as he felt her leg up against his. "Educate me, country girl."

"You can't just go out there and rip off a leaf and roll it up into a cigar and smoke it. Or put it in a pipe or anything else. It doesn't work like that. I had a friend back in high school that tried that. We were all out riding around one night and he decided that he wanted to start smoking. So we pulled over and he walked out into a tobacco field that bordered the road, tore off a leaf, rolled it into a homemade cigar and then lit it up. After a few puffs of his homemade cigar he turned green, fell down on his hands and knees and started moaning and groaning, saying the world was spinning around him. Then he puked up his cheeseburger and fries. We all laughed so hard that we almost pee'd in our pants. After that night he never tried smoking again, either with homemade cigars or store-bought ones."

Logan began to laugh. "So I take it they do something to the tobacco before you can smoke it."

"Yep, city boy. It has to be picked and cured. It takes a while. You can't just smoke it right out of the field." Colby then rolled her eyes and smiled at Logan. It was all he could do to not grab her and kiss her.

"I was only kidding. I have no plans to ever start smoking," Logan said.

"So since you live in a haunted house, I'd thought I take you on the official ghost tour of Starlight. Sound good?"

Logan thought anything sounded good if it meant being with Colby. As far as he was concerned even a game checkers would be enjoyable with her. Anything that involved spending time with her was okay with him.

"Sure. Where are we going?"

"It's a secret. I'll tell you when we get there. We can take my car but you can drive. Where we're going isn't far from here."

"A cherry-red 1969 Chevelle. Where in the world did you get it?" Logan said as he looked at Colby's car. Colby's mouth dropped open when he said this.

"How did you know the year?" she said as she looked at Logan and then at her old car.

Logan looked at the car and then back at Colby.

"You're not serious, are you? I am a used car salesman after all." Logan then winked an eye at Colby.

"And a tobacco kingpin," Colby replied. "My dad left me the car." Colby then looked down at her feet. Logan knew what that meant and decided not to ask Colby about her father.

§§§

The noonday sun was directly overhead as Logan and Colby drove down the road. After leaving his house they had driven along the main road and then turned onto an adjoining road that led into the countryside away from town.

"I take it we're not going into Starlight?" Logan said as he looked over at Colby.

"Nope. Normally a place like we're going would be in the middle of town but because this is tobacco country it's located outside of town," Colby said as she rolled up her window and began to fiddle with the air conditioner.

Just then they drove past an old warehouse that looked like it hadn't been used in fifty years. Grass was growing up through the broken asphalt that surrounded the solitary building. Up ahead Logan could see a bridge approaching.

"The river?"

"Yep. The Skeleton River," Colby replied. "I hated that name when I was a little girl. It just scared me for some reason. I would never swim in that river when I was little because the name of it just gave me the heebie jeebies."

"Where did the name come from? That's a pretty strange name for a river," Logan said. Just then they drove onto the bridge crossing the Skeleton River.

"You don't want to know," Colby replied.

"Come on, tell me."

Colby sat for a few seconds while she watched the river pass underneath them. Logan could tell that she wasn't lying when she had said the river bothered her. She seemed to be lost in thought as she looked down at the water passing under the bridge. After a long pause, she spoke.

"Legend has it that the slaves that worked the surrounding fields back before the Civil War were buried in the river when they died. Their bodies were weighted down with rocks and rope and then tossed into the river. It makes me want to cry every time I think about it. After enough time went by their bodies would decompose and the ropes would rot away. The bones would then wash up on the banks of the river. They say the river had some other name originally but when everyone in town started calling it the *skeleton* river the name just stuck."

Logan suddenly thought about the story Harmon had told him about the soul of a slave wandering the Shaw Fields. It seemed that Starlight had a dark history

Just as they left the bridge, another old abandoned warehouse drifted by.

"What's with all the old warehouses?" Logan said as he looked over at Colby. He could tell she was still upset about telling him the story behind the name of the river. He wanted to change the subject.

"Back in Starlight's heyday they were all full of tobacco ready to go to market. And other stuff too. Lots of cotton was grown around here. Now they all just sit empty."

"So where are we going? Are you gonna make me guess or are you gonna tell me?" Logan then took his finger and poked Colby gently on her leg.

"The old train station. It's been abandoned now for decades. Spooky as all get out. We used to come down here at night when I was in high school and tell ghost stories while sitting inside the old Pullman parked on the tracks."

"Starlight's train station was out here and not in town? That makes a lot of sense, country girl. In the big city where I'm from, the train station isn't out in the boondocks."

Colby raised an eyebrow at Logan and smiled. "It makes perfect sense if the main thing the train hauled away was tobacco. Why would they haul all the tobacco into town when it's grown out here?"

"Good point," Logan conceded.

"Turn here," Colby said as she pointed to a narrow road up ahead on their right.

Logan turned the car onto the road as Colby had directed. It was paved for the first ten feet or so and then turned into red dirt. Logan felt a bump as they left the pavement and before long the road began to get even narrower as it led deeper into the woods. After a few minutes, another wooden bridge appeared.

"The river again? That thing must turn and snake its way all over the place," Logan said as he looked out of the side window as the car moved onto the short bridge. The river wasn't as wide as it had been when they saw it before and the water below them was still and the color of mud.

"Makes me shiver to think what might be at the bottom of it." Colby folded her arms across her chest and then looked down into her lap to avoid seeing the river below them.

"Hey it's okay," Logan said, trying to comfort Colby. "That was a long, long time ago. There can't be anything left after all these years."

Colby thought about it and then said, "Yeah, but it's not the bones I worry about. All Southern land has its share of restless souls. I don't know about where you're from, but out here in the country they just seem to never rest."

"In the city it's the muggers, burglars and rapists that we have to worry about, not restless souls. I think I'd take a burglar over a ghost. A burglar can be shot. I wouldn't have any idea of how to get rid of a ghost." Logan then smiled and winked at Colby. He wanted to lighten things up. He knew that seeing the river had really bothered her.

Colby gave Logan a halfhearted smile. "I guess. They say ghosts can't actually touch you and all they can do is scare you. But I don't know if I agree with that crazy theory. And I don't want to find out. Like I said before, ghosts around here, at least one of them, can hack a person into little pieces."

"So tell me about this train station. I assume we're getting close?"

Colby suddenly perked up and forced the thoughts of the river out of her mind.

"It's really cool. I hope the Pullman is still there."

Logan rounded a curve and the road opened up into a small clearing. On the edge of the woods sat an old decrepit building with one end that looked like it was about to fall in on itself. In front of the station sat an abandoned railway car, the kind used to carry passengers.

"Holy shit that's creepy looking. You used to come out here with your friends when you were in high school? And at night?"

"Well, we might have had a little strawberry wine to give us courage," replied Colby as she grinned. "We'd light a bonfire and sit around it drinking wine out of Mason jars."

"Strawberry wine?" Logan said as he raised an eyebrow at Colby. She was staring out across the small field reminiscing about the bonfires.

"Yep," Colby said. "Beats store-bought wine any day of the week," she said with a grin.

§§§

Chip McPhale brought his truck to a stop at the entrance to the road that led to the train station. He had lost sight of Colby's car because he had let them get too far ahead of him, but he knew where Colby was taking Logan and the cloud of red dust floating over the dirt road confirmed his suspicion. They had driven down the road for sure, and now Chip knew he was finally going to be able to teach Logan Shaw a lesson about coming into town and trying to take his land and his girl. Logan, Chip knew, was about to learn firsthand how things were handled out in the country. And then when he was done with Logan, Chip knew he would have Colby all to himself in the old train station.

Chip turned his truck onto the dirt road and drove slowly until he reached the bridge that led over the river. Once he crossed the bridge he pulled his truck off the road and into an opening between the trees. Then he got out of the truck and began to walk through the woods. He had been deer hunting in these woods since he was a boy and knew them like the back of his hand. He planned to work his way through the woods and then up to the rear of train station. Then he would surprise Colby and Logan when the moment was right.

§§§

Logan brought the car to a stop close to the old train station. He and Colby got out and then he walked up to the tracks that ran in front of the building. When he looked to his left he noticed that the tracks ended not far from the station. The wooden ties were still down but the steel rails had long since been removed. Then he looked over at the old railway car sitting solemnly on the tracks near the front of the station just as Colby walked up beside him.

"I thought you said this station was out here because it was used to haul away tobacco and cotton. That train car is for carrying people. What's it doing here?"

Colby's face tensed slightly. "Well, the station was used mainly for freight, but sometimes a people train would come into town." Colby paused for a second and then looked down at her feet. Then she brought her eyes up to meet Logan's. "Usually they were orphan trains."

"Do tell," Logan said as he frowned at Colby.

"An orphan train," Colby replied.

"What the hell is an orphan train?" Logan said. "We don't have those in the city. At least I don't think we do, or did, I mean."

Colby looked up at Logan and gave him a hint of a smile.

"I'm sure they never had those kinds of trains in the city. I mean, there's no tobacco to pick so why would they need an orphan train."

Logan paused for a second and looked at Colby. The frown on his face conveyed his confusion.

"Well," Colby said, "the story goes that the town would get an orphan train every now and then. They were a big thing a hundred years ago. Orphans from the cities up north were loaded onto the trains and sent out west or down south to work the farms. Starlight would get one every now and then. And it would come to this station."

"How do you know all this?" Logan said.

Colby slid her hands into the front pockets of her shorts. Logan couldn't help but be reminded again at how attractive she was.

"My family has lived around here since the town was founded. I've heard all the stories that have been passed down through the generations. You know us Southerners, we like to have big meals on Sunday and then sit out on the back porch and talk. It's a way of life. I can tell you anything about Starlight that you want to know."

"So tell me about the orphan trains," Logan said as he looked at the old railway car. His curiosity was getting the best of him.

"The orphans were cheap labor for the tobacco fields. When the orphan train came into the station local families that needed help with their farms would come out here and take custody of a few of the kids that had come in on the train. They would adopt them right into their families and take them home. Then the kids would work the fields with the rest of the family. Back then they didn't have all the fancy machinery so everything was done by hand. And the more hands the better."

"Child labor?" Logan replied, trying to hide the disgust in his voice.

"Well, yes and no. I mean, the story goes that these kids were basically homeless and had been living on the streets or in the orphanages up north. Yeah, they worked the fields but they also were given a home and food.

Some people didn't have a lot of kids and they needed the extra help. Back then everyone worked, even the children. People didn't sit around pecking on cell phones like the do nowadays."

"Hey, I like my cellphone," Logan said as he placed a protective hand over the cellphone on his belt. He didn't know why he was carrying it; he had barely been able to get a signal since coming to Starlight.

"I'm just saying that back then if you didn't work you didn't eat. That's all. Even the kids had to work."

"They picked tobacco?" Logan said as he looked at the old railway car again.

"It's called a Pullman, city boy."

"Gotcha," Logan said as he continued to examine the car.

"The little kids would pull the flowers and the hornworms off the plants. When you pull the flower off the top it causes the plant to grow higher and have bigger leaves."

"They did what?" he said has he looked away from the Pullman back to Colby.

"They pulled the flowers and the hornworms off the plants."

"The flowers? What do those flowers look like?"

Colby couldn't figure out why Logan cared what the flowers looked like. This was reflected in the look on her face. "It's just sort of a yellow flower about the size of the palm of your hand. They grow on the tobacco plants but have to be pulled off so they won't stunt the plant's growth."

Logan suddenly remembered the flower he had found lying on the bedroom floor. But when he stuck his fingers into his shirt pocket he realized the flower was gone.

"What's the matter?" Colby said as she watched Logan fumble with his pocket.

"Uh… Nothing," Logan said as he removed his fingers from his shirt pocket while trying to hide the look of surprise he was feeling.

Colby and Logan then looked back at the Pullman.

"Sandy's great-grandmother came in on one of those orphan trains. And she's not the only one in town like that.

"Sandy?"

"Yep. But don't go onto her about it. I don't think she likes to talk about her family's history."

The sun had dropped down lower in the sky. Logan squinted as he looked at the Pullman. The day was passing quickly and Logan knew it was because he was with Colby. He was enjoying every minute of her company. He knew he could get used to being around a girl like her.

"Let's check out the station. And can we get into that, what did you call it? That Pullman?"

"The doors were always locked on the Pullman but I know how to get inside of it. Follow me," Colby said as she took off towards the old rail car.

Logan and Colby walked up to the Pullman and when Logan checked the doors on each end and on the sides, all of them were padlocked. Colby was standing near the middle of the car with her hands on her hips.

"About done, city boy?"

"Sorry. Just checking the doors. So how do we get in this thing?"

Colby motioned for Logan to join her near the middle of the car. Then she squatted down and crawled under the Pullman. In the middle of the underside of the car was a trapdoor. Colby pushed up on the door and smiled when it opened, its rusted hinges screaming in protest. Then she pushed the trapdoor the rest of the way open and stood up in the opening. Logan watched as her upper body disappeared into the Pullman, followed by her legs. Once she was inside she stuck her head back down through the opening and grinned at Logan.

"Well I'll be damned," said Logan.

Once inside the car, Colby and Logan walked from the front to the rear looking at the old seats. The inside of the car was hot and smelled of old leather and mildew. In the end seat was a small pile of what looked to be the remnants of homemade cigarettes.

"Looks like tobacco isn't the only thing they smoke out here in the boonies," Logan said Colby walked up beside him. Looks like the country kids and the city kids have found common ground."

"I never touched that crap," Colby said. "The strawberry wine was always enough for me." Colby then looked up at Logan as she moved so close to him that their bodies touched.

Logan threw caution to the wind. The heat of the railcar, combined with being so close to Colby was making him lightheaded. He looked into Colby's eyes and then reached up and put his hands on her cheeks. Then he kissed her, softly at first and then with more passion. Just as he moved his hands from her face down to the sides of her arms, both he and Colby were jolted out of the moment by the crashing sound of something hitting the side of the Pullman.

Logan stopped kissing Colby and gasped. "What the fuck was that?" Colby then turned her head to see the large star in the middle of one of the Pullman's side windows.

"Did something just hit this car?" Logan said as he scanned the length of the Pullman. Then he saw the window. "Was that window broken before?"

"I don't remember," Colby said, panting as she reached for Logan's hand.

"Let's get out of here," Logan finally said. He led Colby back to the trapdoor. He dropped through first and then helped her climb down.

Once outside of the Pullman, Colby and Logan both stared at the broken window. Logan saw a large rock about the size of a baseball lying on the ground directly below the window.

"Who the hell do you think threw that?" Logan said as he looked at the rock.

"Colby had her suspicions. She knew more about the land around Starlight than she was letting on. But she decided Logan probably wasn't ready to hear about it. She had already told him so much that she was afraid that he might just leave town and say to hell with all of it, the town, his house and her. She didn't want that to happen. Colby liked Logan. In fact, she could not ever remember being around a man that made her feel like he did. Finally she said the only thing she thought would sound logical to Logan.

"Probably just some kids. Teenagers, most likely. There's a path behind the station that leads down to the Skeleton River, to one of the better swimming holes. Kids walk through here all the time on their way to it. They probably saw us and just wanted to scare the bejesus out of us."

"Well, it worked," Logan said. Then he was immediately sorry for his comment. The last thing he wanted to sound like in front of Colby was a scared city boy. Colby looked at him and frowned.

"I mean, they didn't scare me. But you seemed like you were scared." Logan squinted in the sun and smiled at Colby. "I was just about to jump out of the Pullman and start whipping ass," he said as he suddenly struck a bodybuilder pose.

"Uh huh. Is that so?" Colby said as she smiled at Logan. "Well if you're up for it, we can check out the station now."

"Let's go. Old abandoned train stations are my thing. Didn't I tell you?"

Logan took Colby by the hand as they began to walk towards the station. Thoughts of what might have happened in the Pullman had they not been interrupted danced through Logan's head as he and Colby walked through the tall grass. The air was hot and Logan could feel the sweat trickling down his back.

None of the doors were locked that led from the platform into the station. Once inside, Logan and Colby walked up to the old ticket counter in the center of what was once the main lobby of the station. Logan walked around behind the counter and tried his best imitation of a railway ticket clerk.

"Destination, please."

Colby smiled. "How about Wilmington?"

Logan knew he had not exactly been on his game lately as far as women were concerned. But he knew the message Colby was sending to him. After the kiss in the Pullman, he knew that she liked him. He had felt her pulling close to him just as the rock hit the window.

"Well you're in luck, fair lady. I have one ticket left. And it's only for you."

Logan walked around from behind the counter and pulled Colby to him. When their lips touched he could feel her responding to his desire. He moved his hands down to her hips and then wrapped his arms around her waist as their kiss grew more passionate.

Suddenly out of nowhere Logan was hit in the back of the head by a wooden two by four. When Logan fell to the ground, Chip McPhale tossed the two by four on the floor next to Logan. His eyes were burning with a mixture of hatred and lust. Colby screamed and took a step backwards just as Chip stepped over Logan's motionless body.

"I thought I told you that your sweet little ass belongs to me. What the fuck are you doing out here whoring around with this city fuck?"

Colby could smell the liquor on Chip's breath mixed with the aroma of chewing tobacco.

"You stay away from me, Chip. I swear I'll have the sheriff throw your sorry ass in jail if you lay a finger on me."

"The sheriff? You mean that sorry sack of shit Patterson? I'll kill him where he sleeps."

Chip moved towards Colby as she continued to back away from him. She wasn't watching where she was going as she was backing up and when her foot hit a loose board she suddenly tripped and fell to the floor. Before she could even try to get back to her feet, Chip was standing over her.

"I've waited long enough and now I'm gonna fuck you like you need to be fucked. I know you want it, you little tease." Chip then ejected a stream of tobacco juice from his mouth and wiped his chin with the back of his hand.

Colby scrambled to try to push herself away from Chip but when he grabbed her by the leg she knew there would be no getting away from him. The smell of the whiskey and chewing tobacco made her nauseous and she felt bile rising up her throat. She continued to struggle as Chip dropped to his knees while trying to hold her legs with one hand and unbuckle his pants with his other hand. Then she began to scream and yell just as her fingernails dug into the soft flesh of Chip's face.

"You little bitch!" Chip yelled as he felt Colby's fingernails dig into his cheek.

"Get off me Chip!" Colby was crying now, tears streaming down her face as the horrible realization hit her of what was about to happen.

Suddenly the two by four came down on the back of Chip McPhale's head. Chip's body went limp instantly. Then Logan hit Chip once again on the side of his head, crushing Chip's right ear.

Colby pushed Chip's limp body off of her and then tried to get to her feet. Logan dropped the two by four and immediately helped her get up. Then he pulled Colby into a tight hug as she buried her face in his chest and began to sob uncontrollably. Logan kept his eyes on Chip's motionless body. He knew he wasn't going to allow Chip to get up and blindside him again.

"I've got you. It's okay. It's okay." Logan hugged Colby tightly until he felt her begin to calm down. Once her breathing was back to normal he pulled back and looked into her eyes.

"He's never going to hurt you again. I'll make sure of it. Let's get out of here and back to the car. I've had enough of this train station for one day."

"Colby could only nod her approval. The tears were still streaming down her face as she took hold of Logan's hand as he led her out of the station and onto the platform above the tracks. She looked back at Chip's body one more time to assure herself that he wasn't trying to get up and follow them.

Once they were back at the car Logan helped Colby into her seat and then walked around and got behind the wheel.

"Do you think you killed him?" she asked as Logan turned the key in the ignition.

"I doubt it. The hardheaded motherfucker is probably just knocked out cold. It will serve him right to lie in there half the night before he comes to. But he'll have one hell of a headache when he wakes up."

Colby smiled at Logan. Then she put her hand on his arm just as he put the car in gear.

"Thank you," she said as she leaned across the seat and kissed Logan on his cheek.

"You're quite welcome. Now let's get out of here and back to my house. Did I tell you that I live in a big mansion?" Logan said as he winked at Colby.

"There's a rumor going around town that you have chicken and dumplings in the refrigerator too," Colby said as Logan began to drive through the field back towards the dirt road that led to the main road. When he was almost to the bridge over the Skeleton River, Logan noticed Chip's pickup truck pulled off into the edge of the woods. He stopped in the road when he was next to where the truck was parked.

"What are you doing?" Colby asked.

"Wait here," Logan said. Then he stepped out of the car and pulled a three inch lock blade from his pocket.

Logan walked over to Chip's truck and snapped the blade open on the knife. Then he proceeded to punch a hole in the sidewall of one of the rear tires. Then he walked quickly around the truck until he had flattened the other three tires as well. When he was finished he walked back to the car and got inside.

"That will slow down that asshole. We'll see how he likes being out here in the dark with four flat tires."

Colby felt an odd attraction to Logan stir inside of her. She had never had a man take up for her before. Logan made her feel safe, and deep down inside she knew that he would never hurt her and more importantly, never let anyone else hurt her either.

18

Logan and Colby were sitting on the back porch of the house watching the tobacco plants sway in the light breeze. Logan could see clouds off on the horizon but for now the sky was clear and the sun was still hot even though it was much lower in the sky. Colby was sitting next to him in the porch swing and she put her foot on the railing in front of them and gave the swing a gently push.

"So tell me what's next on the Starlight ghost tour. I enjoyed the old Pullman but the train station, well, not so much." Logan then took a sip from his glass of tea. He didn't want to rehash what had happened with Chip McPhale.

Colby smiled. She was feeling better now despite what had happened with Chip at the station. Even though she had just met Logan yesterday she felt like she had known him for years. He had a way of making her feel safe and she liked it.

"Oh, I could take you somewhere pretty spooky, and we don't even have to ride in the car."

"Really?" Logan said as he took another sip of tea before sitting the glass down on the table next to the swing."

"Yep," Colby said. Then she stood up and walked over to the stairs leading down into the yard. "What are you waiting for?" she said as she looked back at Logan still sitting in the porch swing.

Logan got out of the swing and joined Colby as she walked down the stairs to the yard. "Where are we going?"

"It's a surprise. And it's been years since I saw it last myself."

"You country girls like surprises, don't you." Logan said as he looked at Colby.

"Us country girls like a lot of things," she said as she turned and began to walk towards the tobacco field. Logan couldn't help but notice how nice her legs looked as she walked across the backyard.

As they walked by one of the old tobacco barns, Colby told Logan a little about how they were used to cure tobacco. Then they walked into one of the long rows of waist-high tobacco plants. Logan looked out across the field and was amazed by the size of it. And he was amazed at the idea that he owned every acre of it. Just the thought of it filled him with both pride and a sense of dread. He had no idea what he was going to do with all the tobacco.

Colby led Logan all the way through the field to the far tree line that ran down one side of the Shaw land. Along the way Logan noticed a flower growing on one of tobacco plants. He felt a stab of fear as he realized once again that the flower on the plant looked exactly like the one the little girl had been carrying the night before.

The daylight was beginning to wane as Colby led Logan into a path that opened up on the edge of the woods bordering the field.

"We should probably hurry since we don't want to be out here after dark. But where we're going isn't far," Colby said as she picked up the pace.

"Are you going to tell me where we're going?" Logan said.

"Nope. You'll see when we get there."

Logan huffed as he walked along beside Colby. The woods around them were noticeably darker than the tobacco field. They had walked less than a minute when Logan looked to his left and saw several old tombstones poking up through the underbrush.

"Check that out," Logan said has he touched Colby's arm. "There's an old graveyard."

Colby looked in the direction of the tombstones. "You find that a lot around here. Back in the old days sometimes they just buried people in their backyard. There are lots of old abandoned graves all around Starlight." Colby looked over at the tombstones again and then grabbed Logan by the hand.

"Come on, we need to hurry," she said as she pulled Logan along the trail.

Before long they came to a small clearing full of knee-high grass. To his left, Logan could see through the trees to another large field. The Skeleton River was close and Logan could see it through the trees to his right.

"No one plants that field anymore. It's not part of the Shaw land," Colby said as she saw Logan looking across the clearing and through the trees to the distant field. Just as she said this, Logan looked back at the old house standing in the middle of the clearing.

"Let me guess, it's haunted," replied Logan as he looked at the house.

"Probably. It's an old sharecropper house. They used to work those fields that you see through the trees and sometimes they would work the Shaw land too. That land you see through the trees has been lying fallow for years. This house is actually on the Shaw land. That field you see through the trees belongs to the McPhales. They say this old house is theirs but it's on your land. Harmon even proved it to them years ago at Rosemary's request but it didn't do any good."

Colby then pointed at the field through the trees. "If you look across that field you can see the McPhale house."

Logan looked in the direction Colby was pointing and after a few seconds spotted a house on the crest of the gently sloping field.

"I don't know about the rest of them, but Chip is an asshole."

"His brother is too," Colby interrupted. "They're both cut from the same cloth."

Logan could tell that talking about the McPhales bothered Colby so he tried to change the subject. He returned his attention to the abandoned house sitting in front of them.

"A sharecropper's house?" Logan said as he looked at the old decrepit house. The boards had been aged by the weather and the windows were fogged with years of accumulated dirt. One of the windows over the front porch was broken and the weathered front door was painted a shade of light blue.

"Yep. There's no telling how many families have lived in that house. Back in old days sharecroppers picked a lot of the tobacco around here." Then Colby looked down at her feet for a few seconds before her eyes met Logan's. "My great-grandparents lived in this house at one time. They were sharecroppers. My grandmother was born in this house. But thank God my family got out of the tobacco business before I came along."

"So this house is part of your family's history?" Logan said as he looked at Colby.

"Yep," Colby said as she looked away towards the Skeleton River. Logan then tugged at her hand.

"Hey, it's nothing to be ashamed of. Sounds like you come from a long line of hard workers."

"Thanks," Colby said as she smiled at Logan. "But my ancestors weren't the only hard workers that lived in this house. Most sharecroppers in the early days were freed slaves. They were hard workers, and superstitious ones at that."

"Superstitious?"

Colby pointed to the front door of the house. "The door is painted haint blue for a reason."

"What?" Logan raised an eyebrow and looked at Colby.

"They call it 'haint blue', city boy. Like I said, most of the early sharecroppers were freed slaves and they had their superstitions about the dead. They believed that the spirits of the dead would not travel across water so they always painted their front door blue. They thought it would trick the 'haints' and prevent them from entering the house."

"Couldn't the spirits just go through an open window?"

Colby turned to Logan and rolled her eyes. "You're funny, city boy."

"That's what I am. I'm a city boy. Where I come from we put a deadbolt and a chain on the front door to keep out the burglars. We don't think much about haints. It's the living people we worry about, like a thug coming through the front door with a 9mm in his hand. Paint won't stop that."

"Point taken," replied Colby. Then they both looked at the house.

"So what happened to it? That house looks like no one has lived in it for decades."

Colby paused and looked down at the ground. Then she brought her eyes up and began to scan the trees around them. It was getting dark and she knew it was time to go.

"We should leave. I'll tell you about the house later". Colby then looked through the trees towards the banks of the Skeleton River and Logan could tell she was getting upset. Just then the wind began to pick up.

Out of the corner of his eye Logan thought he saw movement in the trees. Suddenly the memory of Chip flashed through his mind. But he knew there was no way that Chip had followed them again. He was probably still laid out cold in the train station.

"Let's get back to your house. We can watch the sun set from your porch," Colby said. She was adamant about leaving.

"What, no tour of the haunted house?" Logan smiled but he could tell Colby was serious.

"Come on, city boy. Southerners know better than to be out in the woods at night, especially the woods around the Shaw Fields. You might run into something out here that could be hazardous to your health."

"Oh baloney. Let's go in the house. It's not that big. It won't take but a few minutes."

Colby grabbed Logan by the hand and pulled him towards the path leading away from the old house. "I'm not joking, Logan. We need to go."

"Okay already. Let's go." Logan knew Colby was getting upset. He thought about what had happened to her at the train station and suddenly felt guilty for trying to get her to explore the old house when it was clear that she wanted to leave.

"Come on, I know the way back." Logan decided to take the lead and get Colby out of the woods and back to his house where she would feel safe. Once they got to the edge of the tobacco field Colby stopped and looked up at the sky. The sun had almost set and the approaching twilight had turned the sky the color of burnished copper. Just then Colby let out a sigh of relief.

"There's no moon yet," she said as she looked up at the sky.

Logan pulled Colby by the hand to get her to step into the row of tobacco plants. He knew she was upset and he wanted to get her back to his house. It took a few minutes to make it across the field but once they made it Logan could tell that Colby was visibly relieved.

"You know, we could have done all that tomorrow. We didn't have to go out to that old house so close to sunset." Logan looked at Colby as she stared out across the fields in the direction of the path to the sharecropper house.

"It's okay. We're okay now. Let's get up on the porch."

Logan and Colby returned to the porch swing just as the sun slipped over the horizon. The air was warm and heavy with the smell of the tobacco field. Colby reached over and put her hand in Logan's and gave the swing a push with her foot.

With the sun gone, Logan could see the large moon hanging over the tobacco field. After a few minutes he finally asked Colby about the sharecropper house.

"So what's the deal with the old house out there in the woods?"

Colby looked over at Logan as a light breeze blew her hair around her face.

"That house has a dark past," Colby said as she pulled some of her hair back and tucked it behind her ear. Then she looked out across the field of tobacco.

"Two sharecroppers that lived with their families in that house were killed working the Shaw Fields. One was killed in the middle of the 1930's. The other sharecropper killed was a kid. I wanna say he was a teenager. His family was living in the house and working the fields in the early 1940's. Both of them were hacked to pieces right out there in that field.

Logan turned to look at Colby after she said this. "Are you serious?"

"Dead serious. Right out in those fields," Colby replied.

Logan watched as sadness flashed across Colby's face. She was looking down at her hands in her lap.

"What is it?" Logan said as he reached over and touched Colby's leg.

A few seconds passed and then Colby looked at Logan. He could see the sadness in her eyes.

"The sharecropper killed in 1937 was my great-grandfather. He was young, like in his early twenties and his name was Franklin. I think that's when my great-grandmother decided she had had enough of working tobacco. She took her children and left the house."

Logan was silent for a moment. He watched as Colby slowly turned her head and looked out over the tobacco field. The moon had finally risen and was beginning to tint the tobacco plants a silvery color.

"And you said my great-grandfather Carson Shaw was killed the same way out in one of those tobacco barns. Sounds like we have something in common."

"Yes, that one down there on the far end of the row," Colby said as she leaned forward in the swing and nodded in the direction of the tobacco barns. I remember my grandmother telling me that it was all over the news that year and was about the biggest thing that had happened in Starlight since the murder of the teenager in the forties.

Logan thought for a minute. "And that's all. Just those people?"

Colby gave the swing another gentle push with her foot. "No, there have been others. The first killing was in 1931. I don't remember the name."

"Damn..." Logan said as he looked out across the field. The only light now came from the rising moon and this gave the tobacco plants an eerie, surreal appearance as the leaves moved in the gentle breeze.

"In the seventies a group of potheads in a van stopped one night out by the road and got the crazy idea that they were going to roll themselves a few homemade cigars. Sort of like what you were talking about doing." Colby smiled at Logan and squeezed his hand. "You'd be surprised at how many people try that stupid homemade cigar idea."

"I'll bet," Logan said.

"Well, they had apparently had a little too much to drink when they decided to drive down Rosemary's driveway. They got out of the van and then wandered out into the fields to get their tobacco leaves. Rosemary must have saw the van out of her window and called the sheriff. But by the time he arrived it was too late."

"Too late?" Logan asked.

"Yep, too late. Once the stoners got out into the field they apparently decided that it wasn't tobacco that they wanted so they sat down in one of the rows to smoke a little weed. Sometime after that one of them apparently wandered off deeper into the field, probably to take a leak or something. The others heard the screaming but by the time they found their friend he had been chopped to pieces. It was a big story at the time and everyone in town remembers it."

"Holy shit..." Logan replied. Then he paused for a moment. "What kind of place is this?"

"I don't think anyone knows, Logan. Something happened here. Something horrible. But no one in town knows what it is."

"And what's with the harvest moon?" Logan asked.

"No one knows why but the killer only strikes under the light of a harvest moon. Harmon told you this, I'm sure. Usually the tobacco has been harvested by late August but sometimes it's still in the field after that. Just depends on the weather. The harvest moon is usually in early September."

"He told me about that. I thought he was just trying to be dramatic. He seems like a character to me. I like him, though. He's a good guy."

"Yes he is. Rosemary liked him too. She might have liked him a little too much when they were younger, but that's none of my business."

Logan frowned at Colby, "None of mine either."

"Harmon said the killings are random and that there is no way to tell when one will happen next."

"That's right. No one has ever been able to find a pattern in the timing of the killings. The last one was in 1996. A guy and a girl from out of town were canoeing down the Skeleton River at night, which is creepy enough if you ask me. I told you why it's called the Skeleton River. Well, I guess they decided they wanted to have sex in a tobacco field for some reason so they pulled their canoe up onto the bank and went into the edge of Rosemary's field where it goes down to the river. It didn't end well for them. And people say the harvest moon was so bright that night that you could read a book by it. That's probably why they were out canoeing after dark."

"Speaking of bright moons, we have one tonight," Logan said as he waved a hand at the tobacco field.

"Yes, we do" Colby replied. "But it's not a harvest moon. We'll probably get one tomorrow night though, if I had to guess. Or maybe the day after."

"So what did you mean when you said it didn't end well for them?" Logan said.

"It's the only known instance where the killer took two victims at the same time. I was just a little girl at the time but I remember hearing the adults talk about it. They said that by the time the killer got done hacking them that you couldn't tell there were two separate bodies. They say the canoe is still locked up down at the sheriff's office as evidence. If that's true it's a waste of space. They'll never find the killer."

"Because the killer is a ghost, right? That's what you're telling me. You don't buy the McPhale story."

"Nope. The McPhale family has always been a bunch of nimrods. They're dangerous but I don't think they're behind the killings. Besides, the killings have been going on for over eighty years."

Colby looked down into her lap. Logan knew she was thinking about what had happened at the train station.

"I hope you killed Chip. Does that make me a bad person?" Colby said. She was clearly ashamed for thinking such a thing.

"Hell no it doesn't. And if he's not dead he will be the next time he tries to lay a finger on you."

Colby turned to Logan and knew that she couldn't hold back any longer. The thought of Logan caring so much for her that he would kill to protect her was more than she could resist. When she threw herself onto him, Logan responded immediately. He knew he had to have her right there on the porch.

As they kissed the passion grew between them. Logan fumbled with

Colby's shirt until he finally pulled it over her head. Before long both of them were naked with Colby on top of Logan as they sat in the swing. Making love to her was more wonderful than he could have ever imagined and he knew her naked body under the light of the moon was the most heavenly thing he had ever seen.

Logan and Colby were lost in each other's arms as they made love in the porch swing. They were in their own world and unaware of anything else. From a distance out in the field of tobacco, a pair of eyes watched Logan and Colby as their bodies moved together locked in the passion of lovemaking.

At that moment, Chip McPhale knew that he would not rest until he killed Logan Shaw. It was all he could do not to walk up onto the porch and do it at that very moment. But that would be too easy. Chip wanted to plan his attack, and make sure that when the end came for Logan Shaw that it would be the most gruesome killing that Starlight had ever seen.

19

Logan could feel Colby's heart beating as she lay against him in the swing. It was almost as if they were one person. The moon was high over the tobacco field and a warm breeze was circulating around them as the porch swing moved slowly back and forth.

Colby knew at that moment that Logan was the man for her. It had been sudden, but her mother had always told her that when the man for her came along that it would happen quickly, and that she would know without a doubt that he was the one for her.

When she lifted her head from Logan's shoulder, Colby looked into his eyes. The moon above them cast sharp shadows on the porch and for a moment it seemed like they were the only two people in the world.

"Well hello there, city boy," Colby said as she grinned at Logan.

"Hello to you too," Logan replied. Then he kissed Colby and held her close. After several more minutes they gathered themselves together, collected their clothes and went into the house.

"Do you mind if I go upstairs and freshen up?" Colby said as she stood naked holding her clothes in her arms. Logan looked at her from head to toe and grinned.

"I like you just the way you are, but help yourself. I'm using the big bedroom at the end of the hall. It has a pretty nice bathroom."

"I'll be right back. And I'm starving too. Do you still have those leftovers?"

"Yep. I'll see if I can warm them up," Logan said as he fumbled with his clothes.

Colby grabbed her purse off the table, disappeared from the kitchen and then made her way upstairs. She found the bedroom Logan was using and then the bathroom. She put on her clothes and pulled a makeup brush out of her purse. She was trying to touch up her makeup in the mirror when she noticed the porcelain doll on the dresser in the bedroom. She could see it over her shoulder in the mirror. She lowered her makeup brush and slowly turned around to look at the doll through the doorway of the bathroom.

The doll was staring straight ahead and appeared to be looking at her. Colby walked out of the bathroom and across the bedroom until she was standing in front of the dresser. The doll continued its blank stare straight ahead as Colby moved close to it.

"Oh how beautiful you are," Colby said as she touched the dark blue material of the doll's dress. Just then Colby was startled by Logan's voice. He was standing in the doorway of the bedroom.

"She likes to watch me sleep." Colby flinched when Logan spoke.

"Oh my god you scared me!" Colby said as she placed a hand across her chest.

"Sorry," Logan said. "But it's true. She likes to watch me sleep. It wouldn't surprise me if she jumped down off of that dresser tonight and walked across the room."

Colby rolled her eyes at Logan. Then she turned to walk back to the bathroom. "I'll be done in just a second," she said as she disappeared into the bathroom.

"Take your time," Logan said as he looked at the doll on the dresser. He expected it to turn its head and look at him. But the doll sat motionless on the dresser instead.

Colby turned off the light in the bathroom and Logan watched as she walked across the bedroom. "Dinner's ready," he said as she approached him standing in the doorway.

"Let's eat," she said as she turned out the bedroom light.

Over reheated chicken and dumplings, Logan and Colby talked about how they had each grown up, him in the city and her in the country. After they finished eating they took their glasses of tea and went back out on the porch. The night had cooled off slightly, and Colby moved close to Logan on the swing.

"Logan, I really don't want to be alone tonight. I'm really scared of Chip. If you didn't kill him with that piece of wood then if I know Chip he's going to want revenge. He might start with me."

"You're not going anywhere tonight. You're staying right here with me, if that's okay with you."

"I'd love that," Colby said as she leaned over to kiss Logan.

§§§

The storm outside was intense. The windows flashed in a strobe-like pattern as the lighting struck in the distance. It was just before midnight and Logan was making slow, passionate love to Colby. She was unlike any woman he had ever been with and he wanted the night to go on forever. When they were finished they fell asleep in each other's arms. Logan could not recall ever feeling so satisfied and happy.

§§§

Logan rolled over and glanced at the clock on the nightstand. The glowing red letters indicated that it was just past 3 am. He raised himself up on an elbow and looked around the room. Colby was sleeping soundly beside him. Something didn't seem right but he couldn't put a finger on it. Slowly he lowered himself back down until his head was on the pillow. But the uneasy feeling would not subside.

Just as Logan felt his eyelids getting heavy, he heard a loud *thump* that seemed to come from the other side of the house. He sat bolt upright in bed just as he heard the sound again. This time it was louder and sounded like something falling over.

Logan knew he was not imagining things. He climbed out of bed as gently as he could to avoid waking Colby. He figured he would have a look around to make sure everything was okay. Then he would come back to bed.

Logan looked down the long hallway outside the bedroom door. He knew that the sound he had heard seemed to have come from down the hall. For some reason this brought him relief. If the sound had come from downstairs then it might have meant someone was trying to break into the house. Logan knew only one person who would try to do that and that person was Chip McPhale. Logan thought about what Colby had said about how Chip would want revenge for being hit with a two by four. And the last thing Logan wanted to deal with at three in the morning was Chip McPhale breaking into the house to settle a score.

The door to the attic stairs at the end of the hall was cracked open slightly. Logan walked gingerly down the hallway while the old wooden floor creaked under his feet. The sound of the floor was much louder in the still of the night than it was during the day. When Logan reached the door, he paused and looked down at the doorknob while his stomach tied itself into knots. Just as he lifted his hand to reach for the doorknob, the door suddenly slammed shut as if someone had jerked it from the other side. Logan recoiled in horror and stepped back away from the door while fighting to maintain control his bowels. Then he closed his eyes and swallowed the rock in his throat. He knew he had to go in the attic, no matter what was on the other side of the door. There was no turning back now.

Slowly, Logan stepped up to the door and placed his hand on the doorknob. He wondered if he would be able to open the door, or if someone, or something, would hold it shut from the other side. Would he have to fight to get the door open? Or would whatever it was that had slammed it shut let him enter through the door and make his way up to the attic.

There was only one way to find out.

Logan put his hand on the cool metal doorknob and closed his eyes. Then he twisted his wrist and was relieved when the doorknob turned freely in his hand. Then he slowly opened the door.

Logan cursed again that there was no light switch on the wall. He climbed the stairs slowly and stopped just before his head reached the level of the attic floor. He took a deep breath and then took one more step up so that his eyes were just a few inches above the attic floor.

The attic was still and the storm from earlier in the night had passed. The glow of the moon outside cut rectangular paths from the dormer windows to the attic floor and at first Logan could not see anything in the attic that could have been the source of the noise he had heard. But then he saw something in the shadows between two of the dormers that made his heard stop cold in his chest.

It was the silhouette of a person.

Logan fought the urge to lower his head and run back down the narrow stairway to the second floor of the house. He knew he had to confront what it was that he was seeing. He tried to focus on the shape of the person on the far side of the attic but his mind told him that something wasn't right. Something seemed off.

Logan summoned every ounce of courage in his body and climbed the rest of the way into the attic. Then he stood beside the top of the stairs and tried to focus on the silhouette of whoever it was standing on the other side of the attic. Then his eyes focused and Logan was hit with the realization of what he was looking at. He could see the face in the glow of the moonlight coming in from the dormers.

Hanging from the rafters by a rope around her neck was the body of Rosemary Abigail Shaw.

Underneath Rosemary's feet was a chair that had toppled over on its side. Logan recoiled in horror at the sight of his great-grandmother and he felt a wave of panic rush through his body. Using every ounce of courage that he could muster, he slowly began to walk across the attic floor towards Rosemary's body.

Rosemary's face was frozen in death. Her mouth was open as if she had tried to take one final breath. Logan felt his dinner boil in his stomach and for a second thought that he was going to vomit. He wanted to reach over and touch Rosemary's hand but could not muster the courage. His hand rose up but then quickly fell back to his side. After a few more seconds, he tried again. Just as he was about to touch Rosemary's hand, her eyes opened and she gasped as if she was trying to pull a breath through the constriction caused by the rope around her neck. Suddenly her body began to shake and her arms began to flail about. Logan gasped and took a step backwards.

As Logan recoiled in horror he took another step away from Rosemary. He continued backwards until he tripped over a box causing him to fall to the attic floor. He scrambled to get to his feet and then turned and ran for the attic stairs. He stumbled and almost fell down the stairs as he tried to make his way out of the attic.

Logan moved quickly down the hallway to the master bedroom. He slipped on the hardwood floor and caught himself with a hand on the wall, knocking a picture off of its nail in the process. The sound of the breaking glass as the picture hit the floor sounded like an explosion in the quiet house. He knew he needed to wake Colby and that they needed to get out of the house. Once he reached the bedroom, he crawled onto the bed and tried to shake Colby awake. She was sleeping soundly with her head underneath the blankets.

"Colby, wake up. Come on, wake up!"

Colby didn't move. Logan pushed against her several more times and then pulled the blanket off of her head.

It was all Logan could do to not cry out in agony.

Colby's body was covered in hornworms. Her eye sockets were empty and Logan watched as worms crawled out of the sunken holes and then down into her open mouth. He turned his head and tried to look away, but when he did he noticed that the doll on the dresser had turned its head and was looking at him. The sight of this was more than he could take and as he tried to get off of the bed he fell backwards onto the floor.

Logan bolted awake and quickly sat up in the bed. He was covered in sweat and his heart was hammering the walls of his chest. He turned to look at Colby and she was lying fast asleep beside him, her face relaxed and peaceful. He turned and looked at the doll on the dresser but its lifeless porcelain eyes were staring straight ahead towards the bathroom.

Logan got out of the bed and went to the bathroom and closed the door. Once he finished vomiting his chicken and dumplings into the toilet he washed his face and tried to get himself together. It had only been a nightmare, a violent, gruesome nightmare, but still just a nightmare.

Or was it?

As Logan stared at himself in the bathroom mirror, he wondered about Rosemary's body hanging in the attic. Of course he had just had a nightmare, but was it more than that? Was his nightmare a fair depiction of how his great-grandmother had killed herself? Logan put this out of his mind. It had only been a nightmare. The fact that he had found Colby in the bed covered in the same worms that eat the tobacco plants was proof that it had been a nightmare. She was sleeping soundly in the bed at this very moment, just as beautiful as she was when he had made love to her at midnight.

Using this logic Logan got himself calmed down and then he went back to bed. It took him more than an hour to get back to sleep but when he finally dozed off his sleep was heavy and dreamless. He awoke several hours later to the smell of coffee floating through the house. Colby was already awake and was apparently making breakfast for them.

"Good morning, sleepyhead," she said as Logan walked into the kitchen. "I was going to make us some breakfast but I forgot there's not really anything in the refrigerator. But we do have coffee, and with coffee all things are possible." Colby smiled and brought her cup to her lips and took a long sip of her coffee.

"I hear ya," Logan said as he walked over to the coffee pot. "I'll have to get some stuff today. Does this town have a grocery store?" Logan yawned as he poured himself a cup of coffee.

"No, silly. We don't have a grocery store," Colby said as she gave Logan a frustrated look. "Everyone in Starlight just grows their own food, raises chickens for the eggs and we drink our milk straight out of the pale after we milk the cow. And we bathe once a month using homemade soap. Of course we have a grocery store. I'll show you where it's at and we can get stuff to make dinner tonight and breakfast tomorrow morning." Colby paused and looked down into her coffee cup. "I mean, if you want…"

"Stop it. Of course you're staying here tonight. Just like last night." Logan walked over and put his cup on the counter and then he took Colby's cup out of her hands and sat it beside his. Then he gave her a hug and a kiss on the neck.

"I have morning breath tinged with coffee breath, so a kiss on the neck is all you'll get."

"Me too," Colby replied. Logan let go of Colby and they both reached for their coffee cups and then walked over and sat down at the kitchen table.

"I'm off work today," Colby said as she took a sip of her coffee.

"So am I," Logan said as he grinned and lifted his cup. "Well, I'm off work from the car business. I do have my tobacco empire to take care of. How I'm supposed to do that is still a mystery to me." Logan then looked at Colby. "You know a lot more about this golden leaf stuff than I do. What am I supposed to do?"

"Nothing, except cash the check when they give it to you," Colby replied.

"Cash what check?" Logan put down his cup and gave Colby his undivided attention.

"Rosemary was too old to work the fields, Logan. She rented out her land and let someone else plant the tobacco seedlings, tend to them, and then harvest them when the time was right. Whoever planted that crop out there will come harvest it when it's ready. Then they'll cure the tobacco leaves and sell them. And that's when you'll get a big cut of the profits. Lots of people around Starlight that have grown too old to work their land do it this way. They make less money, but they don't have to lift a finger. Harmon didn't explain this?"

"I'm sure he probably did but I wasn't listening. He tends to babble sometimes."

"Yes he does," replied Colby. "And he loves to puff on that pipe."

"So I just wait for someone to come and pick the tobacco?"

"Yep. I don't know who it is but I would imagine Harmon can tell you. He's been Rosemary's lawyer since Moby Dick was a minnow so I'm sure he knows all about her business."

"Moby what?"

"Never mind, city boy. I'm hungry. Are you hungry?"

"Very," replied Logan.

"There's a little store just down the road. It's sort of a gas station combined with a snack bar. It looks like something out of the 1950's. We can ride down there and get a sausage biscuit. I really don't want to go into town to the diner."

"Sounds good to me. Let's go," Logan said as he pushed himself away from the breakfast table.

It took about fifteen minutes to drive down to the gas station, order a couple of biscuits and then get back to the house. Logan and Colby poured themselves fresh cups of coffee and then sat down to eat their biscuits, which were wrapped in paper.

"Wow," Logan said as he took a bite. "That's good."

Old man Crawford owns the place. He's had that little gas-n-go store since I was a kid. His wife cooks the sausage. They raise their own pigs and make the sausage themselves." Colby then took a bite out of her biscuit.

"I could get used to this simple country living," Logan said as he took another bite of his biscuit.

"Is that so?" Colby said. "Lots of city people say that until they find out that living in the country means having a septic tank and a well for water."

"Wouldn't bother me," Logan said.

§§§

It was only eleven o'clock in the morning but Chip McPhale was already on his third beer. But it wasn't affecting his pool game, and he was three shots ahead of his brother Ethan as they shot a game at Ben's, a pool hall on the edge of town. Just as Chip sank the eight ball, several of his friends walked up to the table.

"Fuck," Ethan said as he took twenty dollars out of his wallet and tossed it on the table near where his brother was standing.

"You play pretty good pool for a man who just got his ass whipped by a city boy from Wilmington." Joel, who had been Chip's friend since grade school then patted Chip on the back. "It's all over town."

"Fuck you," Chip said as he pushed Joel's hand away. "I'm gonna kill that city fuck if it's the last thing I do. And then I'm gonna take what I want from Colby, the little fucking tease."

Joel and the rest of the young men standing around the table knew that Chip had a temper. They didn't doubt for a minute that he would carry through on his threat.

"Yeah, you do that Chip," Joel said as he nodded towards Chip and then Ethan. "You go right ahead and do that and you'll end up being somebody's bitch in prison." Then Joel and the other men walked away from the pool table to the other side of the bar. They knew better than to be around Chip when he was in this kind of mood. But Chip's brother Ethan was a different story. He shared his brother's temper and wouldn't mind at all if Chip taught Logan Shaw a lesson or two. And he wanted to spend a little time of his own with Colby as well. He had been dreaming about her ass in a pair of tight jeans ever since high school. But he had never let on to his brother about it. Ethan knew that Chip considered Colby to be his property and even though they were brothers, Ethan knew that Chip was probably the meanest person he had ever known. Sometimes Ethan had his doubts that sharing blood with his brother would be enough to temper Chip's anger if he ever made a move for Colby. So over the years he had kept is affection for her a secret from his brother.

"Rack 'em up, little brother. Give me a chance to win back my twenty," Ethan said as he began to rub chalk on his pool cue.

"The loser does the racking," Chip said as he tossed the triangular rack towards Ethan.

Ethan was able to win his twenty back from his brother, and also to win an extra twenty in the games that followed. The more Chip drank, and the more he thought about what he was going to do to Logan, the less he was able to concentrate on beating his brother at pool. By the time the afternoon rolled around, Chip was good and liquored up and had settled on a plan in his mind. But he didn't tell his brother Ethan. Chip knew there were some things that a man had to do alone and he didn't want Ethan tagging along and getting in the way.

§§§

Colby pushed the small shopping cart down the aisle at the grocery store while Logan followed along beside her. The store was small and was nowhere near as busy as the grocery store Logan shopped at near his trailer park in Wilmington, nor was it as large. Once they left the potato chip aisle, where Colby had promptly grabbed a bag of her favorite chips, they moved to the aisle that contained the refrigerated items.

Logan placed bacon and sausage in the cart, along with a gallon of milk.

Then they walked down the freezer aisle where Colby grabbed a half gallon of ice cream. She had already placed everything else she needed to make peach cobbler in the cart.

"We'll have peach cobbler on the porch tonight while we watch the moon rise."

"I doubt we'll do much moon watching if I get you on the porch but peach cobbler sounds great. I don't know what a cobbler is but I'm sure it's delicious," Logan said.

Colby rolled her eyes at Logan and grinned. "You city people are savages."

Once back at the house Logan and Colby put the food away. Then Logan had an idea.

"Say, how about I get a hammer and a few tools and we go up in the attic and see what's in that old trunk? I'm sure I can find something around here to use to get inside that thing. I forgot that I needed to buy bolt cutters when we were in town."

"I'm game," Colby said. "Let's look through all the kitchen drawers. There's bound to be a junk draw that might have a hammer in it."

It didn't take Logan long to find an old hammer. It wasn't in the kitchen but he found it in the downstairs bathroom in the bottom drawer of the cabinet under the sink.

"Follow me," Logan said as he motioned to Colby as he came out of the bathroom.

Once in the attic, they sat down in front of the old trunk. Logan began to examine the lock to see if he could yank it open without hitting it with the hammer. But the lock was sound and would not open. But it only took three hits with the hammer to get the lock to give way. As he removed the lock from the trunk he looked over at Colby, whose eyes were as big as half dollars as she watched him remove the lock. Neither of them knew what was going to be inside.

Logan blew the dust off of the top of the trunk and then slowly opened the lid. The dim light from the solitary bulb spilled down onto the trunk and cast a yellowish glow over the contents.

The trunk looked like it was mostly filled with small boxes. Colby picked up a box and opened it. It held several old pieces of jewelry, including two rings, a broach and a necklace.

"Looks like something a floozie from the Roaring Twenties would wear," Logan said. "Very gaudy."

"I think they're pretty. I love jewelry. Especially old estate jewelry like this," Colby said as she tried on one of the rings.

"Consider it yours," Logan said as he patted Colby on the knee.

"Really?" Colby said as she raised her eyebrows at Logan, who only smiled and nodded.

Most of the other small boxes in the trunk held trinkets of various types – more jewelry, a few bracelets, an old pair of reading glasses and several hat pins. One small oblong box held an old pair of shoes that looked like they had belonged to a little girl.

"I wonder who these belonged to." Logan said as he examined the old shoes. "They still have dried mud on them."

"Whoever it was did a lot of walking. They look worn out," Colby said as she took the shoes away from Logan and looked at them. Then she sat them down beside the trunk.

The next thing Logan found in the trunk was an old brown envelope. He opened the envelope and slowly removed an aged black and white photo of a family standing in front of a train. The station could be seen in the background of the photo.

"That's our train station, the one I took you to see yesterday. That's what it looked like in its heyday," Colby said as she pointed to the building in the photo. Logan looked at the photo and then recognized the station.

"Well I'll be damned, it is the station. Look at that train. It looks like something out of the Old West," Logan said as he gently handed the photo to Colby. It was very old and he didn't want to tear it.

"So who are those people?" Colby asked.

"Hell if I know," Logan said as he looked at the photo of a man and a woman standing behind two young girls.

"Those adults are not Rosemary and Carson," Colby replied.

"I know," Logan said as he studied the photo."

"Wait a minute," Colby said as she turned over the photo and looked on the back.

Someone had penciled the date on the back of the photo. It had almost faded completely away but Colby was able to make out the date – *1929*.

"Holy shit that's old," Logan said. "Damn... So who could those people be?"

Colby grew silent. She frowned at the photo as she held it in between them.

"Wait a minute. I know what that is. Look at the kids in the background standing on the platform of the station. And you can still see some of them in the windows of the passenger cars." Colby took her finger and pointed to the windows of the cars behind the locomotive.

"So?" Logan said.

"I'll bet that's an orphan train," Colby said as her eyes grew wide. "It has to be. Why else would there be so many children in the photo? And the year on the back seems about right. Those trains stopped coming sometime in the 1930's."

Logan looked at Colby and raised an eyebrow. "You sure know a lot about this stuff. How is that?"

Colby continued to stare at the children in the photo. "Like I said, my family has lived in this town since it was founded. The stories get passed down through the years."

Logan took the photo and stuck it back into the envelope and then set it aside. Then he reached down into the trunk and pulled out another item. This one was wrapped in cloth. Colby drew in a breath as Logan removed the cloth to reveal a child's doll.

"Look at that," Colby said. "I'll bet it's handmade. You can always tell by the stitching."

The doll was stuffed and was dressed in an old plaid skirt and had hair made out of brown yarn. The face was smooth cloth with no eyes, nose or mouth and the arms ended as nubs instead hands. Small hand-sewn cloth shoes were stitched onto each foot. Logan held the doll and then tried to straighten out some of the tangles in the yarn.

"It looks like it has seen better days," Logan said as he pulled at a few tufts of stuffing that were coming through one of the seams."

"Looks like somebody loved it," Colby said. "I had a favorite doll when I was little. It was a Raggedy Ann."

"I was more the G.I. Joe type," Logan said.

"Let's see if we can find a name on it. I wrote my name on my doll. Lots of little girls do that."

Colby took the doll and looked it over in an effort to find a name somewhere on the doll.

"There," Logan said as he pointed to one of the doll's feet. In faded letters was the word "Clara".

"So this was Clara's doll," Colby said.

"But who was Clara?" replied Logan as he took the doll from Colby and stared into its blank face.

20

Logan was lying on his back in bed. The clock on the nightstand read a few minutes before midnight. The moonlight coming through the windows made Colby's naked body seem to shimmer as she moved slowly up and down.

The lovemaking was slow and passionate. Colby leaned forward and Logan took her face in his hands and kissed her just as he felt her body tremble. She slid her arms around Logan's shoulders and pulled herself to him as he began thrust deeper into her. The moonlight cut sharp shadows through the room and the only sound in the house was the sound of their lovemaking. Then Colby cried out as the orgasm ripped through her body. Logan followed quickly and then both of their bodies went limp, completely spent and exhausted.

§§§

Logan bolted awake just after two in the morning and the house was eerily still.

Logan knew something was wrong. He knew there was a reason he had been jolted awake and that there was no way he could go back to sleep until he found out why. He turned and looked at Colby sleeping soundly beside him and then decided that he needed to get out of bed and have a look around the house.

Once out of bed Logan walked slowly across the bedroom until he came to the door to the hallway. The thought of Chip McPhale breaking into the house flashed hot through his mind again, but Logan knew that Chip was the least of his problems when it came to the house. There were far worse things right now than an angry redneck wanting to settle a grudge.

There was the attic, for one thing.

Logan looked down the hallway towards the door that led to the attic. But this time the door was closed. Logan felt a wave of relief wash through his body when he saw that the door was closed and not cracked open like it had been in his nightmare. This gave Logan enough courage to step into the hallway.

The floors creaked and groaned and Logan moved slowly down the hallway. When he reached the attic door, he placed his hand on the knob but then thought better of it. He suddenly felt like he was being watched. Logan stared at his hand on the doorknob and then slowly released it. Then he turned and looked down the hall towards the master bedroom where Colby was sleeping.

Someone was standing in front of the window at the far end of the hall.

Logan swallowed hard as he stared at the silhouette of the person standing in front of the window at the end of the hall, the dark shape highlighted against the moonlit drapes covering the window. It was obvious to Logan the silhouette was that of a tall and muscular man and that he was wearing a brim hat. He was holding something in his hand that dangled by his side.

Logan took a step backwards until his back touched the attic door behind him as the dark figure slowly began to walk down the hall towards him. Logan thought about Colby in the bedroom all alone but the dark figure did not seem to pay any attention as he passed by the master bedroom door. He seemed to be focusing his attention on Logan as he moved towards him from the other end of the hallway. The shoulders of the man were so wide that it almost seemed that they were about to touch the walls of the hallway.

Logan could hear no sound as the figure moved towards him. The wooden floorboards were silent as the man slowly closed the distance between them. Logan felt his heart racing in his chest and he wanted to escape, but knew that he had nowhere to go, and even if he did he knew that he could not leave Colby all by herself.

The man stopped within a few feet of Logan and was close enough that Logan could see he was holding some sort of leather strap or belt in his hand. But before Logan could move, the man lifted his hand and then brought the leather strap down violently across Logan's chest. Logan screamed out and fell to the floor as a white hot bolt of pain shot through his body. He raised his arms in an effort to shield himself from the next blow. Then he instinctively curled up into the fetal position in the anticipation of more strikes from the leather strap. His eyes were shut and his jaw was clenched as he tried to absorb the pain from the first strike, while readying himself for the next strike that he knew was coming.

Logan waited for what seemed like an eternity but there was no second strike from the leather strap. Terrified, Logan slowly opened his eyes.

The man was gone.

Logan pushed himself up onto his elbows and then he sat straight up and leaned his back against the attic door. There was a burning hot stripe across his bare chest. The pain was unbearable and when he reached up and touched the welt that had formed where the strap had hit him, a sharp pain knifed through his chest. Logan felt his head begin to swim from the pain and then his world went dark as he passed out and fell sideways back onto the floor.

§§§

Logan was unsure of how long he had been lying on the floor of the hallway. His eyes were closed and the skin on his chest felt like it was on fire from where the leather belt had blistered his skin. It was dark in the hallway and Logan wanted to open his eyes but was afraid to. He squeezed them shut tighter as the pain from his chest continued to rage. Then through his clinched eyelids, Logan could tell that all of a sudden there was light in the hallway. After a few seconds passed, he slowly he opened his eyes.

The lights in the hallway were off, but there seemed to be some sort of light coming from the bedrooms that lined the hallway on the back side of the house. Logan pushed himself up onto his elbow and stared down the hallway towards the door to the closest bedroom. A greenish-yellow light was pouring through the doorway and into the hall. Logan squinted and tried to focus on what he was seeing. After a few minutes, he slowly pushed himself up until his back was against the attic door behind him.

As Logan looked down the hallway, he could see the greenish-yellow light coming from each bedroom door. Slowly he got to his feet and gathered what strength he had. He knew Colby was in the bedroom at the other end of the hallway and he wanted to go to her so that he could protect her. But what he was seeing was surreal, and for all he knew he was just dreaming. But when he reached down and touched the welt on his chest and felt the pain needle every muscle between his neck and his waist he knew that he was not dreaming. No one could sleep through that kind of pain.

To Logan it felt like he was in another world, a world trapped between the physical world and what lay beyond. The greenish-yellow light seemed to shimmer on the walls opposite of the bedroom doors as he slowly approached the first room. Once there, he stood in the doorway and looked into the bedroom. The light he was seeing was pouring in through the windows and even though it was the middle of the night, the fields he saw through the windows were bathed in the harsh noonday sun. But the sunlight had a strange color to it and gave the landscape of the tobacco fields an ethereal appearance.

Logan walked slowly over to the window and looked out into the tobacco fields behind the house. People were working in the fields, walking between the rows carrying armloads of tobacco leaves. To Logan the people looked like they were from a different era, with clothes that seemed out of date. On the far end of the field, Logan could see a mule pulling a cart loaded with tobacco. In the rows he could see adults along with children moving aimlessly down the rows picking the leaves as they went.

Logan studied the scene below him as his mind raced to find a conclusion. He realized that he was looking back in time to what the Shaw Fields had probably looked like a hundred years ago. Unable to process what he was seeing, Logan began to move slowly backwards away from the window. He stopped when his back touched the edge of the doorframe of the bedroom door. Then he moved around the doorframe and back out into the hall. Just as he did, the windows in the bedroom went dark. Then after a few seconds, they turned silvery-white again from the moonlight.

Behind Logan was a closed bedroom door. It was across the hallway from the door he was standing in. Logan turned and looked at the door and could not remember if it had been closed when he had first saw it on his way to the attic door earlier in the night.

Logan placed his hand on the doorknob of the closed door. He knew he had to look inside. This was the only bedroom door that was closed in the entire hallway. He turned the knob and slowly pushed the door open.

The bedroom contained only one piece of furniture and two small beds that looked like they were sized for children. The room had only one window. Logan could see a small door in the corner that he knew was probably the closet. His eyes scanned the room until they settled on the bed. At first he thought the bed was empty but when his eyes focused on it in the dim light he could see that someone was sleeping in it. The small outline of the shape under the blankets told Logan that whoever it was they were not nearly as large as the man that had hit him with the leather belt.

Logan gathered his strength and stepped into the room. He paused to see if the person in the bed was going to stir. But there was no movement under the blankets. Logan took a few more steps towards the bed and then froze solid in his tracks when a board in the floor suddenly squealed under his weight. But there was still no movement under the blankets.

When Logan reached the side of the bed he studied the small outline of the person lying under the covers. Whoever it was had pulled the covers over their head to the point where all Logan could see was the very top of their head. He reached over and slowly pulled the blanket back until he could see the face of a little girl. She was holding a doll close to her face and appeared to be sound asleep.

Logan looked at the little girl and then at the doll. It didn't take him more than a few seconds to realize that he had seen the doll before. It was the one he and Colby had found in the trunk in the attic. The blank cloth of the doll's face contrasted with the face of the little girl.

Suddenly the little girl's eyes opened. Logan gasped and stepped backwards when she looked into his eyes. Then she pulled her doll closer to her in an effort to hide her face from Logan. She seemed to be afraid that he was going to hurt her.

Logan stepped backwards a few more feet as he stared down at the little girl. Suddenly a voice filled his ears.

"Logan?"

Logan turned to see Colby standing in the doorway to the bedroom. She was rubbing one of her eyes.

"What are you doing?"

Logan turned and looked back at the bed, which was now made up and looked as if no one had slept in it in years. Then he looked back at Colby.

"I…"

"Are you okay?" Colby said, a note of apprehension in her voice.

"I guess…" Logan paused and looked back at the bed. "I guess I'm sleepwalking."

"You're not sleepwalking," Colby said. "Maybe you were, but you're awake now. Let's go back to bed."

Logan looked at Colby and then back at the bed one more time. Tomorrow he would tell her all about what he had seen, but now was not the time. Then he thought about the welt on his chest. What would Colby think about that? How would he explain it? Just then he brought his hand up to his chest to feel for the welt but when his hand touched his chest the welt was gone. Confused, he paused for a moment while looking down at his chest. With only the moonlight coming in from the window it was hard to see clearly but he could still tell that the welt was gone.

"What the matter?" Colby said as she watched Logan run his hand around his chest like he was trying to feel for something.

"Uh, nothing. Never mind. Let's go to bed."

Logan and Colby walked back down the hallway to the master bedroom. Then they climbed back into bed. Logan was on his back and Colby laid her head on his chest and within minutes was fast asleep.

For Logan Shaw the rest of the night was a combination of lying in bed wide awake or in a shallow state of fitful sleep. As he laid there in the bed he thought about the house and how it now belonged to him. But something was wrong with it. He had no doubt about this whatsoever now. And Logan realized that he not only owned the house, but apparently everything from its past as well.

Logan finally drifted off to sleep. When he woke up the clock said 9:32 am. He turned his head and looked next to him but Colby was gone. On her pillow was a note. He picked it up and read the handwriting.

Logan, I had to go to work. Come see me later.

Then he read the next line and felt a smile cross his tired face.

I love you. Colby.

21

Harmon Blackwell was sitting in his office when Logan walked through the door.

"Sandy said I could come on back, Harmon. We need to talk."

Harmon leaned back in his chair. He had expected Logan to come in this morning. He knew that Logan had now spent several nights in the old house and by now had no doubt realized that everything is not as it seems with the place.

"Good morning, Logan." Harmon then reached into his desk drawer and produced his bottle of whiskey. "Drink?"

"No thanks," Logan said as he closed the door to the office and then sat down across from Harmon.

"Suit yourself," Harmon said as he poured whiskey into his empty coffee cup. Then he turned up the cup and took a healthy swig. Logan watched as the old man winced as the whiskey went down his throat.

"So I inherited a fucking haunted house, Harmon." Logan paused. "Haunted is not a big enough word to tell you the truth."

"No it's not, Logan. Not nearly big enough. And yes, the house has its... its past. It has a history, I should say."

"I'll say it does," Logan snapped. "I can look out of the windows and night and see back a hundred years. I saw my great-grandmother hang herself in the attic, there's a little girl that wanders the hallways at night, and last night a man whipped me across the chest with a leather belt. Not to mention someone was sleeping in one of the other bedrooms. So yeah, the house obviously has a past. But you didn't tell me that past would come for a visit every night."

Harmon took another pull of whiskey and looked at Logan. Then he took another swig and emptied the cup.

"I'm sorry, Logan," Harmon said as he cleared his throat. "But look at the bright side. The house might have a history but it also comes with five

142

million dollars. That's gotta take the edge off."

"Like that whiskey takes the edge off?" Logan said as he looked at Harmon's coffee cup.

"Exactly," Harmon said. "I'd rather have the five million to tell you the truth. I'll trade you the whiskey for it."

"Sure. But you have to live in the house. Do we have a deal?"

"No thanks," Harmon said quickly as he reached for the whiskey bottle. He poured another shot into his cup as he felt the warmth starting to spread through his body. He had been dreading this conversation with Logan since meeting him.

Harmon leveled his eyes on Logan. "Don't go in the damn fields at night, Logan. Especially when the harvest moon comes this week. We never know when the next murder will happen, but the last one was almost twenty years ago. If I were a betting man I'd say we're due. I'm telling you right now that you're a dead man if you go out there under a harvest moon. There won't be a piece of you left bigger than a shot glass if the killer gets hold of you."

"I know about the fields. You told me all about that and so did Colby. It's the house I want to know about now."

Harmon leaned back in his chair. "Yes… The house." Harmon paused and then reached for his pipe. He lit it and puffed until his head was surrounded by a cloud of blue smoke.

"Well?" Logan said. He was growing impatient with Harmon. He could tell the old man was stalling.

Harmon gave Logan a serious look. "Logan, originally that land was worked by slaves. I told you a little about that already. That's probably where the problem started. Hell, if I had been one of those slaves and forced to work the fields you can bet your bottom lip that I'd be rattling chains in the attic."

"I haven't seen the ghost of any slaves or heard any chains in the attic. What I did see when I looked out the windows last night was something that looked like a scene out of the Great Depression. And Colby and I found some old photos in the attic. The people in the photos were dressed like the people I saw out in the field through the window. Very old, like Grapes of Wrath old, or something like that."

"Children?" Harmon said as he raised an eyebrow.

Logan paused for a few seconds. "Yes. When I looked out of the window I saw children working the fields. Why?"

"And you said a little girl wanders the halls at night?"

"Yes, Harmon. And she looks like she lived a hundred years ago. So what gives?"

Harmon paused for a few minutes. He knew if he drank any more whiskey that he would lose control of his tongue so he puffed on his pipe instead. The nicotine was almost as soothing as the alcohol.

"Logan, Rosemary has lived in that house since she was a little girl. She inherited it from her parents when she was older. After they passed, I should say."

Logan leaned back in the chair. He knew he was finally going to get some answers to what was going on in the house.

"I became friends with Rosemary a few years after Carson died. I was a young college kid and needed money for school so I worked on things around her house for her during the summers. We became friends. The money I earned helped with law school. She paid very well, Logan, much more than my services warranted. She knew I was paying my way through school and I guess she just wanted to help me. And I think she wanted company in the house. When I graduated and came back to Starlight and started this firm she was my first client."

"I've heard that she was more than a client. What age would she have been around that time? About forty or so?" When Logan said this he saw a flash of guilt on Harmon's face.

"Well... That's neither here nor there, Logan."

"I could care less to tell you the truth, Harmon. But if you were Rosemary's yard boy and then her lawyer, and if you, well, spent a few nights in her house then I'm sure you knew what was going on."

"I've seen some of the very things that you have seen, Logan. That little girl... I woke up one night and she was standing beside the bed. And I've seen scenes from the past through the windows just like you did. I once saw slaves working the fields. And one night I even saw Union soldiers passing close to the house. Rosemary didn't like to be in the house alone. I've spent many a night in that house Logan, and I don't think I ever got a wink of sleep. And not for reasons you might expect. I don't know how anyone can sleep in that house to tell you the truth."

"And you didn't tell me this when we first met? What the fuck, Harmon?"

"And how would that conversation have went, Logan? It was hard enough to tell you about the harvest moon killings. I guess I could have said, hey by the way, spirits walk the halls of the house at night and if you look out of the windows you'll be able to see back in time. Come on, Logan. You would have bolted for the door and the house would now be sitting empty."

"So do you know about the things in the attic? Those photos I told you about, do you have any idea who the people are?"

Harmon picked up his empty coffee cup and looked into it. He frowned and put it back down on his desk.

"You need to join AA Harmon, if you don't mind me saying."

Harmon laughed. "What I need Logan is a cold grave to crawl into. I'm old and things weigh heavy on me. The whiskey helps. It will get me through until I take my last breath."

Logan felt bad for telling Harmon he drank too much. It was none of his business and who was he to judge Harmon? There was no telling what burden the old man was carrying around with him. And besides, Logan knew he had a bottle just like Harmon's back in his desk in Wilmington.

"So who are the people in the photos?" Logan asked.

"Probably Rosemary's parents," replied Harmon.

"What?" Logan snapped. "You mean my great-great grandparents?"

Harmon cleared his throat. "That's what I would call them, but Rosemary was always vague about that. She always referred to them as the previous owners of the house. And she got angry every time I tried to talk to her about her childhood and her parents. It's almost like she didn't want to admit they were her parents. I never could understand it and I never could get much out of her about it. And I doubt there's anyone alive in town that knows more than that either. That was a long time ago. And really, what damn difference does it make? You own the house now free and clear and I have all the paperwork to prove it."

Logan thought about this for a minute. He was angry at Harmon but then his anger began to subside. Harmon was right, what difference did it make? Logan decided to let it go and continue with his questions about the photos.

"One photo was of two adults and a child." Logan said as he leaned back in his chair and tried to calm his nerves.

"I have no idea, Logan. If the child wasn't Rosemary then I have no idea who it was," Harmon said as he felt the nicotine wind through his bloodstream. "I heard a story once that a child had died in the house but I never could find out much about it."

§§§

Colby was wrapping silverware in napkins just as the last customer left the diner. The lunch rush, if it could be called a rush, was over and she was eager to finish her shift and go see Logan. She couldn't understand why he had not come by the diner for lunch but then she figured that he was probably at Harmon's office finishing the details of his new inheritance. She felt a pang of sadness in her heart but she knew that he would have come by to see her if he had been able to. But now that her shift was almost over she knew she could finish up her side work with the silverware and then be off for the rest of the day. After that, she wasn't due back at the diner until tomorrow morning.

The only trouble at lunch had come from visit from Chip McPhale. Colby shuddered as she remembered the mark on the side of Chip's face from where he had been hit by Logan with the two by four.

Colby thought about how Chip had simply walked into the diner and sat down at the bar. He ordered from another waitress and did not speak a word to her the entire time he was in the diner. But he had watched every move she made while he ate his lunch, and Colby remembered how it had chilled her down to her bones as his eyes followed her. A few times when they had made eye contact, Colby had to look away after Chip gave her his characteristic grin. It was a cross between a grin and a smirk and it said to Colby that he knew that Logan had gotten the best of him at the old train station but that he would not stop until he had himself a healthy dose of payback.

The worst part of the lunch rush was when Chip had gotten up to leave. He tipped his hat at Colby and gave her a wink while silently mouthing the words *see you later* as he walked past her standing behind the counter near the cash register. She knew Chip McPhale, and she knew that he wasn't kidding.

Colby tried to clear her thoughts of Chip as she walked to her car. It felt good to be out of her waitress uniform and in a pair of shorts and her favorite button-up shirt. She didn't like changing in the diner's restroom but it was easier than going back to her apartment. She had parked in the rear of the diner with several of the other employees and even though it was broad daylight she felt uneasy walking down the sidewalk to the parking lot. No one could see her from the road once she walked past the Dumpster and this made her even more afraid. She fumbled with her keys and then dropped them as she tried to pull them out of her purse. She picked them up and almost had the key in the lock when Chip McPhale walked up beside her and put his hand on her throat. Then he grabbed her by the arm and turned her around so that her back was pressed up against the driver's side door.

"You just don't seem to listen, do you?" Chip then let go of Colby's arm but kept his other hand on her throat. He had his body pressed against her and she knew he was much stronger than she was and that there was no way she was going to be able to break free. Chip tightened his grip on Colby's throat and this caused her to gasp for air as she tried to inhale.

"Chip... *Please...*" Colby could barely speak. Her words were hoarse and could barely get past the constriction in her throat caused by Chip's hand.

Chip then dropped his free hand to Colby's thigh. Then he pulled his hand up slowly and forced it between her legs. Then he tightened his grip on the soft skin of her inner thigh. She tried to cry out but Chip's hold on her throat was too tight. Then Chip leaned in so that his mouth was close to Colby's ear.

"You tell your fucking little boyfriend that I'm coming for him. I'm going to beat his head in with the same two by four that he tried to kill me with. Once his sorry ass is out of the way I'm going to fuck you in that old

Shaw woman's bed. I'm going to give it to you like a real man. Once I get done pumping you I'm going to burn that fucking house down. And if your pussy is as good as I think it's going to be, I might let you live so that I can fuck you again. But if you don't please me then I'll kill you and burn your damn body up with the house right along with that city puke. Do you understand?"

Colby could not breathe much less say anything to Chip. She felt herself getting lightheaded from the lack of oxygen. Chip sensed this and released his grip on her throat. She responded by sucking a huge gulp of air into her lungs.

"You tell him, Colby. Tell him there is nowhere to hide. Tell him I'll find his sorry ass if he decides to skip town. He got a lucky shot at the train station, but you tell him that I'm going to make him pay for it."

Colby held her hand across her throat over the spot where Chip's hand had been. She watched as he walked off past the Dumpster and then back to the street. Then he turned around the edge of the building and disappeared. A few seconds later Colby heard a truck engine start. Then she watched as the truck drove slowly past the diner parking lot. Chip was in the passenger's seat and his brother was driving.

They both looked over at Colby just as Ethan hit the brakes. He backed the truck up and then turned into the diner parking lot where he brought the truck to a stop near the rear end of Colby's car. When Chip opened the door and stepped down onto the pavement, Colby could see the rage in his eyes.

"I've got a better idea," he said as he took a step towards her.

§§§

After Logan finished with Harmon he walked to the diner. He felt a wave of relief when he saw Colby's car in the parking lot. Maybe he hadn't missed her. Harmon had droned on for hours about the old house and its dark past. After they had finished Logan had excused himself as quickly as he could. He had had enough of the ghost stories about the old house and now only wanted to see Colby.

Once inside the diner Logan felt his heart sink when he didn't see Colby. Just then a waitress walked by carrying a pitcher of tea in one hand and a coffee pot in the other.

"Excuse me, have you seen Colby?" Logan didn't remember the waitress's name even though Colby had introduced him to her just the other day.

"Yep. She left about thirty minutes ago. Said she was going to see you." The waitress then winked at Logan.

"Thirty minutes ago? But her car is still out back."

This seemed to puzzle the waitress, who then frowned like she was suddenly deep in thought.

"Maybe she went back to our place. She shares an apartment with me and another friend of ours that works over at the Post Office. You can walk to it from here. Maybe she just decided to walk back to the apartment and then come back for her car later." The waitress, satisfied that she had just solved the mystery, shrugged her shoulders and smiled again at Logan.

"Can you tell me how to get to the apartment?" Logan asked.

The waitress suddenly seemed apprehensive. She knew that Colby liked Logan but that didn't mean that he needed to know where they all lived. But after a few seconds she put the thought out of her mind. She decided Logan looked harmless enough.

"Sure, just down the street. You'll see the building on the left. The number is 247." The waitress then pointed out of the window of the diner to the street out front.

"Thanks," Logan replied. Then he turned and left the diner. Once outside he ran into the street without looking and was almost run over by a car. Logan tried to smile and play it off while the driver cussed him from behind the wheel. He waved politely and made his way across the street and then began to walk briskly down the sidewalk. He was anxious to find Colby and he was also worried about her since Harmon said that he had just seen Chip McPhale in town. Logan felt pang of regret that Chip has survived the blow to the head from the two by four. He wished he had finished him off. Sheriff Patterson would have ruled it self-defense and Colby could have backed him up on it.

Logan walked past the old movie theater now serving as a church. The windows were dark but he could hear music playing and he thought he could hear a choir singing. Then the music stopped and he heard someone talking over a PA system. But then the sounds began to fade away as he continued on down the sidewalk. Up ahead he could see a small building sitting in the middle of a gravel lot. He knew it had to be Colby's apartment building.

It didn't take Logan long to find the door marked 247. It was on the second floor. As Logan stood outside the door he looked down into the parking lot. There were only a few cars in it and this led Logan to think that the apartments were mostly vacant. He turned and knocked on the door and waited for someone to answer. Then he knocked again. After several minutes he decided that no one was home. But Colby had to be there. Where else could she be? Why would her car be at the diner if she had not walked back to her apartment?

Logan leaned to his side and peered through the small window beside the door. But the shade was pulled and he couldn't see inside the apartment.

"Colby? It's me, Logan," he said as he knocked on the door again.

After calling out Colby's name a few more times while knocking on the door, Logan finally gave up and walked back down the stairs to the gravel parking lot. Then he walked out to the sidewalk and looked both ways down the street. Maybe Colby had stepped into a store for some reason. But most of the storefronts were boarded up, and the ones that were open for business didn't look like the kind of stores Colby would be interested in.

"What a depressing town," Logan said as he looked down the street. He had no idea about what to do so he just turned and started to make his way back to the diner. Maybe the waitress he had talked to would have another idea about where Colby might be.

Once back in the diner, Logan was disappointed to find out that the waitress had no other theories about where Colby might be, other than she might have walked over to the Post Office. Logan figured if she had done that then she would be back by now so he dismissed the idea.

"Where else could she be?" Logan asked the waitress. He was growing frustrated.

"She might have walked down to the law office looking for you. Other than that, I have no idea. Sorry."

The waitress then turned and disappeared into the kitchen leaving Logan standing alone by the cash register. Out of the corner of his eye, he saw the sheriff sitting near the end of the bar sipping on a cup of coffee. There was an empty plate in front of him.

"Sheriff Patterson," Logan said as he walked up and sat down on the stool next to the man. The sheriff took a sip of coffee and looked at Logan.

"Thought you'd have high-tailed it out of town by now. How's uh, how's your new house?" The sheriff looked at Logan and gave him half a smile while nodding his head. Apparently he knew the stories about the old house. Logan looked back at the sheriff while trying to figure out if the man was on his side or not.

"The house is fine, sheriff. If you just ignore the lost souls wandering the damn halls at night the place isn't all that bad to tell you the truth. I'm trying to find Colby. I'm worried about her." Logan was trying to gain the upper hand with the sheriff. Logan knew he was on the man's turf and he also had a good suspicion that the sheriff could really care less about helping him. So Logan tried to center the conversation on Colby.

The sheriff put down his cup and looked at Logan. Logan couldn't tell if the sheriff was just a lazy country boy that didn't take his job seriously, or someone who had his shit wired and would not hesitate to lock up a stranger from out of town if he thought that stranger was a threat. Logan silently decided it was the latter of the two.

"Find her? Is she missing?" Sheriff Patterson said as he picked up his cup again and took a sip. Then he stared through the opening in the wall behind the counter. He watched the cook working on an order while waiting for Logan to answer him.

"Well, yes. I think she is. Her car is parked outside and I just checked her apartment. She's not there."

The sheriff smirked and looked into his cup of coffee. Then his eyes met Logan's.

"Come on, Mr. Shaw. You watch TV, right? You know I can't file a missing person report until she has been gone for forty eight hours."

Logan knew his case was thin. The sheriff was right. Colby was hardly a missing person when she had just been seen about an hour ago by everyone in the diner. But this didn't help Logan understand why her car was out in the parking lot and she was nowhere to be found. Then he reminded himself that the sheriff didn't know about the fight at the old train station. If he did he might consider Colby's car out in the parking lot to be a little more suspicious. But Logan knew better than to tell the sheriff that he had hit Chip McPhale with a two by four and then left him to die. For all Logan knew, the sheriff and Chip were related. He had heard enough about small towns to know how that worked.

Sheriff Patterson stood up from the stool and took a couple of dollar bills from his wallet. He tossed them on the counter beside his plate and then turned to Logan.

"I tell you what, Mr. Shaw."

"Call me Logan."

"I tell you what, Logan. I'll keep my eyes open."

Logan exhaled, trying to hide his frustration. "Thanks, sheriff."

Logan nodded to Sheriff Patterson as he walked past him to the cash register. He watched as the sheriff paid for his meal and then left the diner. Then Logan walked over to the waitress, who had watched the entire exchange between the two men.

"Do you have Colby's phone number?" Then Logan thought to himself how bad that sounded. He didn't even know her phone number. Logan pulled out his phone and, amazed the he had service for once, punched in the number as the waitress recited it for him. Then he smiled and thanked her. As he was walking out of the diner he listened into his phone. There was no answer.

Outside, Logan tried to figure out what to do. He knew he should be worried about Colby and then again he thought that maybe he was overreacting. But when he thought about Chip McPhale, Logan knew that he had every reason to worry that something bad had happened to her.

With no idea about what to do, Logan did the only thing he could think of. He walked back to Harmon's office and got in his car. Then he drove up and down Main Street again in the hopes that he might see Colby. When he didn't see any sign of her he headed out of town towards his house. He figured that she might show up later, or she might at least call him. Then

Logan thought about spending the night in the old house all alone and felt a sense of dread begin to percolate in his gut.

22

Logan was sitting on the back porch of the house watching the moon rise over the tobacco field. Colby had been right when she said she thought they would get a harvest moon sometime this week. He watched as the huge yellow ball rose up above the tree line. He missed Colby and was terrified that something had happened to her. She had not shown up at the house, and she hadn't even called. Deep down in the pit of his stomach, Logan knew that somehow his worst fears were going to come true.

Logan felt anger flare inside him. If Chip McPhale harmed Colby, Logan knew he would kill him if it was the last thing he did. He thought about this as he watched the harvest moon begin its trek to its place in the night sky. He missed Colby. He missed her badly.

Logan got up from the porch swing and walked back into the house. He had to do something to occupy his time. He tried to tell himself that Colby would show up and everything would be fine. He pulled his cellphone out of his pocket but noticed that he didn't have a signal. Since coming to Starlight his cellphone had alternated from being barely useful to totally worthless. Service this far out in the country had been sketchy at best.

As Logan walked into the kitchen he stopped dead in his tracks in front of the sink. Then he listened. He thought he had heard a noise coming from somewhere in the house. He looked up as if he was trying to see through the ceiling to the hallway above him but the house fell silent. He waited a few more seconds and had just about convinced himself that his mind was playing tricks on him when he heard the sound again. It was a swift *pat pat pat* and it seemed to be coming from upstairs. Logan stood frozen as he listened to the sound. It seemed to grow louder and then fade away before growing louder again.

With his heart hammering in his chest, Logan turned and walked quickly through the kitchen until he was in the foyer. The sound continued above him.

Pat pat pat...

Logan stopped at the foot of the stairs. He didn't want to go upstairs; he didn't even want to look up the stairway to the second floor but he knew he had no choice. It was fight or flight, and Logan knew he couldn't just run from the house and hope everything would get better. He knew he had to fight. But against what?

Pat pat pat...

Logan swallowed hard and looked up the stairway towards the second floor hallway. He could hear the noise but it seemed to be at the other end of the house. But then the noise stopped and Logan felt a brief moment of relief. But then the noise resumed and started to get louder.

Something was coming down the upstairs hallway from the other side of the house.

Logan took a step backwards but continued to look up towards the second floor hallway. It took all the strength he had to stand there while the sound grew louder. Suddenly there was a flash of motion as someone ran past the top of the stairway. Logan gasped and took another step backwards.

"Hey!" Logan yelled up the stairway. Suddenly the sound stopped.

For what seemed like an eternity Logan stood at the bottom of the stairs afraid to move. Time seemed to slow and then stand still. He heard a floorboard creak from somewhere down near the end of the upstairs hallway, near where the master bedroom was located. Then there was silence followed by another creak of a board. Whoever had just run down the hallway was now walking back towards the top of the stairway.

Logan waited as the skin on the back of his neck started to tingle. The front door was just a few steps away. He knew he could bolt for it and then run out into the front yard. But that would be the cowardly thing to do and Logan desperately wanted his days as a coward to be over with. It was time to confront whatever was in the house.

Logan heard another creak as nausea began to ferment in his intestines. Then there was movement at the top of the stairs. Logan drew in a sharp breath as the little girl with the flower stepped into the dim light at the top of the staircase.

Logan stood paralyzed with fear as he looked up at the face of the little girl standing at the top of the stairs. Her dress was varying shades of gray and seemed to be made of scraps of cloth sewn together. It hung down to her knees, leaving the bottom of her legs exposed. Logan could see what looked like scratches and scars on her legs below her knees. The little girl's hair hung down onto her shoulders and her face was solemn. She was peering down the staircase and looking directly at Logan. Her eyes were dark and lifeless. Just as before, she was holding a flower in her hand.

Logan watched as the little girl twirled the flower in her fingers. Then she dropped it and stepped to the side out of sight. Logan listened as the old floorboards in the hallway creaked and groaned as the little girl made her way back down the hallway. Then the sound stopped and the house grew silent.

With every ounce of courage Logan could muster he took a few steps forward and placed a foot on the bottom step. Then he slowly began to climb the stairs, stopping every few steps to listen for the sound of the little girl's footsteps. But the house remained silent.

Once at the top of the stairs, Logan paused and tried to gather his strength. The only light in the hallway was the yellowish glow of a small lamp on a table near the entrance to the master bedroom. Logan closed his eyes and swallowed hard, and then he leaned forward and peered down the hallway in the direction the little girl had gone.

The hallway was empty.

Logan knew the ordeal was far from over. The little girl could be in any of the rooms off the hallway. But when his eyes settle on the door to the attic, Logan knew immediately where the little girl had gone. The attic door was cracked open and the faint light from inside traced a thin yellow line across the hardwood floor.

When Logan stepped onto the top stair a board groaned under his feet causing him to curse under his breath. He promised himself at that very moment that if he made it through the night he was going into town tomorrow and buy a box of nails and then put a nail through every damn squeaky board in the hallway. The thought was merely a diversion to the problem at hand, an attempt by his mind to find something rational to process. But when Logan looked down the hallway at the attic door he regained his focus. He knew what he had to do.

Logan walked slowly down the hallway until he came to the first door to a bedroom. He looked into the shadowy room but only saw the dark silhouette of the bed. The window shades were open and he could see the moonlit field behind the house through the glass. Just as he was about to step away and continue down the hallway, the light coming through the window flared and changed color. Suddenly the walls of the bedroom were bathed in a kaleidoscope of colors that moved and swirled through the room. Then as quickly as it had started, the brilliant show of colors died out. When Logan looked through the window he could see that now the fields were awash in the late afternoon sun.

Standing in the doorway Logan knew that he had to walk to the window and look outside. He didn't want to think what would happen if he just ignored what was happening and the continued on down the hallway. The house wanted him to see what was outside and he knew he had no choice but to go look.

Logan walked slowly into the bedroom past the foot of the small bed and then to the window. He looked out across the sunlit tobacco field and felt a sudden sense of relief when he realized that nothing had changed and that he was just merely looking out into the daytime version of his tobacco fields. Mercifully, he was not going to be treated to another scene from the house's grisly past. Logan stood at the window and surveyed the fields and the row of tobacco barns situated in a straight line off to his right. Then something about the tobacco barns caught his eye.

The barns were bathed in the golden haze of the late afternoon sun but something looked different about them. At first Logan couldn't put a finger on what it was. It took him a minute of studying the barns until he realized the difference.

The tobacco barns he was looking at seemed new, like that had just recently been built. Smoke was coming from each chimney, rising slowly into the afternoon sky. Logan had not noticed the smoke before and now that he saw it he knew that he was looking out into a scene from the past.

The fields were still, the leafless tobacco plant stalks sat motionless in the sun. Apparently in the scene the harvest was complete and the tobacco was now being cured in the barns. Logan scanned the distant tree line and realized that it looked different too. He could see the Skeleton River shining through an opening in the trees. And rising up from the distant tree line was another plume of smoke. Logan tried to figure out where the smoke was coming from but it took him a few seconds before it came to him.

The sharecropper's house.

Logan figured that the smoke had to be coming from the sharecropper's house, obviously the lived-in version of it and not the abandoned one that Colby had taken him to. Logan scanned the field and the barns, and then his eyes returned to the smoke rising from the tree line. He knew what he was seeing was another scene from the era of when sharecropper's worked the Shaw land.

Movement caught Logan's eye, off to the left near the far edge of the field. He wanted to step away from the window when he saw it but his legs would not obey his commands. Instead, he stood still at the window as he watched a horse-drawn cart followed by a group of people moved down the far edge of the tobacco field headed towards the woods. On the cart was an oblong wooden box. A solitary horse pulled the cart guided by a man in dark suit wearing a brim hat.

Logan watched as the procession moved along the edge of the field and then turned onto a wide path cut through the trees. When the cart turned it allowed Logan a better view of the wooden box. It was then that he realized that the rectangular box was a coffin.

The small group of people followed the cart into the woods and before long the entire procession disappeared from view. Logan frowned and turned the scene over and over in his mind trying to figure out what he had just witnessed. It was obvious that it was a funeral procession. But whose funeral procession was it? Whose body was inside the coffins? Why was he being allowed to see this?

Suddenly the entire scene disappeared in swirl of light. Logan had to squint as the kaleidoscope of light returned. But after a few seconds, the brilliant lights disappeared and Logan was once again staring out into a moonlit tobacco field. The harvest moon had now moved farther above the distant tree line. Logan knew he was now looking at the present-day version of the fields.

Logan took a step backwards and slowly turned around. Then he let out a gasp.

Standing in the doorway was the little girl. Logan instinctively moved backwards until he felt his back touch the window. But suddenly the little girl turned and ran down the hallway, disappearing from sight. Logan listened to her footsteps as they moved quickly away.

Logan walked slowly to the bedroom door. Then he leaned out and looked down the hallway towards the attic door. He turned and looked in the other direction but there was no sign of the little girl.

The attic door was still cracked open and Logan knew right then what he had to do. He felt his heart pounding in his chest as he stepped out of the bedroom and into the hallway. Once at the attic door, he reached down and grasped the cold doorknob and slowly pulled the door open.

He could see up the narrow staircase to the attic above. The light of the moon was streaming in through the dormers as Logan slowly climbed the stairs. He stopped when his eyes were level with the attic floor.

Logan felt every nerve ending in his body fire in unison when he saw the old woman sitting on the floor in the middle of the attic. He thought for a moment that his legs were going to give way and that he would fall back down the stairs. But he held onto the edge of the attic floor as he kept his head low. He finally regained his composure enough to study the woman's face. It was then he realized that he was looking at his great-grandmother Rosemary. She was sitting in the middle of the attic floor surrounded by porcelain dolls. The dolls reminded him of the one that was sitting on the dresser in his bedroom.

Logan watched as Rosemary picked up a doll and began to stroke its dress with her hands. She then ran her fingers through the doll's hair before pulling the doll close to her chest. Then Logan watched in horror as Rosemary held the doll with one hand and used her other hand to twist off the doll's head. She then took the head and placed it beside her on the floor. Rosemary then dropped the headless doll and picked up another one lying close to her legs. Logan watched as she repeated the same actions with the new doll, placing its head in the pile with the others.

Just as Logan was about to call out Rosemary's name, she suddenly became aware of his presence. He watched as she lifted her face and looked directly at him. When their eyes locked Logan felt the blood drain from his face. He knew right then that Rosemary could see him and knew who he was.

"Rosemary?" Logan's voice rattled through the attic breaking the silence.

Logan could see tears running down her cheeks as she sat in the middle of a swath of moonlight pouring in from a dormer. After a few seconds she returned her attention to the doll in her lap. She stroked the hair, adjusted the dress and then slowly twisted the head off and placed it in the pile like she had done before. It seemed as if she wanted Logan to watch what she was doing.

Suddenly the light from the dormers flared and the walls were awash once again in brilliant colors. Logan brought his hand over his eyes and once the light died down he dropped his hand and scanned the attic.

Rosemary was gone. Left in her place was the pile of doll heads. The bodies of the dolls were gone as well.

Logan summoned what courage he had left. He took a step up, then another. His eyes slowly scanned the attic as he rose to the top step. But Rosemary was gone and he was now in the attic alone.

Logan walked slowly over to the closest dormer, continuing to scan the attic around him as he went. The dormer was on the rear of the house and looked out over the backyard and the fields. As Logan stepped up to the window glass, he had to squint to adjust to the daylight outside. When he looked down onto the fields he noticed that the tobacco was gone. In its place he could see freshly plowed rows of sandy dirt.

Outside several young men were plowing rows on the far side of the field, each one walking being a single plow pulled by a mule. The sun was high overhead and Logan could tell that the weather was hot. He watched as the men behind the plows wiped the sweat from their foreheads underneath their brim hats.

Logan knew the scene he was seeing had to be very old. The presence of the mules proved this. On the far edge of the field, through an opening in the tree line, Logan could see the banks of the Skeleton River, its surface shining brightly in the noonday sun. To the left of the Shaw Fields Logan could see the adjoining fields. He could see other workers busy plowing those fields as well, each one guiding their plow behind a mule.

Logan noticed a man sitting on a horse at the edge of the field closest to the house. He had to look down at an angle to see the man who seemed to be watching the laborers plow the fields. He was holding something in one of his hands but Logan could not make out what it was.

Logan studied the man and then got the feeling that he had seen him before. Just then the man turned and looked up at the dormer as if he knew

Logan was watching him. As the man's eyes looked up at Logan from underneath the brim of his hat, Logan noticed the leather strap hanging from the man's hand. It was at that moment that Logan recognized the man. It was the man that had hit him across the chest in the hallway.

Before he could study the man further, the lights flared and an instant later Logan found himself once again staring out into the moonlit tobacco fields. The harvest moon was now higher above the tree line and its light was illuminating the fields bright enough to cause the tobacco plants to cast shadows between the rows.

Logan was about to step away from the window when movement in the tobacco field caught his eye. He strained to see through the window glass as his eyes followed the rows of tobacco to the far tree line. But whatever he had seen was gone, if he had seen anything at all. After a few more seconds of scanning the field he gave up and turned away from the window and then made his way across the attic and down the stairs to the hallway.

Logan realized at that moment that if he wanted to find Colby the first place he needed to look was at the McPhale house. He knew that it would be almost suicidal to drive onto the McPhale land and pick a fight with Chip and his brother, but Logan knew that he had to find Colby and he was certain that Chip McPhale had to be behind her disappearance. Logan knew that Chip wanted revenge for being hit with the two by four at the old train station and that the best way to get it was to take Colby and force Logan to come to him and fight him on his terms.

The thought of doing that terrified Logan but he knew he had no other choice. He knew at that moment that he loved Colby and that nothing would stop him from finding her. He felt a hot flash of anger blaze across his forehead when he thought about Chip McPhale harming her. Logan knew that if he had to kill Chip McPhale in order to save Colby, then that's exactly what he would do.

23

Chip McPhale leaned back against the old table and turned the knob on the Coleman camping lantern until the flame grew bright enough to cast sharp shadows around the room. His brother Ethan sat across the room on the stone hearth of the old fireplace. Colby sat tied to a chair in the middle of the room. She had long since given up on struggling against the ropes that bound her hands and legs to the chair. It hadn't taken her long to realize that it brought Chip pleasure to see her squirm and twist against the ropes.

"Come on, baby. Struggle for me. Be a good little whore and try and free yourself."

Hatred flared in Colby's eyes as she glared at Chip but she refused to pull against the ropes. The last thing she wanted to do was give Chip McPhale what he wanted. When she didn't obey Chip's command to struggle, he pushed himself off of the table and walked slowly over to her. When he bent down close to her, Colby could smell the bourbon on his breath. Then he touched her chin with his finger causing her to jerk her chin away in revulsion.

"I said struggle, you little hussy."

Colby knew better than to anger Chip. With what strength she had left, she pulled at the ropes that held her hands behind the back of the chair. Then she watched as a look of pleasure washed over Chip's face.

"That's a good girl. Things will go better for you tonight if you do as you're told."

After Chip said this he stood up and took a step backwards from Colby. The sight of her tied to the chair with a rag crammed in her mouth to keep her quiet excited him. But he wanted to savor every moment. He had waited for this for a long time and he was in no hurry to rush. But before he could have his way with Colby, he knew he had to get rid of his brother. Chip knew Ethan wouldn't have the stomach to go much further and that his brother might even try to stop him once things got physical.

"Ethan, you run along back to the house. Keep an eye out for that city fuck in case he comes snooping around."

Ethan looked at Chip with surprise. "He ain't gonna come around our house."

Chip shot a look at Ethan. It was enough to terrify Colby as she looked at Chip's face. The hatred boiling in the man was unbelievable. Colby knew that he was accustomed to getting his way with no backtalk from anyone.

"I said run back to the fucking house. I have some business to take care of with my little kitten here," Chip said as he stepped beside Colby and put his hand on her shoulder.

Ethan looked at Colby and knew that he shouldn't leave her alone with his brother. But Ethan also knew that even though Chip was his younger brother that he would stand little chance against him in a fight. And if Ethan did manage to outfight his brother he realized that it would not be the end of it. Ethan was well accustomed with his brother's taste for revenge and he knew that his brother would win eventually. Ethan realized he could never go to sleep if he got on his brother's bad side.

"Come on, little brother. Let it go. Let's go back to the house and finish off that bottle."

"I said go back to the house and keep an eye out for the city boy. You know he's gonna come looking for his little whore. It won't take him long to figure out where she's at."

Ethan balked at this and continued to try and reason with his brother.

"He might know where we live but he damn sure ain't gonna come down here, little brother. He believes that bullshit story about the killer and the moon and there's no way his pussy ass is gonna cross his field at night to get down here. And why would he? How would he know we're down here?"

Chip was growing impatient with his brother. And he didn't like Colby seeing Ethan stand up to him. He knew in her eyes it undermined his image of authority.

"I'm not going to tell you again, Ethan. Run along." When Chip said this he lifted his shirt and tucked it behind the small revolver stuck in the front of his pants. Colby's eyes grew wide when she saw the gun.

When Ethan saw the handle of the gun sticking out from behind Chip's belt, he knew he had lost the fight and that Colby was on her own. Ethan knew that when it came to his brother Chip that nothing meant more to him than getting his way, not even family.

Ethan gave Colby a wary look as he crossed the room to the front door. He knew what was going to happen to her and he felt bad about it, but not bad enough to do anything about it. He knew Chip wasn't going to kill her, but he knew that what Chip had planned for her would probably make her wish that he did.

"Come on, Chip. Turn her loose and let's get out of here." This was Ethan's last attempt to change his brother's mind.

"I said go the fuck back to the house, Ethan. This is your last warning."

Ethan glared at his brother. Then he decided that the battle was lost.

"Suit yourself, Chip." Ethan then let out a long sigh and looked at Colby one more time. Then he stepped through the front door of the old sharecropper's house and closed it behind him. Once outside he cut through the woods following the trail that would lead to the house his parents had left him and his brother after their mother had died and their father had been put in a nursing home.

Ethan knew that the Shaw land and his family's land met somewhere in the thick stand of woods that formed a border between the fields. As he walked through the woods along the trail he looked up through the canopy of the treetops at the yellow disk of the harvest moon. Then he pulled his bib hat down close over his eyes and quickened his pace. He knew better than to wander off the trail and onto the Shaw land. Even if his brother didn't believe in the ghost of tobacco road, Ethan had always believed in the legend of the ghost and because of that he made sure that he didn't cross over into the Shaw Fields.

Ethan wanted to get as far away from the old sharecropper's house as he could. To his left through the woods he could see the lights of the Shaw house. He knew at this very moment that Logan Shaw was probably pacing in the house worried sick about the whereabouts of Colby but Ethan was confident that Logan would never think to check the old sharecropper's house. In fact, Ethan was sure that Logan would probably try to find Colby by following Harmon's directions to their house. This had been the primary reason behind taking Colby to the abandoned sharecropper's house. Logan would never think to look there.

Ethan realized that the best thing to do now was to make his way home and wait for Logan to show up. He tried to put the thought of what was happing to Colby out of his mind as he moved through the woods and then out into the open field behind his house. He could see his house in the distance, a welcome sight bathed in the yellow glow of the harvest moon.

24

The house was small and sat well off the road. Logan pulled slowly down the gravel road towards the house watching for a sign that would show him that someone was home. But the lights were off in all of the rooms and the windows were dark. Logan stopped near the halfway point to the house and pulled off into the tall grass that lined the gravel driveway. He decided to walk from this point on.

It had taken him less than fifteen minutes to find the house of Ethan and Chip McPhale. Harmon had told him roughly where their house was located and he had used common sense to fill in the gaps. There weren't that many roads that branched off the main road towards where he knew the house had to be and before long Logan had found it. He was still unsure if it was the right house when he had first pulled into the driveway but now he was close enough to see Chip's old pickup truck sitting in front of the house. Once he saw this, Logan knew he was in the right place.

Driving to the house had been Logan's only choice. He could see the distant McPhale house from his own house but he would have had to cross his fields on foot to get to it. He had promised Colby that he would never go into his fields at night and tonight he felt like the least he could do was to honor the promise he had made to her.

The trees that lined the gravel drive to the house cast large shadows under the light of the harvest moon. Logan thought about the stories Colby had told him about the ghost but she had also told him that the killings were random and followed no set pattern other than they always occurred under the kind of moon that now hung overhead. But Logan knew he was on McPhale land and not Shaw land so he tried to convince himself that he was safe. He wasn't sure if he believed it or not.

Logan wished he had a gun, but he was painfully aware that taking a gun onto someone's property in the middle of the night and then killing them with it would hardly look good in the eyes of the law, no matter how well-intentioned his motives were. But he knew he had to find Colby and he was sure she had to be in Chip and Ethan's house. He would just have to fight for her the old fashioned way and hope that the McPhale brothers would face him in the same manner. Hopefully one of them wouldn't cut him down with a shotgun the minute he entered the house and later claim that they thought he was a burglar.

The McPhale house was an old brick rancher with a dark carport. Logan moved slowly up the driveway past Chip's truck before stepping into the cave-like carport. He felt his nerves calm a bit as he was swallowed by the darkness. Somehow it made him feel more protected to be in the shadowy carport than out in the bright moonlight. The carport was empty, which led Logan to believe that either Ethan was gone or the two brothers only owned the one pickup truck.

Logan's heart was thundering in his chest as he moved close to the door that led into the house. He could feel the adrenaline rushing through his veins. Logan thought he had to be crazy. Here he was about to break into someone's home in the middle of the night to try and rescue a girl that he wasn't even sure was in the house. He wished he could count on Sheriff Patterson to take care of this but he had his doubts as to what kind of lawman Patterson really was. Logan knew that not only could he not trust Patterson, he had no time to call him and try to explain the situation. Logan had a good mind as to what the McPhale brothers would do with Colby and he knew the time to save her was right now.

Logan slowly put out his hand and placed it on the doorknob. Then a thought hit him. What was he doing trying to sneak into the house? Maybe the direct approach would work better. With this in mind, he let go of the doorknob and took a step backwards. Then he balled up his fist and gave the door several hard knocks.

"Open up Chip! Ethan! I know you two are in there. Open this fucking door!" Logan was so scared that he felt like his bowels were going to empty into his pants. Openly trying to pick a fight with two men like Chip and Ethan McPhale was the most insane thing he had ever done. But he loved Colby, and Logan knew he was her only hope of rescue.

Before Logan could knock on the door again, Ethan McPhale came up behind him in the darkness. He raised the baseball bat in his hands and brought it down violently across Logan's shoulders, just barely missing the back of his head. Ethan's miscalculation in the darkness had saved Logan's life. Had the baseball bat found the back of Logan's head instead of the top his shoulder blades, the blow would have split his head open and killed him instantly.

Logan fell to his hands and knees as the pain rocketed through his upper body like a charge of electricity. He managed to turn just enough to see Ethan's shadow figure standing over him. Logan watched as baseball bat rose in the darkness, its shape silhouetted against the backdrop of the moonlit opening of the carport.

Ethan brought the bat down again across Logan's shoulders. This second blow caused Logan's arms to give way and he collapsed onto the concrete floor of the carport.

"You stupid fucking prick! You just couldn't leave well enough alone, could you?" Ethan's voice boomed in Logan's head as the pain cut through his upper body like a blade. But he knew he had to fight, and that if Ethan got the best of him then Colby would be left to her fate. With all the strength he could muster, Logan pushed himself up off the concrete until he was back on his hands and knees.

Just as Ethan brought the bat down again, Logan shifted to the side. The bat crashed hard against the concrete and flew out of Ethan's hands. Logan knew this was his only chance. With every ounce of strength he had left he kicked his right leg towards Ethan, hitting him right above his ankles. The blow took Ethan's legs out from under him. He fell hard onto the concrete just as Logan rose to his feet.

Logan took his right foot and kicked Ethan violently in the side of his body just above his belt. The resulting impact caused Ethan to cry out in pain. Before he could gather himself Logan was on top of him. He grabbed Ethan by the hair and began to pound the back of his head into the concrete. After three hits, Ethan's body went limp. Then Logan rolled off of him and onto the cold concrete. His chest was heaving and his shoulders were throbbing from the two hits of the bat.

After a few moments, Logan collected himself and managed to get to his feet. Ethan was still lying motionless on the floor of the carport. Logan suddenly realized that he might have killed Ethan but when he placed his fingers on the side of Ethan's neck he could still feel a pulse. He was not dead, he was just unconscious.

Logan thought for sure that Chip had to be inside the house. But then he thought about it and knew that there was no way he would have let Ethan come outside to fight without him. Logan knew that Chip would not have gone down as easily as Ethan had. But where was Chip? He obviously was not in the house and that meant that Ethan was alone. Logan knew that if Chip was not in the house then neither was Colby. So where were they?

Logan walked over to Ethan and kneeled down beside him. Ethan began to stir slightly and then he started to moan and groan.

"Where are they Ethan? Where the fuck is Colby and your brother Chip? You better fucking tell me or I'll finish your ass off right now and dump your body in the Skeleton River where no one will ever find it."

"Fuck you." Ethan's words were slurred and barely understandable.

Logan winced as the pain shot through his shoulder blades but he managed to grab Ethan by the hair again and lift his head up several inches off the concrete.

"Tell me where Colby is or I'll crack your fucking skull open."

Ethan knew better than to resist. This was his brother's fight and not his. He gave in and then uttered one word to Logan.

"Sharecropper's…"

Logan didn't need to hear the word 'house'. He knew what Ethan was trying to tell him. Suddenly it all made sense. How could he have been so stupid? He looked down at Ethan and then let go of his hair. Ethan's head dropped to the concrete and Logan watched as his eyes slowly rolled back in his head. He knew Ethan was out again and would probably stay that way for hours.

Now that he knew where to look, Logan knew it was time to find Colby.

25

Chip McPhale turned the chair around and sat down in it so that he could lean forward against the backrest. He was only a few feet away from Colby and she could smell the liquor on his breath and see the fiery look in his eyes as he studied her from head to toe. Then he reached into his pocket and removed the small flask. He unscrewed the metal cap and took a long swig of whiskey. Then he screwed the cap back on and tossed the flask over his shoulder. Colby flinched as the metallic flask bounced across the floor and came to rest against the far wall. She could tell by the sound that the flask was empty.

"Now now, angel. No need to be so nervous. We're just going to get to know each other a little better. You play along and I'll make sure you enjoy yourself."

Colby felt warm bile rise in her throat. The thought of Chip McPhale putting his hands on her, or doing something even worse made her feel nauseous. Even though she knew better she pulled against the ropes that held her to the chair. Then she chided herself when she saw desire flash in Chip's eyes. She knew that she was giving him what he wanted when she struggled against the ropes. She made a silent promise to herself that from that moment on she would do her best not to try and get free, if for no other reason than to deprive Chip of the pleasure he so craved.

Chip stood up and pushed the chair to the side hard enough that it fell over onto its side with a loud clank. Colby flinched again at the sound of it.

"Don't worry, kitten. No one can hear us out here, least of all that dumb shit city boy that you've been fuckin'. Yeah, I know what you two have been doin' in old lady Shaw's house. But he'll never find you out here."

Colby tried to remain calm but she felt her chest begin to heave as Chip took a step towards her. Then he stopped and she watched as he pulled a pocketknife out of his pants pocket. A glint of reflected light bounced off the blade as he snapped it open. Then a smile crept onto his face as he looked down at the blade.

Colby closed her eyes as Chip walked around behind her chair. He put his hand on her shoulder and then with his other hand ran the dull back edge of the blade along Colby's upper arm. She quivered when she felt the cold steel touch her skin.

"I'd hold still if I were you, kitten," Chip said as he leaned down and whispered into Colby's ear. She turned her head to the side to escape the smell of his breath. This angered Chip and he grabbed her by the chin and pulled until she turned her head back towards him. Then he adjusted the handkerchief that was crammed in her mouth to keep her quiet.

"Don't you look away from me you little bitch!"

Chip moved around to the front of the chair so that he could get an eyeful of Colby's body as drunken desire flared in his veins. He knew that he was going to get what he had been craving for so many years and that he was going to have all the time he wanted to enjoy it. The only person that knew where they were at was Ethan, and Chip knew that his brother would keep his mouth shut at all costs.

Chip took the pocketknife and brought it up to the first button near the neckline of Colby's shirt. He worked the blade in between the folds of fabric and then cut the button free, listening as it bounced on the wooden floor at their feet. After a few seconds he brought the blade down to the second and third buttons before cutting them free as well. This was enough to allow Colby's shirt to open so that Chip could see the tanned skin underneath.

"Very nice, kitten. I'm going to take my time undressing you. You've made me wait all these years so now I'm going to make you wait. Deep down inside I know you want it, but all in good time."

Chip continued down Colby's shirt until he had cut all of the buttons free. Then he took the tip of the knife and flipped open each fold of her shirt exposing her chest. Colby could not hold back any longer. She tried to stop herself but she couldn't help but begin to cry. Chip watched as a teardrop traced a trail down her face. He took his finger and ran it up the side of Colby's cheek and wiped away the tear.

"There's no need for that, kitten," Chip said as he raised his finger to his mouth and tasted the salty tear. "No need at all."

Chip turned his attention to Colby's legs. She was wearing shorts and her skin was the color of caramel under the light of the camping lantern. Chip folded the knife shut and dropped it back into his pocket. Then he leaned down and ran his hands along the tops of Colby's thighs. It took everything in her not to recoil against his touch. If it was the last thing she did, she wasn't going to give Chip McPhale the pleasure of seeing her resist him.

Chip stood up and looked at Colby. He could see her trembling in the dim light of the lantern. He reached over and slowly pulled the handkerchief out of her mouth.

"Now if you scream so help me I will cut your tongue out of your mouth with my fucking pocketknife. Do you understand, kitten?"

Colby swallowed hard and slowly nodded yes. Then she felt her heart sink as she watched Chip reach for the zipper on his pants.

"You're gonna use that pretty mouth for something other than screaming. And you better be good about it and take your time or I swear I'll bleed you out right here in this fucking run-down house."

Before Chip could completely unzip his pants the front door of the old house burst open. Suddenly Logan Shaw stepped into the room and locked eyes with Chip. In Logan's left hand was the baseball bat.

"Well look what we have here," Chip said as he zipped his pants shut. "Looks like we've got ourselves a hero."

"You got that right you stupid fuck," Logan said as he lifted the baseball bat and moved into the room towards Chip.

As Logan stepped into the room Chip moved away from Colby and the chair. He wanted to be ready when Logan lunged at him. He watched as Logan moved across the dimly lit room, raising the bat as he walked. Chip felt the whiskey working on his head but knew that he was still sharp enough to take Logan down. And he wanted Colby to see it. He wanted her to know that the last man that could save her was about to be beaten senseless. And Chip knew that as soon as he got done with Logan that he would take care of Colby because there would be no one left to stop him.

Logan felt a sharp pain in his shoulders as he raised the bat in the air. Ethan had hit him hard and had probably done a lot of damage. The shot of pain caused Logan to hesitate, and this was the opportunity that Chip was waiting for.

As the bat came down, Chip stepped quickly to the side. Logan swung but missed, and this caused him to lose his balance. Chip drew back and swung hard, his fist catching Logan right below his sternum. This was enough to cause Logan to buckle over and fall to the floor.

"Chip no!" yelled Colby from the chair. But he ignored her and walked slowly and deliberately over to Logan who was lying on the floor trying to regain his breath. Chip drew back his right foot and kicked Logan hard in the stomach. Then he reached down and grabbed Logan by the hair and lifted his head several inches off of the floor.

"You're gonna wish you had left town when you had the chance, city boy." Chip then drew back his fist and slammed it into Logan's face. Colby watched in horror as Logan's body when limp.

Chip stood up and admired his handiwork. Logan was out cold on the floor and for the time being would not be able to stop him from taking care of his business with Colby. When he looked over at her sitting in the chair, he could see the fear in her eyes. The last person that could save her was lying unconscious on the floor. Colby knew that now there was little anyone could do to stop Chip from doing whatever he wanted with her.

Chip took one more look at Logan and then nudged him with his foot. But Logan didn't stir. He was out cold. This brought a smile to Chip's face as he slowly turned his head to look at Colby. He knew it was the time to take what he wanted.

Colby's eyes grew wide as she watched Chip walk across the room towards her. When he stepped beside her he leaned down and whispered into her ear.

"Looks like you're fresh out of heroes, kitten. So I think it's time we get back to our business."

Colby knew her only chance was to try to reason with Chip, or to at least try to outsmart him. She knew that Chip was the kind of man that wanted a woman to fight against him so she tried to use this in her favor.

"Just take what you want and get it over with Chip. I'm not afraid of you. Just go ahead and take whatever you want. I'm sure it will be quick."

The last remark inflamed Chip. He stood up and looked at Colby as anger flared through his body. Then he slapped her across the face.

"Don't you fucking sass me you little whore. I promise you it will be anything but quick." Chip then looked over at Logan lying motionless on the floor. The baseball bat was lying beside him.

"Looks like your little hero boy will be out for a while. It'll take him at least an hour to sleep off the ass whippin' I gave him. That gives us plenty of time."

"Just untie me, Chip. I'll do anything you want." Colby was trying to speak in a calm voice so that Chip would not sense her fear. "I promise I'll make it good for you if you'll just untie me." Then Colby looked into Chip's eyes. "A girl needs to use her hands to please her man."

Chip smiled and exhaled a long, whiskey-laced breath. Then he slowly untied Colby's hands and then her feet. He knew she had nowhere to go and that no one was going to save her now that Logan was lying unconscious on the floor. Once the ropes were free, Chip stood up and admired Colby's body. Her legs were long and slender and her shirt was still pulled open from where he had cut the buttons off with his pocketknife.

The whiskey was beginning to catch up with Chip. When Colby brought her right foot up violently into his groin he was slow to try and block it. The resulting pain shot though his abdomen like a sharp nail. Then he fell down onto his knees.

Colby pushed Chip backwards as she got out of the chair. She turned and tried to run towards Logan but Chip managed to grab her by the ankle as she turned. But she broke free before stumbling and falling to the floor. Rather than try and get to her feet Colby crawled on her hands and knees as fast as she could towards Logan. All she needed was to get her hands on the baseball bat lying at his side.

Just as Colby put a hand on the bat, Chip grabbed her again by her leg just above her ankle. She felt his grip tighten and she knew there was no way that she would be able to break free again. He was too strong. Instead of trying to wrestle free from Chip's grasp, she wrapped both hands around the handle grip of the bat. Then with every ounce of strength she could muster she rolled over onto her side and swung the bat down towards Chip, catching him on the forearm right between his wrist and elbow. He shrieked in pain as he let go of her leg and withdrew his arm. But then his rage returned and he rose up on his knees while holding his arm against his stomach.

"I'm gonna kill you, you little bitch!"

Colby was crying now but she forced herself to gather her strength. She pushed herself up and quickly got to her feet just as Chip was trying to get his balance. He was holding his arm and this caused him to have trouble getting to his feet.

Before Chip could get his balance, Colby drew back with the bat and then swung at his head. The tip of the bat caught Chip in the chin and caused him to fall back down to his knees. Then he collapsed onto the floor, squirming from the pain.

"I swear… I'm going to…" Chip's words were garbled from the impact of the bat on his chin. He was still conscious but Colby knew that it wouldn't take him long to collect himself. She looked over at Logan and ran to him. Then she got down on her knees and tried to wake him.

"Logan! Logan! It's me!" Colby patted the sides of Logan's face until he began to stir. Then she heard Chip moan and roll over onto his back. "Logan! You've got to wake up now!"

Logan slowly regained consciousness. When his eyes flickered open he gasped when he saw Colby leaning over him. He was groggy and weak but he brought both of his arms up and put them around her. Then he tried to pull her close. But Colby knew they had to move, had to get out of the house before Chip regained his wits. She knew that neither she nor Logan would survive his rage once he regained his composure and realized what was going on.

Colby pulled and tugged at Logan until she got him to his feet. Once up he began to come out of the haze from being unconscious. He looked around the room and saw Chip lying on the floor.

"There's no time. We have to get out of here while we can!" Colby screamed. "Come on!"

Colby then pulled at Logan's hand as they both moved in unison towards the front door of the old sharecropper's house. Just as they exited the door and stepped out into the night, Colby heard Chip moan from inside the house.

Maybe they could get back to the Shaw house before he regained his strength and came after them.

26

Colby and Logan moved quickly through the woods on the trail that led away from the sharecropper's house towards the edge of the Shaw tobacco fields. The moonlight cut through the overhead canopy of tree limbs and provided enough illumination for them to see their way through as they followed the trail. Once they got to the edge of the field, Colby stopped and grabbed Logan by the hand causing him to stop as well.

"What are you doing? We need to move," Logan said as he looked at Colby with a befuddled look on his face. His head was pounding and he could feel the hot bruise on his face from Chip's fist.

Colby didn't say anything. She looked out over the moonlit tobacco field and then at the Shaw house sitting on the distant rise above the far edge of the field. She knew better than to step out of the edge of the woods and into the field.

"Come on, Colby. Let's go! That crazy fuck will be after us before long. In case you didn't notice, you didn't knock him out. It won't take him long to recover."

"Shhhh…" was Colby's only reply. Then she brought her hand up and put it across Logan's mouth. "Stop talking, Logan. Just stop talking."

Logan reached up and pulled Colby's hand from his mouth. "What the hell is wrong with you?"

Colby didn't immediately respond. She seemed to be entranced by the moonlit tobacco field in front of them. Finally she snapped out of it and then looked up at Logan. He could see the fear in her eyes.

"Logan, look at the moon." Colby then pointed across the field to the yellow moon hanging in the sky above the distant Skeleton River.

"Colby, jeez. Now is not the time for ghost stories. Right now it's the living that we need to be afraid of, as in Chip McPhale."

Colby scanned the field and then brought her eyes to Logan again.

"Just run fast, Logan. We need to run fast and we can't stop until we get to your house. Promise me we won't stop no matter what."

Logan looked at Colby and saw fear burning in her eyes.

"Yeah yeah. But can we go please? Let's just go. Follow me." Then Logan grabbed Colby by the hand and they both stepped out of the woods and into the tobacco field.

Behind them, Chip McPhale stumbled out of the old sharecropper's house and began to make his way along the trail towards the fields. He knew where Logan and Colby were going and he planned to catch them both. His first order of business would be to beat Logan Shaw unconscious again and then kill him. Then he would resume his business with Colby, and after he had his fill of her he would kill her too. The thought of this brought a crooked smile to his face as he made his way through the woods. Just as he reached the end of the trail he looked out into the tobacco field and saw two dark shadows moving up one of the rows heading for the distant Shaw house.

Colby and Logan... Chip thought as he watched them move in unison along the row. Then he stepped into the field.

Logan and Colby had made it almost halfway across the field when Colby stepped in a depression in the dirt and fell face first to the ground. She felt a sharp pain knife through her ankle as it twisted underneath her. When she fell, Logan immediately stopped running. Then he came back and knelt down beside her. She was lying on her side holding her ankle.

"Oh my god, Logan I think I just broke my ankle!"

"Probably just sprained it," Logan said as he tried to catch his breath. "Come on, let's get you up and I'll carry you."

Colby yelped in pain as Logan lifted her to her feet. She wrapped her arms around his shoulders as he picked her up and cradled her in his arms. Then he resumed his pace down the tobacco row. They were moving much slower now and Logan knew that Chip could very well catch up with them if they didn't try to move faster. But in the moonlight he could barely see the shadowy ground between the tobacco plants and this made it hard to keep his footing.

Logan slowed just a bit so that he could look behind him as he ran with Colby in his arms. His worst fear was confirmed when he saw the dark outline of Chip McPhale closing in on them. Logan knew if he didn't hurry that Chip would catch them before they managed to get across the field.

Logan turned his head and looked down into the dark gulf between the two rows of tobacco plants. Then he quickened his pace in order to open the distance between them and Chip. But he hadn't traveled more than ten paces when his foot caught a baseball-sized rock sticking out of the soil. When his foot hit the rock he stumbled and he and Colby both tumbled to the ground.

"Fuck!" Logan hissed as he and Colby hit the dirt.

Just as Logan pushed himself up and got to his feet, he turned to see the dark hulk of Chip McPhale standing over him. Before Logan could react, Chip swung the baseball bat, the tip of it catching Logan squarely on the jaw. Chip watched in satisfaction as Logan fell sideways across a tobacco plant, out cold from the impact of the bat.

Colby was on the ground and trying to push herself away from Chip. The pain shot through her ankle and all the way up her leg to her hip as she tried to move. Tears were streaming down her face as she tried to scramble away from Chip. She knew there was no way she could get to her feet and run. She looked back over her shoulder and could see the Shaw house. It was closer but she and Logan had still only made it a little more than halfway across the field.

Colby continued to push herself down the row in an effort to get away from Chip. Her hands sank into the sandy soil and this made it hard to get any traction. Panic engulfed her as Chip began to take slow steps toward her while holding the bat in his hand. His skin seemed to glow in the yellow moonlight as he moved and Colby knew she was not going to be able to escape him this time.

Chip looked behind him and could see the faint outline of Logan's motionless body lying in the shadows between the rows. He knew that he now had all the time he needed to finally take care of Colby. She belonged to him once again, but then that had never really changed. She had always belonged to him.

"There's no need to try and get away, kitten," Chip said as he moved closer to Colby. The pain in her ankle cut all the way up her leg as she tried to push herself away from him. But the effort was futile. As Chip moved closer to her, he lowered the baseball bat. He knew he wouldn't need it to handle Colby now. He had other things in mind besides hitting her with the bat.

"I think it's time that you and I get busy," Chip said as he let go of the handle of the bat. Then he took a step towards Colby while his hands moved to his belt. He removed the small revolver and dropped it beside the bat. He was now standing directly over her.

Colby made a fist in the sandy soil and then threw a handful of it in Chip's face. The sand filled his eyes and caused a stream of profanities to come out of his mouth.

"You fucking little bitch!" Chip yelled as he brought his hands to his eyes. The sand grated his eyeballs like emery cloth. He drew back his leg in anger and then kicked Colby violently in the side of her shin. She screamed out in pain as he tried to clear his eyes of the sand.

When Chip could finally see again he realized that Colby had scrambled farther down the row away from him. This filled him with rage. He quickly closed the distance between them and once he caught up to her he reached down and grabbed her by the ankle. The resulting bolt of pain felt like it was going to split her body in half.

"I don't know where the fuck you think you're going!" Chip hissed as he pulled Colby to him. Then he dropped to his knees and grabbed Colby by both legs, pulling her across the dirt until she was close to him.

"I said we're going to get to know each other. And you better take it like a good little whore if you know what's good for you."

Chip began to unbuckle his belt buckle with one hand. He used his other hand to reach down and grab the top of Colby's shorts. She was kicking and screaming and using both fists to hit Chip across his arms and chest but none of it had any effect. He was too strong and she knew that there was no way she was going to get away from him this time.

Colby continued to push against Chip but her strength was leaving her. The pain in her leg burned from her ankle all the way to her waist. She was crying and begging Chip to stop.

"Please, Chip! No! *Please!*" Chip ignored her as he leaned forward and pulled at the waistband of her shorts. Her open shirt was bunched up around her shoulders as she used what strength she had left to try and fight him off.

The tears flowed down Colby's cheeks and onto the sandy dirt underneath her. She knew what was going to happen and that Chip would not stop until he got what he wanted. She knew that she would never be able to win the fight with him. He was just too strong.

"Now you're gonna take it like a…"

Chip suddenly choked on the words in his throat as the tobacco axe cut deep into the side of his neck, almost severing his head from his body. Colby gasped as Chip's limp body fell forward onto her. She screamed and began to convulse as she tried to get out from under Chip's lifeless corpse. His head, attached only by a bloody rope of flesh and tendon, rolled backwards at a grotesque angle when she pushed on his body. Fighting the urge to vomit, Colby finally managed rid herself of Chip's corpse and then scramble backwards until she was a few feet away from it. Then something caught her eye. She wiped the tears from her face with the back of her hand and tried to focus on what she was seeing.

Standing at the foot of Chip's lifeless body was a young girl not much taller than the surrounding tobacco plants. Colby began to shake all over as fear, hot and acidic, churned in her abdomen. The young girl was holding a tobacco axe in her hand, its blade covered with Chip McPhale's blood.

Before Colby could move, the girl lifted the tobacco axe high in the air and brought it down violently into what remained of the connective tissue between Chip's head and his body. Colby gasped as Chip's head broke free and rolled across the soil to the base of a nearby tobacco plant. Then the killer lifted the axe again and again, over and over, each time burying the head of the axe deep into Chip's lifeless corpse.

Colby let out a bloodcurdling scream that pierced the night sky over the tobacco field. Her body was stiff with fear and she was unable to move, unable to push herself farther down the row away from the grisly scene unfolding before her. She watched as the girl continued to hack and chop at Chip's body until it was nothing more than a mound of bloody flesh and bone mingled with the shreds of fabric from his clothes.

But as quickly as it had begun, the slaughter ended. The girl then stepped back away from Chip's body while still holding the tobacco axe firmly in her hands. Then Colby felt the blood drain from her face when the young girl turned and looked directly into her eyes.

The killer walked slowly past the mound of flesh that had once been Chip McPhale and then to within a few feet of Colby. Bathed in the light of the harvest moon, Colby could see the dress, the shoes, and the long, unwashed hair. The appearance of the little girl reminded Colby of old photos she had seen of people who had lived a hundred years in the past.

The killer did not drop the tobacco axe as she looked down at Colby. After a few seconds, she moved it from one had to the other as she continued to study Colby lying in the dirt a few feet away.

"Who... Who are you?" Colby croaked as she pushed herself up against the stalk of the closet tobacco plant. The little girl did not respond. Her eyes were lifeless and black, set against skin tinted yellow from the light of the moon.

"You stay away from me!" Colby yelled as she raised a hand. She grabbed another handful of sandy dirt with her other hand and threw it at the little girl, but it had no effect.

Then the killer took a step forward. Colby watched as the young girl turned her head to look at Chip's body. After a few moments she turned her head back to Colby.

Colby felt her entire body begin to tremble. She knew no one had ever seen the ghost of the Shaw fields and lived to tell about it. She knew that she was no more than a few seconds away from the fate that had befallen Chip McPhale. And after the killer was done with her, Colby knew she would then turn her rage on Logan who was still lying unconscious down the row towards the middle of the field.

Suddenly a moan echoed through the still air. Colby jerked her head in the direction of the noise and waited. After a few seconds, she heard it again. This time she recognized the sound as Logan's voice. He was calling out to her.

The little girl seemed to be able to hear Logan calling out in the night. She turned her head in the direction of Logan and then back to Colby. Then she took a few more steps forward and stopped. She was only inches away from Colby's feet. Colby then watched as the little girl lifted her arm and opened her hand. In her other hand she held the bloody tobacco axe.

Colby thought for a second that the little girl wanted her to take her by the hand. But then she realized that the little girl wanted something instead, but Colby had no idea what it was. After a few seconds the little girl dropped her hand back to her side.

Paralyzed with fear, Colby knew that her time had come. The little girl slowly raised the tobacco axe into the air but then seemed to hesitate just as Logan's voice rang out again from down the row. Once again the little girl looked in Logan's direction and then back down at Colby. Then she lowered the axe and took a step backwards. Colby remained still, afraid to move or make any sort of noise as the little girl continued to look at her with her black, coal-like eyes. Then suddenly the little girl turned around and walked through the row of tobacco plants and disappeared from sight.

After a few seconds, Colby sat up and tried to see where the little girl had gone. But there was no sign of her. Then she heard Logan's voice again. She knew she had to get to him and that they had to get out of the field. She managed to lift herself up and get to her feet. Then she limped past Chip's dead body until she finally found Logan lying in the dirt farther down the row. She bent down and wrapped her arms around him and began to cry.

"Colby... Are you alright? What the hell happened?" Logan was groggy but managed to sit up so that he could see Colby's terrified face. The fear burning in her eyes was like nothing he had ever seen before.

"Hey, talk to me," he said as he held Colby tightly against him. But she didn't speak at first. Then suddenly she seemed to snap out of it.

"Get up, Logan. We've got to move. Chip is dead. The killer got him. I saw the whole thing. I saw the killer hack Chip to pieces. Get up! We've got to get out of here!"

Logan got to his feet and picked Colby up along with him. He put her arm around his neck so that he could help her walk on her ankle. Then they began to make their way up the row towards Chip's body.

"Holy fucking shit..." Logan said as he and Colby went past Chip's mutilated body.

"I saw it happen, Logan. I saw the killer."

"We need to get out of this field," Logan said as he began to shuffle faster up the row. Colby grimaced in pain but continued along with him trying to lift some of her weight off her ankle by holding onto Logan. In a matter of minutes they were out of the field. Once clear of the tobacco plants, they collapsed on the grass near the back porch of Logan's house.

27

Logan and Colby stood on the back porch of his house and stared out into the moonlit tobacco field. Colby was still trembling but she had finally collected herself enough to be able tell Logan what had happened after he had been knocked out with the baseball bat by Chip McPhale. The pain in her ankle was beginning to subside.

"It's a little girl, Logan. All these years and the killer is a little girl. The ghost of tobacco road is just a little girl. I saw her with my own eyes."

"Colby, come on. Are you serious?" Logan looked at Colby in disbelief and then out into the tobacco field. The harvest moon had moved higher in the sky and was now bathing the tobacco plants in a bright, silvery light.

"I'm telling you I saw her, Logan. I watched her chop Chip McPhale to pieces. He was about to rape me before she took his head off with one swing of her tobacco axe. You saw his body. We need to call the sheriff. We need to call him right now."

"Just hold on, Colby. We'll call him. But let's get our story straight before we do that." Logan was embarrassed that he had been knocked out cold by Chip. He wished he had been conscious so that he could have maybe seen the killer along with Colby, or even better, took care of Chip McPhale himself.

"She's just a little girl, Logan. She looks like she lived a hundred years ago. She's wearing an old handmade dress, old shoes and her hair is long and dirty. Her eyes are lifeless black holes in her face. And…"

"And what?" Logan said.

Colby paused for a second, unsure of how to tell Logan what had happened.

"And she… She seemed to want something. She extended her hand like she wanted me to give her something but I didn't know what to do. When she realized I didn't have anything to give her she raised her axe and I thought that my time had come. But then you called out and she seemed to change. When she heard your voice she lowered her tobacco axe, turned and then disappeared into the tobacco plants. If you hadn't called out…"

"Hey, hey, it's alright. It's alright, Colby. I'm here." Logan pulled Colby close and held her tightly as he looked out into the field.

"What do you think she wanted?" Logan said as he turned and looked down at Colby's face. She was lost in a trance, staring out into the moonlit tobacco field.

"I don't know. But she thought that I had it, whatever it was. I just can't believe it. I can't believe she didn't kill me, Logan. No one has ever seen her and lived to tell about it. All these years… You should have heard some the stories that have gone around this town. Everyone had their own theory about who the killer was. But I can tell you no one ever thought it was a young girl."

Colby looked up at Logan and then back out into the field.

"She couldn't have been more than ten years old."

"Do you think she's still out there?" Logan didn't know what else to ask. He was sure that Colby was telling him the truth, at least as she remembered it, but her story was more than just a little outlandish. How could a little girl like that kill grown men out in the fields? And if she really was a ghost, if such a thing existed, then why? Why was she here in the Shaw Fields? Logan had no answers to his questions.

Logan looked out into the tobacco field and then asked Colby a question.

"Colby, has anyone ever been killed outside of the boundaries of the field?"

Colby frowned as if in deep thought.

"Not that I've ever heard of," she finally answered. "Carson was killed in one of the tobacco barns but at one time tobacco grew where that barn is located."

Logan exhaled. "That's good. I guess we're safe then standing up here on the porch."

Colby pulled herself closer to Logan. She liked the feel of his arm around her. Despite knowing that Chip McPhale's lifeless, mutilated body was lying out in the fields directly in front of them, she felt safe standing next to Logan.

"So she wanted something?" Logan said as he rubbed Colby's shoulder. "What could it be?"

Colby didn't know what to make of the tone of Logan's voice. He was seriously trying to figure out what the ghost wanted when it had reached out to her. As for Colby, she didn't care. They were safely out of the fields and that was all that mattered to her.

"Why does it matter, Logan? What difference does it make?"

"Because there will be more killings, Colby. You said yourself that they've been going on for over eighty years. If she wants something, maybe she will leave if she gets it."

"That's crazy talk, Logan. Think about what you're saying. It sounds ridiculous. What could we have that she would want? We don't even know who she is. I mean, she's a…"

"A ghost… I get it. But we need to try and figure it out, Colby."

Colby frowned and looked at Logan. He had a determined look in his eyes that scared her.

Suddenly Logan had an idea. He looked down at Colby with a look of astonishment.

"You said she's a little girl dressed in old clothes, right?"

"Yes," Colby replied nervously.

Logan looked back out into the field.

"You're scaring me, Logan. What are you thinking? We don't have time for this. There's a dead body out in your field, or what's left of a dead body, and we need to call the sheriff. We didn't do anything wrong. We have nothing to worry about. So let's go call Patterson."

Logan acted like he had not heard a word Colby had just said.

"Come on. I have an idea." Logan took Colby's arm and put it around his neck so that he could help her walk. Her ankle was still throbbing from being twisted out in the field as Logan led her off the porch and into the house.

"Where are we going?" she said as they moved through the kitchen on their way to the front door. She thought for a moment that Logan was going to lead them through the front door and that maybe he wanted to get in the car and leave. But when he turned and began to lead her to the stairs she was even more confused.

"Logan, where are we going?" Colby said as she let go of his shoulder. "I think I can make it okay," she said as she put weight on her ankle.

"Are you sure?" replied Logan. "Just let me help you up the stairs."

"Okay, just tell me what we're doing first."

"I've got a hunch," Logan said. "And only you can help me. After all, you said you saw her."

"But you're scaring me, Logan. This house scares me too."

"You said no one has ever been killed outside of the fields, so we'll be fine. But come on, we've got to hurry. The moon is rising higher and if the little girl you saw really is the ghost then we don't have much time."

Logan helped Colby upstairs and into the hallway. Then they walked down the hall to the attic door, Colby wincing as she put weight on her ankle. The door squeaked on its hinges when Logan pulled it open.

"We need to go look at something."

"Logan, I don't want to go up there."

"It's okay. I'll go up first. You just stay close behind. I can't do this without you. You're the only person that has ever seen her, Colby."

Colby huffed and shook her head. "Okay, but let me stay close to you."

Logan helped Colby along as they ascended the narrow attic stairs and once they got to the top Logan fumbled around until he found the pullcord to the light. It clicked when he pulled on the string and the attic was suddenly bathed in the dim incandescent glow of the solitary light bulb above them.

Logan moved to the old trunk in the corner of the attic. Colby came along behind him and then they sat down on the floor. He opened the lid and began to pull the contents from the trunk one piece at a time. When he found the old photo album he sat backwards on his heels and pulled Colby close to him.

"Help me find her," he said as he flipped through the pages.

"Help you do what?" Colby said as a look of disbelieve bloomed on her face.

"I've got a hunch. You saw her so you know what she looks like. Just help me look through the photos until you see her."

"Have you lost your mind?" Colby said as she looked down at the first page of the album. She didn't know what else to do but humor Logan. As crazy as it sounded, he seemed to really believe that there would be a photo of the ghost in the old album.

"Suit yourself," Colby said as Logan laid the photo album on his thigh and then put his arm around her as she looked down at the old photos taped by the corners to the first page.

"Nope," was all Colby said after she examined the two photos on the first page of the album. One photo was of Rosemary when she was probably middle-aged and the other one was of a Labrador retriever. "Cute dog," Colby said after she examined the photo. Then Logan flipped the page.

Colby examined the photos and shook her head as Logan turned each page. When Logan was almost to the end of the album, Colby grabbed his hand just as he was about to flip the page. She opened her mouth and drew in a quick breath. Then she looked at Logan and back at the photo.

Taped in the middle of the page was a single photo of two young girls standing side by side on the edge of a tobacco field. One girl was slightly shorter than the other one and looked to be just a few years younger than the taller girl. Colby put her hand on the page to steady the album and Logan could see that she was starting to tremble again.

"Logan..." was all Colby could manage to say. She fell silent as she studied the photo of the two girls. Logan could see a mix of astonishment and fear cloud Colby's face as she looked at the photo. After a few more seconds she spoke.

"The... The taller girl, Logan. That's her." Colby then moved her hand to the page and traced her finger across the photo. "And she was even wearing that same dress," Colby said as she pointed to the old gray patchwork cloth dress the girl was wearing in the photo.

"Are you sure?" Logan said as he looked at Colby.

"I'm positive. How did you know there would be a picture of her in this old album?"

"Call it a hunch."

"A what? A *hunch*? Are you serious?" Colby said, making no effort to hide her disbelief.

"Come on. We don't have much time." Logan said as he started to close the photo album.

"Wait!" said Colby. She opened the album again and pointed to the second girl in the photo.

"Do you recognize the other little girl?" Colby asked as she looked at Logan.

Logan frowned as he looked at the photo. At first he had no idea who the other girl was but then it slowly dawned on him that he was looking at a very young version of his great-grandmother.

"That's Rosemary," Colby said.

Logan's eyes grew wide as he recognized his very young great-grandmother. He paused as he studied the photo and then finally spoke.

"So if that's Rosemary who is the other girl?"

"I'll bet the other girl is her older sister," Colby said. "My grandmother was friends with Rosemary. I remember her telling me once that Rosemary had a sister who died when she was young."

"Well I'll be damned," replied Logan. "Harmon mentioned a sister but he didn't say much else.

"Talk about being damned. For some reason the soul of Rosemary's sister returns to the Shaw Fields every now and then. But why? Why does she want to kill?"

"She's looking for something, for one thing," replied Colby. "Why she kills, I don't know. She could be angry."

Logan looked into Colby's eyes. "You said she wanted something from you. But thank God she didn't kill you when you couldn't give it to her. I wonder why she spared you"

Colby thought about this for a minute, trying to find a reason why her life was spared by the ghost of tobacco road. She knew she was the first person to see the ghost and live to tell about it.

"She was about to kill me, Logan. Then she heard your voice and she stopped."

Colby drew in a breath when she realized that she had just answered her own question. She put her hand on Logan's knee.

"Logan, she's family to you. If she's Rosemary's sister then she's your aunt, your great-aunt. She's your blood, Logan. That's why she spared me when she heard your voice."

Logan brought his hands to his face and then ran his fingers through his hair. Then he exhaled and looked at Colby.

"Why can't I have a normal family like everybody else?" he said, exasperated.

"No one has a normal family, Logan. But I will say yours is stranger than most." Colby gently poked Logan in the ribs but it didn't seem to lighten his mood.

"Rosemary's dead sister is the ghost of tobacco road..." Logan said as he touched the photo one more time.

Logan lifted his eyes from the photo and looked at Colby with a look of bewilderment. It took a few seconds for him to speak.

"So what happened to her? How did she die?"

"I don't know. We might never know," Colby said.

"Wait a minute," Logan said as he began to shuffle through the pile of things they had removed from the trunk. When he found the large envelope he was looking for, he removed the photo from inside of it.

"Remember this photo? The one taken at the train station?"

Colby took the photo from Logan's hand and examined it closely. Then she compared the two girls standing with the adults at the train station to the two girls photographed on the edge of the tobacco field.

"They're the same two girls," whispered Colby.

"Damn..." Logan muttered under his breath as he leaned over and examined the two photos. "You're right, it's them. And I'll just bet the taller girl's name is Clara."

When he said Clara's name, Logan suddenly remembered there was business at hand. He took the train station photo from Colby and stuck it into the photo album and then closed it up. Then he began to put all the items back in the trunk. Colby felt a chill run through her body and looked nervously around the attic to make sure they were alone. For some reason she felt like they were being watched. When she turned her head Logan stuck one of the items from the trunk in the back waistband of his pants and then pulled his shirt over it to hide it from view. He had another hunch and knew that he would have to act on it. Then he finished repacking the trunk and closed the lid.

"Come on, Colby. We need to hurry."

"Now where are we going? I thought you found what you were looking for."

"There's one more thing I need to do. Let's get back out to the field before it's too late."

28

Logan Shaw stood on the back porch of his house and looked out into the moonlit tobacco field. Colby was standing next to him.

"You can't go out there, Logan. I won't let you. Have you completely lost your mind?"

"Colby, this could be my chance to end all of this. Maybe I can help her find peace. We can't live in this house worrying about the next harvest moon and if she will return. We have to put an end to this. I mean, I have to put an end to this. You have to stay here. You can't come with me into the field."

"Logan Shaw you are certifiably insane if you think I'm going to let you walk back out into that field knowing that the ghost is out there. She has already killed one person tonight."

Logan turned and looked at Colby. He knew that she had to love him if she was so worried about him going out into the field. He gently took her face in his hands and kissed her.

"I love you, Colby. I want you forever. But we can't have that until I take care of this. If this is going to be our home then I have to help that little girl's soul find peace. Think of how bad we'll feel if we don't fix this and she kills again. It will be on us."

Colby was on the verge of tears. "We can go away, Logan. We don't have to stay here."

Logan shook his head. "You said yourself that she's my blood. She won't kill me, Colby. I believe that."

"Well I don't", snapped Colby. "I know I said that she's your blood and that's why she didn't kill us but what if I'm wrong, Logan? And we both agree that she wants something and neither of us know what it is. What if you get there and she finds you and realizes that you don't have what she wants? What will you do then? She's angry, Logan. And she kills because of it. She even killed her own sister's husband, your great-grandfather. Have you forgotten about what happened to Carson?"

"He wasn't her blood, Colby. I need to go. The moon is rising higher every minute. Who knows how much longer she'll be out there."

"Logan no!" Colby cried as Logan pulled away from her and walked down the steps to the backyard. She grimaced in pain as she tried to follow him down the stairs. Logan had stopped in the yard and was looking out into the field when she caught up to him. She wrapped her arms around him and held him tightly.

"Please don't go, Logan! She'll kill you. She'll hack you to pieces just like she did Chip."

Logan knew he had to find some way to make Colby believe that what he was about to do was the right thing.

"Colby, the fact that she killed Chip should tell you something. There is some good in her. I just know it. She knew what Chip was about to do to you and she killed him before he could do it. I have to help her, Colby. She deserves to rest in peace."

Colby reached up and wiped the tears from her eyes. Logan squeezed her hand and then turned and began to walk towards the tobacco field.

When Logan reached the edge of the field he stopped and surveyed his surroundings. Had he really lost his mind? What if Colby was right? The idea that the ghost would not harm him was just that – an idea. And it could be a foolish one at that. What if he was wrong and she killed him? Colby would be alone and he would miss having a life with the kind of girl he had always dreamed of having. Logan thought about this but then quickly put it out of his mind. He knew he had to take a chance; he had to be a man and take care of this problem. If the ghost of tobacco road really was his kin then it fell on him to end this. After all, he was Rosemary's only living relative. There was no one else.

Logan took a deep breath and stepped in between the two closest rows of tobacco plants. Then he stopped and stood still. A gentle breeze rolled across the field causing the plants to sway in unison. He looked over his shoulder and saw that Colby had retreated back to the porch and was watching him from there. He could tell that she was terrified out of her wits.

With fear boiling in his stomach Logan began to slowly walk down the row. As he moved he reached behind him and felt for the bulge in his shirt near his waist. When his hand found it he felt a sense of relief wash over him. He hoped like hell that he was right and that what he had brought from the trunk would appease the ghost. If it did not, Logan knew he would never live to see the light of another day and that Colby would have to go on without him.

Logan continued to walk down the row until he was almost halfway across the field. He knew Chip's body was lying somewhere close by but in the confusion of running out of the field with Colby he had forgotten exactly which row it was on. But after he walked a few more paces he suddenly smelled the sweet, metallic scent of blood. He knew right then that he had to be close to Chip's body and the spot where Colby had seen the ghost.

Logan stepped through several rows of tobacco plants and tried to follow the smell of the blood. After he crossed several more rows he finally found what he was looking for. Lying in the middle of a row was the ruined body of Chip McPhale. Logan walked up to it and could see what remained of the torso and legs. Then he saw Chip's severed head lying close to the stalk of a tobacco plant, its blank expression frozen in the moonlight.

"Serves you right, you fucking prick," Logan said as he looked down at Chip's body. Then he scanned the tobacco field around him.

The harvest moon was high in the sky. Logan hoped that the spell was not broken and that the ghost would appear soon. He wasn't sure if he was right about the ghost's name, but he decided that calling out to her might be worth a chance.

"Clara," Logan said softly. There was no response. Then he said the name again, this time a little louder.

"Clara!"

A breeze combed through the tobacco plants causing the broad leaves to rustle against each other. It sounded like a whisper wafting across the field. Logan scanned the field around him but the ghost was nowhere to be seen. Then he called out again.

"Clara!"

When Logan turned his head back in the direction of the bank of the Skeleton River, he thought he caught movement down the row towards the far side of the field.

Logan felt the hackles on the back of his neck rise as his eyes focused on the dark shape coming towards him. He took a step backward but then caught himself. He knew it was time to stand his ground and that even if he tried to get away he would never make it out of the field alive.

As the shadowy figure approached, Logan looked down at the ruined mound of pulp that had once been Chip McPhale. He wondered if his foolish bravado was about to earn him the same fate as Chip. Logan tried to purge these thoughts from his mind as the ghost slowly approached, moving closer with every agonizing second. When she was less than ten feet away, she stopped and stood still. In her hand he could see the small tobacco axe, the moonlight glinting off of the sharp blade.

"Clara?" Logan croaked as fear, raw and toxic bubbled up into his throat. His voice brought no response or movement from the ghost. She merely stood still and stared at him through lifeless, empty eye sockets.

Then Clara took a step forward and Logan had to fight the urge to turn and run. When she raised the tobacco axe every ounce of courage left him, and he began step backwards down the row behind him. He knew right then that he had been a fool to assume that she wouldn't kill him.

In his haste to retreat Logan forgot about the body of Chip McPhale. As he moved backwards he tripped over Chip's body and fell to the ground. The impact knocked the wind out of him.

Clara slowly moved past the body of Chip McPhale and closer to Logan, who had managed to push himself backwards into the row of tobacco plants behind him. He wanted to get up and run, he wanted to save himself from what he knew was about to happen, but his body would not obey. His strength was gone, choked out of him by the impending doom that awaited him.

Logan felt his entire body tremble as the ghost walked to within several feet of him. Then she stopped and stood still. Her long, matted hair hung down across the front of her face and Logan could again see the empty eye sockets set against pale skin. In her right hand was the tobacco axe. Her left hand was empty.

Logan watched as Clara extended her empty hand towards him. When she did, he felt a strange sense of relief wash over him. Clara was asking him for something and he knew that he might very well have a chance to live if he could produce what she wanted. He prayed that his assumption about what she wanted would be correct.

Logan closed his eyes and took a deep breath. Then he reached behind him and pulled the doll out of his waistband of his pants and out from under his shirt. He held the doll in his hand and slowly extended it towards the ghost.

At first Clara made no effort to take the doll and for one long terrifying moment Logan thought that the doll was not going to satisfy her. But suddenly she dropped the tobacco axe and took the doll from Logan using both of her hands. He watched as she slowly brought the old, handmade doll to her until she was holding it tightly against her chest.

Then something strange began to happen.

Logan drew in a deep breath as he watched Clara's face slowly begin to change. In the bright moonlight he could see the color return to her skin. The empty eye sockets slowly faded away and were replaced by the bright eyes of a child. The matted hair around her face began to move in the breeze, free of the dirt and grime that had weighted it down for decades.

Clara looked at Logan and smiled. Then she pulled the doll close to her face and closed her eyes. After a few moments she opened them again and looked at Logan one more time. Then she slowly turned around and walked through the adjoining row of tobacco plants. A moment later, Logan watched as she faded away and then disappeared. He started to call out her name but caught himself. He knew she would not answer, nor would she return.

It was then that Logan realized that the ghost of tobacco road was gone forever.

29

Sheriff Tom Patterson stood stoically at the edge of the tobacco field watching the two men from the county coroner's office do what they could to get the remains of Chip McPhale's corpse into a body bag. He shook his head and looked down at his feet just as Logan and Colby walked up to him. The rising sun was just barely above the distant tree line and the morning air was crisp and carried the scent of tobacco leaves and the Skeleton River.

"Good morning," Logan said. Colby nodded at the sheriff as she came to a stop and looked out into the field at the men working on Chip's body.

"It's a busy morning," replied the sheriff. Logan could sense irritation in the man's voice. "I've got a dead body out there in that field that looks like it's been run through a wood chipper. Ethan McPhale got the shit beat out of him last night by an intruder, and if that's not enough, Harmon Blackwell decided to nibble on the end of his thirty eight last night. He blew his brains all over the wall of his office. Damn near sent Sandy into cardiac arrest when she found him this morning. Is there something you want to tell me, Logan?"

Logan was speechless. Why in the world would Harmon kill himself?

After a long pause, Logan finally spoke. "Uh, no Sheriff Patterson. I have no idea. Why would you think I would know anything?"

Patterson rubbed his chin. "He's your lawyer. I figured you might have some sort of insight into why he would take his own life."

"I have no idea, sheriff. I wish I could help but I have nothing to offer you."

Patterson looked at Logan. "Harmon had an old picture of your great-grandmother in his lap. It was taken a long time ago. I figured you might know something about that too."

Logan hesitated and then thought better of it. What could it hurt to tell the sheriff what he knew? Rosemary and Harmon were both dead.

"All I can tell you sheriff is that I think Harmon and Rosemary had something going a long, long time ago. He told me a little about it but not much. The times I met with him he drank and smoked the whole time. He seemed happy, but only on the surface."

The sheriff thought about this and then turned his head and looked across the field at the McPhale house sitting on the top of the distant rise.

"So he wanted to be with his long lost love? Is that what you're telling me?"

"I guess," replied Logan. It was the best he could do considering the circumstances. He suddenly remembered that Harmon had said that all he needed was a cold grave to crawl into. Now it appeared that the old man would finally have what he wanted.

Patterson shook his head and then looked back out into the tobacco field. "Sandy said that last week Harmon went to see a doctor in Raleigh. She said he got a phone call a few days later and she didn't think it was good news. She said Harmon had a different look in his eyes after that call. Maybe that's the reason he took his own life." Patterson then looked at Logan again. "He did enjoy the leaf more than most people."

Logan nodded his head and frowned. Then he looked at Colby before looking back out into the field where the men were still working on Chip's body.

Patterson paused for a moment. "Ethan McPhale is in the emergency room at County. But he'll probably be released today. His injuries aren't life threatening." Then the sheriff looked at Logan. "Exactly where were you last night, Mr. Shaw?"

Logan picked up on the shift in the sheriff's tone and the fact that he had suddenly switched to using last names. He was about to say something when Colby spoke up.

"He was here with me, Tom." Then she paused for a second. "All night long."

Logan could see the jealousy flash hot across the sheriff's face. But then it passed and the sheriff regained his composure.

"I see," Patterson said as he looked at Colby. "Well I'll still need a statement from both of you."

"There's not much to say, sheriff. I came down this morning to make coffee, looked out the window and saw buzzards circling over the field. I got a little curious and that's when I found the body. Then I came in and called your office."

"We found the bat," the sheriff interrupted. "We'll be fingerprinting it later this morning."

Logan felt his stomach tense. He knew he had to say something.

"Hopefully you'll get some leads, sheriff. And I hope Ethan is okay. As for his brother out there, well…"

Then Patterson spoke. "I guess this puts an end to the rumors about past members of the McPhale family being behind the killings over the years. And Chip and Ethan too."

"I think we all know what killed Chip McPhale," Colby said.

Patterson looked at Colby when she said this. Then he looked out over the field towards the river. "It's been almost twenty years since someone died out in that field. Let's hope it's another twenty before it happens again."

The three of them were silent for a minute. Then the silence was broken by one of the men working on Chip's body. He was yelling from out in the field and waving his arm in an attempt to get the sheriff's attention. When Patterson noticed, he looked at Logan and Colby.

"Excuse me for a second," he said as he turned and walked out into the field towards the men.

Logan watched as the sheriff walked out into the middle of the field. Once he reached the men one of them handed him something. But at this distance Logan couldn't tell what it was. He watched as the sheriff examined the item and then began to walk back up the row and out of the field.

"What is it?" sheriff, Logan asked as Patterson walked up to him and Colby. Then Logan got a good look at what the sheriff was carrying and felt his heart palpitate in his chest.

In Sheriff Patterson's hand was a small tobacco axe. The blade of the axe was covered with a thick layer of rust and the wooden handle was nearly rotten from years of exposure to the weather.

"What do you make of that, sheriff?"

Despite asking the sheriff this question, Logan knew what he was looking at. It was the tobacco axe Clara had used to kill Chip McPhale, and most likely every other victim over the years. Logan remembered her dropping it when he had handed her the doll, and in his haste to leave the field last night after she disappeared he had not thought to pick it up.

"Do you mind, sheriff?" Logan said as he held out his hand. He wanted to hold the axe and examine it.

Patterson paused but then thought better of it. "I guess not. I doubt it's going to be entered into evidence. I mean, look at the damn blade. It's so rusted and dull that there's no way in hell it could be used to hack someone to pieces. And the handle is about rotten. One good swing and the head would probably break off. I don't see how it can be considered the murder weapon. But they did find a .38 revolver close to the body. It will go into evidence even though it's loaded but hasn't been fired." After Patterson said this he handed the axe to Logan.

Logan took the axe and ran his thumb along the surface of the blade. It was rough and covered in a thick layer of reddish brown rust as if it had been lying in the field for decades. He offered it to Colby and she took it gently in her hands and then turned it back and forth to examine it. She tried to hide her astonishment at holding what she knew was the murder weapon of the ghost of tobacco road. After a minute or so she handed it back to Patterson.

"If you don't mind, sheriff, I'd like to have this back when you're finished with it. There's no telling how many past members of my family have used that axe. I've got an old trunk full of family heirlooms up in the attic. This will make a nice addition to it."

Sheriff Patterson thought about this for a moment. He looked at Logan and then at the old rusted tobacco axe. There was no dried blood on the axe and by the looks of it he knew that it probably had nothing to do with Chip's murder. It probably was just an old artifact left in the field long ago by someone working the tobacco. Perhaps it had been uncovered the last time the field had been plowed.

"Take it, Logan. I have no use for it," Sheriff Patterson said as he handed the old axe to Logan.

30

Logan held Clara's tobacco axe in his hands and looked at it one more time before wrapping it in the cloth. Then he laid it gently into the attic trunk. Colby was sitting on the floor underneath the light reading the old diary they had found in the trunk. The sun was setting outside and the dormer windows of the attic were the color of lavender.

"What's its say?" Logan asked as he sat down and leaned up against the trunk. He could tell by the expression on Colby's face that she was upset. Even though they had spent most of the day trying to forget the events of the previous night, Logan knew it would take her more than a day to get over it, if she·ever got over it.

"It's awful. I don't know if I can read much more. Those poor little girls…"

"What little girls?"

"Rosemary and her sister, Clara. This diary apparently belonged to the woman who adopted Rosemary and Clara from the orphan train. She signs her name Florence". Colby looked up at Logan. "You're great-grandmother and her sister were orphans, Logan. They were adopted right from one of the trains."

"They were orphans? I'll bet Harmon didn't even know that. He said Rosemary never liked to talk about her parents." As Logan said this, Colby returned her attention to the diary and began to read again.

Logan watched as Colby frowned and then looked away from the diary again, like she had just read something that disturbed her.

"What is it?" Logan said as he looked at Colby.

"She writes about bringing Rosemary and Clara home from the orphan train on the day they adopted them. Apparently back then people just showed up at the train station and picked the children they wanted. So Florence and her husband, she doesn't give his name, went to the station and picked out Rosemary and Clara. She writes that her husband wanted boys because they were better farmhands but all the boys were taken when they got there that day so they chose the two girls. The people on the train said Rosemary and Clara's mother had died of tuberculosis in New York City and their father had abandoned them. They were found living on the streets and taken into custody as wards of the state."

"For the love of God," replied Logan. "How horrible."

"It gets worse. You might not want to hear it," Colby said as she studied a page of the diary.

"Considering the events of the past twenty four hours, I think I'm probably up to hearing just about anything at this point. What does it say?"

Colby inhaled and then put her hand over her mouth. What she was reading in the diary was bothering her deeply.

"Florence writes about how her husband beat the girls. He was an abusive man, it seems."

Logan felt his stomach turn. "I'll bet he beat this Florence lady as well."

"Probably," replied Colby, visibly shaken by what she was reading. "Apparently one night Florence confronted her husband when he was beating Clara. He apparently let go of Clara and turned his attention to Florence. But she writes that she was afraid to tell the police because she knew she couldn't handle the farm if they took her husband away. So she must have just decided to live with it."

"I'll be damned," replied Logan.

Colby flipped through a few more pages of the diary and then her eyes grew wide when she read what was written at the top of the page.

"Now what?" Logan said as he leaned in towards Colby.

"The next entry in the diary starts out *We buried Clara today.*"

"So the old man beat her to death?" Logan said.

"It doesn't really say what happened. It just says they buried her," Colby said as she looked up from the diary at Logan who was frowning in disgust.

"That explains the funeral procession," he finally said.

Colby's face grew serious. "What?"

"The funeral procession. I saw it last night. This house has a way of showing you things that it wants you to see, like scenes from its past. I watched a funeral procession out of one of the upstairs windows. There were people following a horse-drawn cart carrying a coffin. It must have been Clara's. The procession went along the far edge of the field and turned into the woods towards that old sharecropper's house."

"Sounds like you found Rosemary's liquor cabinet is what it sounds like. You're telling me you watched Clara's funeral procession. That page of the diary is dated 1930, Logan."

"Yep, I watched it." Logan said matter-of-factly. "And Rosemary doesn't have a liquor cabinet. I've already looked. But I saw the funeral procession. And I saw other scenes from the past too."

"This explains everything," Colby said. "All the killings over the years…

The brutality of them. It seems Clara's ghost had a score to settle." Colby then began to flip through the remaining pages of the diary.

"The last entry is dated 1948. Florence must have died that year," Colby said when she got to the last page.

"And Rosemary was left alone with the house and the land," replied Logan.

"Yep," Colby said. "She was grown by then and she must have married Carson not long after Florence died. They raised tobacco on the land and made a living for themselves."

Logan thought about this and nodded his head.

"Let's hope that now she can rest in peace," Logan said as he got to his feet. Colby handed him the old diary and he placed it in the trunk on top of the tobacco axe wrapped in cloth. Then he closed the lid of the trunk.

§§§

Logan listened to the grandfather clock chime from the downstairs foyer. It was two o'clock in the morning. Colby was sleeping soundly beside him. The lovemaking from earlier had been heavenly and Logan could tell by her breathing pattern that Colby was in a deep sleep. He slowly got out of bed, being careful not to wake her. Once on his feet he crept slowly out of the bedroom and into the hallway. He took a few steps forward and then stopped and waited.

Suddenly the walls of the hallway were bathed in swirling light. Logan waited for the light show to die down and then walked to the first bedroom that overlooked the backyard of the house. Once inside the bedroom he walked to the window so that he could view the scene that was being offered to him by the house.

A harvest moon floated high over the fields, illuminating the tobacco plants with a silvery glow. Logan scanned the field but didn't see any movement. He couldn't understand why the house wanted to show him an empty tobacco field in the middle of the night. He was about to step away from the window when movement below the window caught his eye.

Logan watched as a grown man appeared in the yard below him. He was walking briskly towards the tobacco field holding a young girl by her arm. She was fighting against him but the man was tall and strong and had no problem controlling her. Logan watched as both of them moved across the yard to the edge of the tobacco field. The man paused and looked down at the girl and then pulled her by the arm and into the field.

The man moved quickly between the rows of tobacco plants with the young girl in tow. Logan watched as she continued to resist as they moved farther into the field. Before long both of them were swallowed up in the sea of tobacco plants and Logan could no longer make out their shapes.

Logan tried to locate them in the field but it was no use. The man and the girl had disappeared from his sight, too far away for him to see them. He stood at the window and waited. His eyes scanned the field from one side all the way to the other, to the edge of the distant bank of the Skeleton River, but he could not see them. Time seemed to slow to a crawl and Logan lost count of the minutes as they passed. He wanted to turn and pull away from the window but he could not move. He knew that the house was not ready for him to leave the window. There was still something left for him to see.

Just then Logan noticed movement in the middle of the tobacco field. He watched as the man came back into view, walking slowly up the row towards the house. Logan looked closely at the man and then realized that the girl was not with him. He was alone.

When the man reached the edge of the field he stopped and stood still. Then Logan felt a shiver run down his body as the man tilted his head back and looked up at the window where he was standing.

"He sees me," Logan muttered under his breath. But before Logan could react, the kaleidoscope of lights suddenly returned causing him to raise his hand over his eyes. After a few seconds the lights died down and Logan found himself staring back out into the present day version of his tobacco field.

The man was gone.

What did it mean? What had the house just showed him? Who was the man, and more importantly, who was the girl? What had happened to her?

Logan knew he had witnessed something horrible. He felt a sense of dread wash over him. He stepped away from the window and tried to clear his mind. Then he returned to the master bedroom and crawled back into bed with Colby, the warmth of her body bringing him comfort as he closed his eyes and tried to go back to sleep. But despite his efforts, sleep would elude him and he would lie awake for the rest of the night.

§§§

Colby was sitting at the breakfast table sipping her coffee while looking at Logan. She could tell something was bothering him.

"What's wrong?" she said as she reached over and touched his hand.

"I didn't sleep much last night."

Colby smiled when Logan said this.

"Well you know what that means don't you?"

Logan raised an eyebrow and looked at Colby. "I can't imagine."

"They say when you can't sleep at night it's because you're awake in someone else's dream."

Logan slowly smiled at Colby. He knew right then that she was just about the sweetest girl he had ever met. She was a far cry from some of the brash women that had crossed his path in the past.

"They say that, do they? And who exactly is *they*?"

"I dunno. But they say it, whoever they are."

Colby grinned at Logan and took a sip of her coffee. Logan's smile faded and the disturbed look returned to his face.

"I know what happened to Clara. And I know why her ghost only killed under the light of a harvest moon."

Colby made no effort to hide her astonishment. She put her cup down on the table, almost spilling her coffee in the process.

"You know what happened to Clara? How?"

"The house showed me," Logan said stoically.

"When?"

"Last night, while you were sleeping. I got up and went to the window in the back bedroom. I saw a man drag a young girl into the tobacco field. The moon in the sky was as big and bright as any harvest moon I've ever seen. He dragged her by the arm into the field. Time passed, I'm not sure how much, but then he reappeared without her. I think he took her out into the field and killed her. First he probably…"

Colby drew in a breath and then covered her mouth with her hand. Logan looked at her and could see tears welling up in her eyes.

"It makes sense now," Logan said. "She was killed under the light of a harvest moon after he dragged her out into the field and took what he wanted from her."

Suddenly a look of wonder crossed Colby's face. Logan frowned as he watched her slowly open her mouth like she had just remembered something important.

"What?" he finally said.

"I'll bet he was her first victim. I don't know the details or his name but now that I think about it I remember my grandmother telling me that the first murder in the Shaw Fields was the owner of the house. This house. It happened in 1931."

Colby then grew silent as she tried to piece everything together.

"The diary said they buried Clara in 1930. Her ghost must have returned the next year and killed him in the field. I'm sure no one at the time connected the dots. No one knew what had happened."

"Well now we do, and as far as I'm concerned we can keep it to ourselves," Logan said as he took a long sip of his coffee. Colby followed suit and then looked across the kitchen towards the back porch and the tobacco fields bathed in the morning sun.

31

It was close to lunchtime when Sheriff Patterson called to tell Logan that Ethan was out of the hospital and had been spotted in town. He advised Logan to steer clear for a while until things cooled off. Sheriff Patterson cautioned Logan about Ethan and reminded him to keep the doors to the Shaw house locked at all times.

"Will do, sheriff," Logan said as he hung up the phone. Colby was sitting in a chair by the kitchen table tying her shoes.

"Are you about ready?" she asked as she stood up and looked at Logan.

"As ready as I'll ever be. Let's go see what we can find."

Logan and Colby went out the back door and onto the porch. Colby waited while Logan locked the door and then dropped the key in his pocket. He picked up the axe handle propped against the doorframe and smiled as he lifted it up to examine it. He had found it in the basement earlier in the morning and knew that it would be handy to have given the fact that Ethan probably considered their business unfinished.

The noonday sun was high overhead as Logan and Colby walked across the backyard to the edge of the tobacco field.

"They should start picking soon," she said as they stepped into a row. Logan had made a mental note of the approximate location of where Chip's body had been found and he made a conscious effort to make sure he and Colby didn't walk down a row that would take them to that spot.

Once they reached the middle of the field, Logan scanned the area around him. It felt as if he was wading through a waist-deep sea of tobacco plants. He couldn't believe how big the field was and the amount of money that would be made from the harvesting of the leaves.

When they reached the far edge of the field they walked along the tree line until they found the trail that led to the sharecropper's house. Colby paused and reached out and took Logan by the hand.

"Are you sure you want to go in there?" Logan asked as he looked at Colby.

"I don't want to go to the house. Let's just go to the graves. I don't ever want to go in that sharecropper house again."

"I'll hire someone to come out here with a bulldozer and tear the place down. How's that?"

"Sounds perfect," Colby replied.

They stepped onto the path with Logan in the lead. It wasn't long until they came upon the spot where they had seen the old tombstones.

"There," Colby said as she pointed into the trees. They could see several tombstones jutting out of the underbrush about fifty feet off the path.

Logan and Colby both found themselves wishing they had worn long pants as they pushed their way through the underbrush. It took several minutes before they finally reached the tombstones. It was then that Logan spotted a footpath that led away from the graves toward the tobacco field.

"Looks like we took the back way," he said as he pointed to the path. Colby smiled and feigned exasperation.

The area around the graves was relatively clear. "Looks like someone kept the brush off the graves," Colby finally said.

Logan nodded his head. "Probably Rosemary until she got too old. Then I would imagine she started paying someone to do it. Probably the same people she paid to keep her yard in order."

Colby bent down to the smallest of the three tombstones and began to rub the surface of the stone with her hand. It wasn't long before she had brushed away most of the embedded dirt to reveal the name engraved in the stone. Logan watched as a look of surprise bloomed on Colby's face.

"This is her, Logan. This is Clara's grave."

Colby looked up at Logan and then back down at Clara's tombstone. "The date of death is 1930."

"Poor little girl," Colby said as she rested a hand on Clara's tombstone.

"I knew we'd find her out here," Logan said. He paused for a second as he looked at the other tombstones. "But who do these stones belong to?"

Colby moved over in front of the next tombstone. It was larger than the other two. Logan kneeled down beside her as she began to rub on the stone.

"Elijah," Colby said as she brushed away the dirt. "I can't make out the last name."

"Who the fuck is Elijah?" replied Logan.

"I don't know," Colby said as she continued to rub at the dirt under the engraved name on the tombstone. Then she suddenly stopped and drew in a sharp breath.

"It's dated 1931," Logan.

"That's the year of the first killing," Logan said.

"You don't think this is…"

"That means Elijah was this Florence lady's husband. They buried that sorry motherfucker right next to Clara," Logan said as he shook his head in disgust. "No wonder her soul couldn't rest."

"That's not funny," Colby said as she and Logan got to their feet.

"I wasn't trying to be funny. I was serious. Why would they do that?"

"They didn't know, Logan. Like I said, I've heard all the stories over the years. I've never heard anyone talk about it. No one knew what he did to Clara, except maybe Florence. You were the one that figured it out."

"I had help," Logan said as he turned and looked through the trees at his house sitting in the distance.

Logan then turned his attention to the third tombstone. "So who could that be?"

Colby stepped in front of the third tombstone. Then she kneeled down and began to rub on the surface of the stone.

"Scarlett," Colby finally said after she had brushed away most of the dirt. "Born 1922. Died 1928."

"Who is Scarlett?" Logan said, frowning as he stared at the stone.

"I dunno," Colby said as she stood up and stepped close to Logan. "The photo in the trunk of Rosemary and Clara at the train station was dated 1929. This little girl died in 1928. Who was she?"

A look of revelation suddenly washed across Logan's face.

"I've seen her."

Colby slowly turned her head and looked at Logan, who was staring down at the tombstone.

"What do you mean you've *seen* her?"

"She must be the little girl that dropped the flower on my front porch the first night I stayed in the house. And she likes to wander the upstairs hallway at night." Logan said this matter-of-factly, which unnerved Colby.

"Have you lost your mind?" Colby finally said. Logan turned and gave Colby a look of frustration.

"What, it's perfectly believable that a ghost can kill people out in my tobacco field but I'm crazy for saying another ghost wanders the upstairs hallway of my house? Seems my house is crawling with the souls of the dead. Same goes for my tobacco field."

"Good point," Colby said sheepishly. "Sorry."

"So Florence and Elijah did have a child before they adopted Rosemary and Clara," Logan said.

"Seems that way," Colby replied. "But she didn't make it. It's says typhoid fever underneath 1928."

"Sad," Logan said as he paused for a moment. Then a question came to mind that he had meant to ask Harmon during their previous meeting.

"By the way," Logan said. "Where are Rosemary and Carson buried?"

Colby looked surprised. "Harmon didn't tell you?"

"Nope."

"Carson was cremated. Rosemary had his ashes thrown in the Skeleton River. They did the same thing with Rosemary when she died. I remember talking to Harmon about it when he came in the diner for breakfast right after she passed away. He said it was in her will that she be cremated and thrown in the river like Carson."

"Well that simplifies things, I guess," Logan said as he reached down and picked up his axe handle. Then he took Colby by the hand as they turned and followed the path away from the graves to begin the long walk back to his house.

32

Logan and Colby spent the rest of the afternoon sitting on the back porch of the house. They made sandwiches for dinner and turned in early. The lovemaking went on for what seemed like hours until they were both so exhausted that they fell asleep in each other's arms.

Outside the tobacco fields were quiet. The leaves of the plants were bathed by the moonlight, which painted oblong shadows from the corners of the tobacco barns sitting dormant along the edge of the field.

Ethan McPhale made it a point to be as quiet as possible as he approached the Shaw house. It was just after midnight and as he moved through the tobacco he tried to put the thought of being butchered by whatever it was that haunted the Shaw Fields out of his mind. He had a score to settle with Logan Shaw and he knew that tonight he would avenge his little brother's death, even if it meant crossing the Shaw Fields to get to the house.

The can of kerosene brushed against the leaves of the tobacco plants as Ethan moved quickly up the row. Once he reached the end of the row he was relieved to step out of the field and onto the grass of the backyard. He paused and scanned the yard and the back of the house. Just then an owl hooted from a nearby tree and almost caused Ethan to drop the can of kerosene.

Ethan could see that all of the lights were out in the house. Even the back porch light had been left turned off.

"Stupid city fuck," Ethan muttered as he began to make his way across the backyard towards the house. "He doesn't even have enough sense to leave a light on."

Ethan crossed the backyard quickly. When he reached the base of the back porch steps he stopped and looked over his shoulder at the dark hulks of the tobacco barns. Then he thought about the story his father had once told him about a man being hacked to pieces in one of the barns. Just as he was about to climb the back porch steps he was startled once again by the owl perched in the tree next to the house. He gritted his teeth in anger at the bird, and at himself for being so skittish.

Ethan moved quickly up the stairs and onto the back porch. He felt relief when he stepped into the dark shadow cast by the overhanging roof of the porch. The moon was bright tonight, but it was not a harvest moon. This brought Ethan a degree of comfort. He knew he was safe. But then he thought about how his little brother had not been so lucky, and how he had been slaughtered the night before last.

"I don't know who or what killed my brother but I'm going to make you pay for it, city boy," Ethan said as he began to pour the contents of the kerosene can down the length of the porch against the back wall of the house. He splashed kerosene on the swing and down the back steps. Then he stepped back and pulled the book of matches out of his pocket. He struck one and dropped it into the puddle of kerosene lying on the bottom step.

The fire ran up the steps and in seconds engulfed the entire back porch. Ethan knew he was only half finished and had to move quickly. He grabbed the handle of the kerosene can and ran around the side of the house to the front porch. To his dismay there was a solitary light burning above the front door, but Ethan knew he was safe. The house was too far away from the road for anyone to see him as they drove by.

Ethan moved up the steps of the house and poured more of the kerosene along the length of the front porch, splashing a good bit of it on the door. He cursed as some of it splashed back onto his clothes and in his eyes. The oily, pungent odor of the kerosene filled his nostrils as he worked but he didn't let it slow him down.

Ethan knew the house only had a front a back door and that by lighting both porches on fire he would effectively close off the escape routes, forcing Logan and Colby to have to jump from the upstairs windows if they managed to awaken before the smoke and fire killed them.

Ethan poured what was left of the kerosene down the steps. Just as he was about to light the puddle at his feet, he looked over at the bottle tree jutting out of the ground close to the porch. He smirked as he remembered that his mother had put one similar to it in their yard when he was growing up. Then he struck a match and dropped it into the kerosene. Within seconds the front porch was ablaze.

Ethan knew all he had to do now was to make a dash back around the corner of the house and into the tobacco field. It wouldn't take him long to make it across the field and back to his house. Then he could climb into bed and in the morning he would wake up and everything would be over. The Shaw house would be gone, and with it Logan Shaw.

Just as Ethan turned to move towards the corner of the house he was startled to see a little girl standing only a few feet away from him. In her hand was a small yellow flower. Ethan had picked enough tobacco in his day to know what the flower was and where it came from. But he had no idea who the little girl was and he was even more surprised that she had been able to approach him without him knowing it.

"Who the fuck are you?" Ethan hissed as he took a step backwards. The little girl only smiled and lifted her arm in an effort to hand him the flower.

"You stay away!" Ethan shrieked as he took another step backwards. He knew something wasn't right about the little girl. In his haste to get away from her he overstepped and put his foot into the burning puddle of kerosene at the bottom of the front porch steps. The fire moved quickly up his leg and onto his upper body. He screamed in agony as the hot fire burned away his clothing and scorched his skin. In a few more seconds he was completely consumed by the fire, his arms flailing as he tried in vain to escape. He fell to his knees and then onto his stomach as the fire quickly took his life.

The little girl was unfazed by the sight of Ethan's burning corpse. She walked past him and onto the steps of the porch. The fire was all around her but she ignored it. She walked up the steps and then through the raging fire to the front door of the house. Standing in the middle of the flames, she turned and looked at Ethan one more time before stepping through the burning surface of the front door.

Logan and Colby were fast asleep in the upstairs bedroom. Both porches were ablaze and the fire was beginning to make its way into the house. It would not be long before the entire bottom floor of the house would be consumed by the fire. Wispy fingers of smoke were already making their way up the stairs to the hallway above.

Logan was startled awake by the touch of a small hand on his face. When he jerked awake he sat bolt upright in bed. It took him a few seconds to gather his wits and orient himself. Once he realized he was awake he looked over at Colby lying asleep beside him. Then he turned his head and gasped when he saw the little girl standing beside the bed. He knew right then that it had been her hand that he had felt touch his forehead.

"You have to get out," the little girl whispered.

Logan frowned and looked at the little girl.

"Scarlett? Is that you?"

"You have to get out now," Scarlett repeated.

Then Logan turned and looked at the windows of the bedroom. He saw the flickering yellow light and then smelled smoke coming into the room. He knew right then that the house was on fire.

33

Logan tried not to panic. "Colby, wake up!" he said as he shook
Colby awake. Her eyes flickered open and for a moment she was
disoriented. Then she focused on Logan leaning over her.
"What's wrong?"

Logan wasted no time explaining. "We've got to get out of the house!"
was all he said.

Logan stood up while Colby climbed out of the bed. Once she was on
her feet he resisted the urge to grab her by the hand and run out of the
bedroom.

"Put your pants on! And your shirt. Cover as much skin as you can. And
put your shoes on." Colby grabbed her clothes lying in a pile on the floor.
She quickly pulled on her jeans, T-shirt and shoes. Logan did the same and
then moved quickly to the old dresser sitting in the corner. He pulled open
a drawer and grabbed an old cotton nightgown that had belonged to
Rosemary. He tossed it to Colby.

"Ball that up and breathe through it." Colby did as she was told just as
Logan grabbed her by the hand. "Let's go. We have to get out of here. The
house is on fire."

Logan pulled Colby to the door of the bedroom. He looked down the
hall and saw that it was quickly filling with smoke. Without hesitating, he
guided Colby out of the bedroom and into the hallway. Within seconds they
were standing at the top of the stairs looking down into the foyer below.

"What are we going to do, Logan?"

Logan looked at Colby. He felt the courage that he had longed for
suddenly explode in his chest. He knew that he had to save her life, as well
as his own. It was all up to him.

"We're going down the stairs. They're not on fire yet so we don't have
to worry about them collapsing. We'll go into one of the rooms downstairs
and try to get out of a window."

"I'm scared, Logan. I don't know if I can do that."

Logan looked at Colby. He raised her hand to her face, the hand holding the old nightgown.

"Just breathe through this. I'll handle the rest." With this, Logan bent down and lifted Colby over his shoulder and wrapped one arm around her legs as they hung in front of him. He used his other hand to grab the handrail to steady himself. Then he began to descend the stairs.

The heat coming from the front of the house was unbearable when Logan got to the bottom of the stairs. He was glad he and Colby had taken the extra few seconds to put on their clothes. Once he was off the stairs he looked to his left and then to his right. The dining room was completely ablaze. The portrait of Carson and Rosemary was already on fire and was almost completely destroyed.

Logan looked to his right and saw that the living room was not quite as bad. He moved quickly into the room and then put Colby down so that he could find something to use to break the window.

Colby began to cough. "Hurry!" she said as she watched Logan pick up one of the antique chairs sitting in front of the fireplace.

Logan lifted the chair and ran towards the only window in the room. It was tall and ran down almost to the floor. He threw the chair as hard as he could towards the glass, which was framed with raging yellow flames. The heavy chair broke through the window with a crash and landed on the porch outside.

Logan then grabbed Colby and threw her over his shoulder again. Without hesitation he moved to the window and pushed his way through and onto the porch. Then he held Colby tightly as he jumped off the end of the porch to the grass a few feet below. When they hit the ground Logan's legs buckled. He dropped Colby and they both rolled over onto their backs.

Logan got up and pulled Colby up with him. He took her by the hand and led her out into the front yard until they were far enough from the house to feel safe. Cool air rushed into their lungs as they moved.

Once they were out in the yard they turned around and looked at the Shaw house, now almost completely ablaze.

Colby grabbed Logan and embraced him. "Logan, you saved my life. I love you."

"I love you too," Logan replied as he held Colby tight. When they released each other Colby looked over her shoulder and saw something burning on the walkway that led to the porch steps.

"Logan, what is that? Look, there's something in front of the porch stairs."

Logan focused on the body lying at the foot of the porch stairs.

"Stay here. I don't want you near the fire." Logan then walked quickly across the yard until he was a few feet away from the burning pile of flesh that had once been Ethan McPhale. The five gallon can of kerosene lying close to the body told Logan all he needed to know. He turned and walked back to Colby.

"Looks like this town is fresh out of McPhales. Seems Ethan got a little too close to his own handiwork and caught himself on fire. Serves him right, the ignorant motherfucker."

Colby looked past Logan at the burning remains of Ethan. "How do you know it's him?"

"I can tell. It makes sense. He probably came over tonight to avenge his sorry ass brother. Now they can both rot in Hell together. They got what was coming to them."

"Logan, your house…" Colby turned her gaze from Ethan's body to the raging inferno of the Shaw house.

"I don't really care, Colby. It's probably better this way. All those restless souls, maybe they can move on now. Besides, I have plenty of land. We can build another one." Logan then pulled Colby to him. "I managed to save the only thing in the house that's important to me." At the sound of this, Colby kissed Logan and held him tight. Then she released him and looked up into his eyes.

"I knew there was a hero in there somewhere," she said as she placed her hand on Logan's chest.

For a moment, Logan and Colby were lost in each other's eyes. Then Logan snapped back to reality and looked at the burning house once again.

"I don't know about you, but I've had enough of this town for tonight. We need to get out of here. We can come back tomorrow or the next day but right now let's just get out of town."

"Where are we going?" asked Colby.

"Just come with me." Logan then took Colby by the hand and led her to his car sitting near the fountain in the circular portion of the driveway. It was far enough from the house that it had not been damaged by the flames. Once in the car, Logan tipped the sun visor. He smiled as the keys fell into his lap.

"I know a place," he said as he cranked the engine.

34

Colby was asleep when Logan pulled into his trailer park. He eased the car up to his mobile home and then brought it to a stop, the headlights illuminating the front door of his trailer in a wash of white light. He looked over at Lowell's trailer and saw that the lights were out. It was just after four in the morning.

"Colby…" Logan said as he gently put his hand on her shoulder. "Wake up, baby."

Colby's eyes fluttered open. She sat up in the car seat and was momentarily disoriented, but when she looked over at Logan she immediately relaxed. She could see him smiling at her in the reflected glow of the headlights.

"Where are we?" Colby said as she looked around her. Then her eyes settled on the mobile home in front of the car.

"Welcome to the Casa de Shaw. The real one. Believe it or not I actually bought this with my own money. Well, insurance money anyway. The trailer's all mine, I just pay rent on the lot. And as far as I know my humble little abode here isn't haunted."

Colby turned her head and looked at Logan, a sleepy grin working its way onto her face.

"I love it. The big old house in Starlight wasn't really you. And to tell you the truth, it wasn't really me either. Can we go inside?"

"Yep. I asked my neighbor Lowell to keep an eye out while I was gone. Looks like he fell asleep on the job." Logan then nodded towards Lowell's dark trailer. "You can meet him and his wife tomorrow."

Logan reached over the seat and grabbed the manila envelope Harmon had given him during one of their meetings. It contained a copy of Rosemary's will and information on how to access the money in the bank.

"What's that?" Colby asked.

"I'll tell you all about it tomorrow. For now, let's go in and try to get some sleep. We only have a few hours before the sun comes up."

Logan got out of the car and walked around and opened Colby's door. Then he took her by the hand and led her to the front door of his mobile home. He had forgotten to leave a light on when he had left for Starlight over a week ago and was apprehensive about opening the door and walking into the dark trailer.

Once inside, Logan patted the wall beside the door until he found the light switch. One flick of the switch bathed the small living room with the warm glow of incandescent light.

Logan locked the door behind them. "Wait here," he said as he let go of Colby's hand. "Just let me give the place a quick check."

Logan moved through the trailer turning on lights as he went. He checked the bedroom windows and then the closet. He switched on the light in the small bathroom as he walked through the narrow hallway back to the kitchen. Colby was still standing by the front door.

"All secure. Let's hit the sack. Tomorrow will be another day."

Colby smiled as she and Logan embraced by the door. Then she followed him to the bedroom. They stripped naked and crawled under the sheets. Then Colby leaned over Logan lying on his back beside her.

"Thank you again for saving my life, Logan." She looked into his eyes as the dim glow from the streetlight outside sifted through the window drapes and cast crooked shadows through the bedroom.

"You're not the only one that has been saved, Colby. You've rescued me too."

Logan pulled Colby on top of him. The lovemaking was slow and passionate. He could feel her heart beating as he held her body to his, her breath hot against his neck. When they were finished they fell asleep curled up together in the small bedroom, a room no bigger than the pantry had been at the Shaw mansion in Starlight. The last thought that went through Logan Shaw's head before he fell fast asleep was how much more like home his trailer felt now that he was sharing his bed with a woman that he loved, and who loved him in return.

§§§

Logan finally woke up just after eight o'clock. Instinctively he sniffed the air for the smell of coffee only to remember that he had not set up the coffeemaker the night before when he and Colby had arrived from Starlight.

Colby was still sound asleep beside him. Logan eased himself out of bed and slipped on his pants and shirt. He knew he didn't have anything to cook for breakfast but he knew he could at least make coffee. That would be a good start. He could always make a biscuit run once Colby woke up.

Logan moved down the hallway to the kitchen and in a few minutes had a fresh pot of coffee brewing. He leaned over the sink and stared out across the trailer park through the kitchen window. In the distance he could hear the sound of the large cranes working the cargo in the nearby port. He knew he needed to call Sheriff Patterson. Now that the sun had come up the news of the Shaw house burning down was probably all over Starlight, as well as the news of Ethan's burnt corpse.

Logan began to run the events of the previous night through his head. He thought about the burning house and how he and Colby had barely escaped with their lives. He thought about the charred corpse of Ethan McPhale and the bloody, mutilated corpse of his brother Chip. Logan thought about how he and Colby had pieced together the puzzle of the ghost of tobacco road and how maybe now Clara's ghost could rest in peace. He thought about how the house had shared its secrets with him during the long nights he had spent there. Now it was all gone. But like he had told Colby, Logan knew they could rebuild the house. Or build another one somewhere else. He could sell the land, or he could keep it. But as long as he had Colby he knew everything would fall into place.

Logan's final thought was about Scarlett, and how her ghost had saved them from dying in the fire. Hopefully her soul was now at peace as well.

Outside the window Logan saw a car slowly drift by on the road in front of his trailer. He watched as the car turned into the short gravel driveway of Lowell's trailer. Logan knew he needed to go out and thank Lowell for watching over his trailer while he had been gone.

The smell of coffee had spread all through the trailer and Logan could hear Colby stirring in the bedroom. He turned his attention once again to the distant cranes working the port. Then he pushed himself away from the sink and walked to the front door. Maybe he could catch Lowell before he went inside his trailer. Then maybe later when he and Colby had themselves together he could formally introduce her to Lowell and his wife.

Logan unlocked the front door and pulled it open. Just as he was about to step through the door he looked down. His mouth slowly opened and he drew in a deep breath, unable to believe what he was seeing. His mind had to be playing tricks on him. Logan knew that what he was seeing had no place in a trailer park outside of an industrial shipping port. And he knew it was not there by accident.

Logan slowly reached down and picked up the small yellow flower. Just then, Colby walked up behind him and almost scared him into the next life.

"What is it?" she said as she rubbed one of her eyes.

"Looks like we had a visitor last night," he said as he handed the flower to Colby.

Thank you for reading this novel.

Please visit my website at www.dalejyoung.com. If you subscribe to my blog you'll receive advance notice of book releases and discount offers, as well as interesting posts about ghost folklore of the American South.

You are invited to leave a review at Amazon.com and share your thoughts about this book with other readers.

ABOUT THE AUTHOR

Dale Young was born in North Carolina. His family has deep roots in the Blue Ridge Mountains, a dark and spooky land where superstitions about  the dead run deep. The ghost stories and tales of wandering spirits passed down through his family over the years inspired him to become a writer at an early age.

BOOKS BY DALE J. YOUNG

Horror novels:
The Ghost of Tobacco Road

The Summerland Trilogy:
Book I - The Ties That Bind
Book II - Wicked Izzy
Book III - Summerland

The Curious Midlife Crisis of Barlow McSwain (short story)

Other novels:
Hanging the Artificial Sun

http://dalejyoung.com

Published by Niner 8 Books

Made in the USA
Charleston, SC
04 September 2015